THE NIGHTSILVER PROMISE

By Annaliese Avery

CELESTIAL MECHANISM CYCLE

Book One
The Nightsilver Promise

Book Two
The Doomfire Secret

THE NIGHTSILVER PROMISE

CELESTIAL MECHANISM CYCLE I

ANNALIESE AVERY

Scholastic Inc.

Copyright © 2021 by Annaliese Avery

First published in the UK by Scholastic Children's Books, an imprint of
Scholastic Ltd., Euston House, 24 Eversholt Street, London, NW1 1DB, UK

This USA edition was originally published in hardcover by
Scholastic Press in 2022.

All rights reserved. Published by Scholastic Inc., *Publishers since* 1920.
SCHOLASTIC and associated logos are trademarks and/or registered
trademarks of Scholastic Inc.

The publisher does not have any control over and does not assume any
responsibility for author or third-party websites or their content.

No part of this publication may be reproduced, stored in a retrieval system,
or transmitted in any form or by any means, electronic, mechanical,
photocopying, recording, or otherwise, without written permission of the
publisher. For information regarding permission, write to Scholastic Inc.,
Attention: Permissions Department, 557 Broadway, New York, NY 10012.

This book is a work of fiction. Names, characters, places, and incidents are
either the product of the author's imagination or are used fictitiously, and any
resemblance to actual persons, living or dead, business establishments, events,
or locales is entirely coincidental.

ISBN 978-1-338-75447-6

10 9 8 7 6 5 4 3 2 1   23 24 25 26 27

Printed in the U.S.A.   40
This edition first printing 2023

Book design by Stephanie Yang

FOR MY GRANDAD BUSTER,
WHO SHOWED ME THE STARS
AND TAUGHT ME THEIR SONG

NON EST AD ASTRA MOLLIS E TERRIS VIA.

SENECA THE YOUNGER

1

DESTINY CALLING

Destiny was calling Paisley Fitzwilliam. She held its summons clutched in her hand.

Walking away from the aerodoc station, she adjusted the strap on her father's old dragonhide satchel, her flame-touched curls twisting out from under her woolen cap, the sound of the aerocopters filling her ears as they lifted into the skies of London.

She glanced up, squinting into the clear winter sky. She could just make out the floating borough of Greenwich Overhead as it sat in the west away from the rising sun. By the time the sun fell this evening, the floating borough would be high in the east, welcoming the night.

A chill north wind had gripped London, its icy fingers extending out over the rest of the Empire of Albion, but Paisley paid it little attention as she walked the frost-covered streets of Lower London. There were more important things at hand than the frozen Thames; this was the day that she had been waiting thirteen long turnings for. Today she would find out what the stars had in store for her. Paisley glanced down at the summons, the mechanized Old Celtic type crisp and black against the cream of the parchment, inviting her to discover what the Chief Designer had planned for her track. Paisley smiled as she crossed Old Broad Street and made her way toward the Mechanist chapel. She was as sure of her future as she was that the sun was made of dragon fire and the Earth of clockwork.

Paisley knew that she was going to be an explorer, just like her father.

She passed a news-smith as he bellowed out the headline from the *King's Herald*.

"Killer comet signals the beginning of the end," he called. "Lady Scientist insists it's *not* a dragon."

Paisley stopped dead at the words *lady scientist*. She snapped her head toward the news-smith and reached out for a paper.

"Oi, this ain't no library—if you wanna read it, you'll have to buy it," the gruff young man said.

Paisley reached inside the folds of her thick woolen coat. As she handed over a silver sixpence, she saw the man look at her left wrist; her sleeve had ridden up to show her thick dragonhide brace-let. Paisley blushed as she tried to ignore the narrowing of the man's eyes and the dismissive way he thrust the change at her. After today, she would never have to wear the bracelet again; her track would be revealed and her stars would shine brightly for all to see.

She walked slowly as she read the paper; her mother's name leaped out at her.

Celestial Physicist Professor Violetta Fitzwilliam, the first and only woman to hold tenure in the floating borough of Greenwich Overhead, has been credited with finding a fast-moving comet, Comet Wolstenholme, named after the Professor's grandfather, who was also a scientist. The comet is set to light up the skies over our glorious Empire and the savage nations of the Northern Realm within the next few days.

The Guild of Mechanists are reassuring concerned citizens that if Fitzwilliam's claims are true, then the comet will be part of the Chief Designer's plan.

However, there are those who believe that all is not well in the Celestial Mechanism.

Concern is growing that this so-called comet is none other than Malgol—the Great Dragon prophesied by the Dragon Walkers.

Given the Professor's own tumultuous track, there may be some truth to this. Readers may remember that Professor Fitzwilliam is the wife of the late Knight of Albion, sworn protector of the George and commander of the League of Explorers, Sir Edmund

Fitzwilliam. Sir Edmund died almost four turnings ago in the Empires to the East while on a diplomatic mission for the George. She is also mother to a crippled son and a teenage daughter, who is reported to be trackless.

The Professor is hosting a lecture this evening on her discovery, which the *Herald* will report on tomorrow. For those wishing to know more about the prophecy, turn to page eight.

Exasperated, Paisley pouted as she folded the newspaper and stuffed it into her satchel. *Great Dragon, indeed.* Mother had been tracking the comet for weeks, measuring its progress as it moved along its unseen track in the Mechanism. The idea that it could be a Great Dragon was utterly unscientific!

And as for her being trackless . . . well, she was about to fix that.

The clock tower struck as she hurried up Wormwood Street; the Mechanist chapel dominated the road with its domed roof and twisting corner spires.

Paisley reached out for the central cog on the chapel's ornately decorated door and paused.

She looked behind her at the busy street, at the people passing, sure and steady on their daily tracks. Her breathing came fast.

What if her stars weren't to her liking?

What if the destiny she had planned for herself was about to be stolen by her stars?

Paisley inhaled deeply, the air filling her lungs with little icy stabs. She held it for a moment, then let it out in one go, her hot breath steaming like a dragon's.

It would have been so much easier if she had just received her stars when she was a baby, like almost everyone else did.

Everyone she knew already had their track. It was customary that a person's destiny was given to them at some time during their infancy. They would grow up, secure in the knowledge of what their track had in store for them.

But not Paisley.

She'd had thirteen turnings of dreaming and hoping. Of working out for herself what her track held. Now she had her own plans for her future. Plans that the Chief Designer had not drawn up.

It was rare for a person to go so long without knowing their track, but not unheard of. The Mechanists only ever revealed a destiny when the stars said it was the right time to do so. For some reason, Paisley's stars had been waiting till this very moment.

But now that she was finally about to be told her path in life, a cold doubt crept over her.

Paisley lowered her hand from the door and chewed her lip.

What if the Chief Designer had something in store for her that she didn't want?

She'd kept the summons a secret from Mother and her younger brother, Dax, for that very reason. She could go home now and no one would know. She took a step back and turned to leave.

Then stopped.

Looking down at the summons letter, she unfolded the envelope and tipped out the small copper disk inside. Not for the first time, she ran her fingers over the grooves at the edge of the disk and the scratches that crisscrossed its surface—these small lines and notches would mark out her fate.

She looked back over her shoulder, toward the news-smith. No one would sneer at her lack of guiding stars again.

She clenched the token in her fist and pushed open the chapel doors, ready to face her future.

Paisley's boots clipped across the stone floor. Her eyes followed the twisting pillars of cogs as they slowly rotated up to an inky black ceiling. The ceiling shone with the light of a thousand false stars, each one a replica of a true star, each one turning in the heavens in the exact position of its counterpart.

She focused on one small bright star, and a flicker of hope burst up inside her. Maybe her stars would be aligned with what she wanted after all—otherwise, why would the Chief Designer allow her to wish for it if it wasn't in her track?

Above the dais hung the Doom. Paisley had often sat in the pews and examined the brightly painted scene while the Mechanist priest read from the Blueprints, the ancient teachings of the Chief Designer.

The Doom depicted two stories. One told of how the Chief Designer had forged the looping golden tracks of the Celestial Mechanism in the breath of the Great Dragons, their fire as bright as the gleaming tracks and glinting in the light of the false stars of the chapel.

She had often heard the tale retold in the reading of the teachings—of how dragon breath had made the sun and the light, and the Chief Designer had invented the night so that the stars might guide us.

The second story showed the fate of the Great Dragons, their punishment for turning away from the Chief Designer and forging their own way in the world: a vibrant image of the First George confronting the Great Dragon, Ealdordóm, the first to be banished. In his hand, the George held his lance, Ascalon. The lance was said to have been designed for the George so that he could fulfill his destiny and rid the world of the Great Dragons, just as the Chief Designer had planned.

Paisley had often felt that the fate of the Great Dragons ought to have been different. They had not deserved to die just because they wanted to live their lives in their own way. Paisley had spent her entire thirteen turnings living her life in her own way; the idea that she would soon be powerless over her destiny made her wonder if it would be better for her to remain trackless.

However, the teachings of the Blueprints were very clear that everyone had a track that must be kept to, and it was finally time for Paisley to receive hers.

The schematica was waiting for her on the dais. Her left wrist tingled in anticipation.

Like most Mechanist machines, the schematica was elegant in its design. The slot at the top was just the right size for the copper disk, and the circular hole at the front was just the right size for her hand.

Paisley could feel the rise and fall of her chest now.

This was it.

The cogs of fate had already turned for her, and she was about to know what her track held. Excitement jostled with fear, and won out.

She held her breath as she placed her left hand into the machine, palm up, and then placed the disk in the slot with her other hand. For a moment, nothing happened, and then the machine closed around Paisley's forearm, trapping her hand and wrist inside.

Her breathing quickened; she felt a clamminess come over her.

Paisley's wrist began to burn. She bit her lip, and tears sprang to her eyes. But the pain subsided in a moment. The schematica opened, and Paisley tentatively pulled her hand out.

She held her arm up to the light, studying the smattering of golden stars on her wrist.

Paisley smiled. She finally had her track. She was just like everyone else in the Empire.

But there was something strange about her stars. In all the charts she had ever seen, the golden dots were scattered over a circle, defining its circumference, filling its surface. But her stars were scattered in a semicircle, as if it was missing its other half.

From the bottom of the schematica came a long piece of parchment. It had Paisley's name typed on it in Old Celtic.

Below her name was a drawing identical to the stars on her wrist.

Paisley looked beyond this at the series of symbols and detailed explanations. She translated each one quickly; they told her what type of person she was and how the cogs of her track would turn.

She smiled broadly, reassured at the strange grouping of her stars as everything she read about herself rang true. Her stars said that she was brave and loyal. That she stood by the truth and would fight for the rights of herself and others. Her stars said that she put the needs of others before herself and that she should be aware of her own needs and interests from time to time. Then she paused.

As Paisley translated the last section of her chart, her mouth became dry. She read the lines once, twice, a third time. Her breathing came fast, and her heart sounded in her ears. Fear gripped her.

You will be brave. You will try your hardest. You will have far to go, but you will not have long to travel. You will suffer great losses. Your stars say that you will fail. Your stars say, Paisley Fitzwilliam, that before the end of your fourteenth turning, your cog will cease, your track will end, and you will die.

2

HERE BE DRAGONS

Paisley did not linger in the chapel. She felt as if the air had become thick and putrid. She needed to be outside. If she could just breathe fresh, cool air, she was sure that the spinning in her head would stop. As her track soon would.

She stifled a sob, tears running down her face as she staggered toward the doors of the chapel. She felt as if the track that had been placed before her was narrow and poorly made. She stopped briefly under the starry ceiling. She wanted to shout up at the false stars illuminating her as they silently turned in the ceiling, to shout at the Chief Designer, "What was it all for? Why give me such dreams if you meant me to die?"

But the words were lodged deep inside her, afraid to come out, afraid to be spoken as the truth. Instead she stumbled outside. The weak winter sunlight gave no warmth; the cold of the North turned her tears to ice.

If she had stayed, she may have seen the teenage boy skulking in the shadows of the chapel.

But she didn't notice him there or as he followed her through the streets.

She walked without direction, wandering in a daze as she stuffed the parchment into her pocket. A short time ago, Paisley had been as sure of her future as she was of the turning of the Mechanism. She had been sure that she would follow in her father's track as an explorer and make him proud. Now she felt as if her cog was dislodged, spinning in ever-slowing circles that made her inhale sharply.

If her stars were right, she thought, then soon she would see him again. She pulled her father's satchel tight to her as fresh tears leaped into her eyes. She thought that he might be disappointed in the shortness of her track and how little she had done along it.

She swallowed her tears back.

Before the end of your fourteenth turning, your cog will cease, your track will end, and you will die.

Sometime in the next nine moons, she, Paisley Fitzwilliam, was going to die. Her track had only just begun, and now it was about to end. Her head swam full of the dreams that she had, all dashed in a moment. She would be no more. She would leave the world and enter the Veil. She wondered if the Mechanists were right, if the Veil was the place where the spark that had made a person went and waited till the Chief Designer assigned them a new track. She hoped that the Mechanists were right in a way she never had before. Father would be in the Veil; she had always believed that this was true and that she would one day see him there, but it was too soon. She still had things to do here and people to love.

In the next moment, Paisley realized that whatever happened, death meant no more Mother and Dax. She balled her hands into frustrated fists, her nails biting into her palms as she wondered what she would tell them, how she would break the terrible news.

She decided that she would tell them nothing. She would cover her stars and pretend they didn't exist.

Her mind spun like a tightly wound spring as she sank deeper into the darkness of her destiny.

She was blind to the world around her, unaware of the commotion ahead or the danger behind as the dark-haired boy knocked into her, stealthily picking the parchment from her pocket as he jolted her into the here and now.

Paisley stopped and blinked, not realizing what she had lost, as she looked around to see that the road in front of her was blocked. The electrica wagons of the Men of the Yard were parked across the street, their red-and-black insignia covering the sides of the vehicles as they surrounded the entrance of a department store.

Paisley slipped to the front of the gathered crowd, awareness creeping back to her.

"What's going on?" a man behind her asked.

A lady to the side of Paisley answered him in a loud whisper, "One of the shopgirls is *Dragon Touched*."

At the mention of *Dragon Touch*, every hair on Paisley's body stood on end.

"No! The filthy half-breed." The man spat on the ground. The lady did the same, warding off the Dragon Touch.

"At least it ain't a boy, what with this dragon comet an' all," another man said, and the other two muttered in agitated agreement.

Paisley felt the small coiled spring of fear that lived inside her begin to twist ever tighter.

The door to the shop banged open, and two Men of the Yard in their red-and-black uniforms strode into the street, dragging the shopgirl out.

Her hands were cuffed behind her back, and around her neck was a nightsilver collar. One of the Yardmen tugged at the chain that led from it, and Paisley felt her blood boil.

The girl yelped as she stumbled forward. That was when Paisley realized that the sleeves on the girl's dress had been ripped off.

Paisley shuddered, not at the thought of the biting cold on the young girl's arms but at the sight of her flesh and fear for what it meant for the girl. From the elbow up, her arms were covered in vivid red scales.

Dragon Touch.

The crowd around Paisley was jeering and calling.

"Half-breed!"

"Kill the dragon!"

"Lance her!"

The girl's terrified face scanned the crowd, her wide eyes red-rimmed, her cheeks tearstained. Paisley realized that the girl was only a little older than she was and felt a burst of fire run hot inside. She took a step forward, not quite sure what she was going to do, but she had to make her stars count for something.

Just then, the shopgirl opened her mouth wide, much wider than Paisley had thought was possible. Her jaw seemed to dislocate and protrude. Then, from deep in her throat, came a roar.

A roar that filled the street, filled the world, even. It flooded into Paisley's ears, and she clasped her hands tightly over them.

She knew that Dragon Touch manifested in different ways, giving each of the Touched different attributes—but it was so rare and so varied, Paisley had never seen or heard of anything like this before.

She watched the girl in awe as the sound dug into her brain, making her knees weak as she all of a sudden felt faint. She closed her eyes tight and doubled over as her ears, her head, her whole body vibrated, and like those around her, Paisley blacked out.

Paisley woke to find herself lying on the cold hard cobbles, looking up at the blue sky. The dark, squat, floating borough of Harrow-on-High drifted overhead.

Standing shakily, with the crowd splayed out around her, she stumbled across the barricaded area, searching for the dragon girl. But she was gone. In the few minutes that Paisley had been unconscious, the girl had vanished. All that remained was a set of keys, along with the empty collar and handcuffs.

Paisley smiled.

The Men of the Yard were coming around too as Paisley slipped into the crowd on the other side. Most people were still unconscious or in various states of confusion.

"Which way did she go?" the Captain shouted.

One of the younger Yardmen threw up on the pavement. The Captain looked at him in disgust and bellowed at him, "Find the filthy dragon. Or it'll be you we hang in her place."

As Paisley moved away, she hoped that the girl could make it to safety. Maybe she'd reach the floating boroughs above London. Maybe the Dragon Walkers would save her.

Paisley hoped that it was in the young woman's stars to survive, and not for the first time, she wondered if the Mechanism applied to the Dragon Touched the way it did to everyone else.

+ + ✳ + +

As Paisley began to think more clearly and set her course homeward, the boy who had stolen her fate began to sink deeper toward what he knew was his own destiny.

He moved through the back streets of the city, in the places where only rats and wrongdoers dwelled.

He paused for a moment to look at Paisley's chart, lifting his own star-covered wrist to the parchment. His stars were scattered across his olive skin, covering the circular tattoo in small groups and pairings. He had never seen stars like the ones on Paisley's chart before, bunched in one half and tightly packed. He guessed that this was why she was so important to his mistress; he certainly hadn't seen anything else about her that marked her as special.

He scanned the Old Celtic script. He had never fully learned the old language but knew enough for Paisley's fate to make sense to him. The girl wasn't going to live past the turning.

He rolled the parchment and placed it in his inside coat pocket, then pulled out his electrica lantern before making his way down into the sewer tunnels.

He took long, sure strides as he walked away from the heart of the city, his neckerchief pulled up over his nose, the stench of the sloshing water around him slowly fading as he turned away from the channels that led to the frozen Thames.

The opening was hard to see in the weak light from the lantern, but he knew where the keyhole was and the right way to turn it.

The tunnels beyond became wider, the air cleaner and the brick-work more elaborate. After a while, a series of electrica lights told him he was close. He pocketed his lantern and stepped into a wide, cavernous space.

The eight ornately laid walls of the subterranean hall all met in a point, which hovered above its center. The twisting pillars and brickwork converged to then push down and form the head of a dragon, openmouthed and expectant.

Raised up on an octagonal platform, below the gaping jaws, was a nightsilver throne, cast in ink-black metal around the white teeth of a Great Dragon. On it sat a beautiful girl. She looked no older than ten, but the boy knew she was as old as the teeth in the throne she sat on. She was dressed in a midnight taffeta coat and dragon-hide trousers. Her hair was as long and flowing as the dark waters of the tunnels.

"Do you have it, Roach?" she called to him, her voice bouncing off the walls.

Roach pulled Paisley's destiny from his jacket pocket and walked toward the throne. He clenched his jaw as he bowed his head and handed over the rolled-up parchment.

The girl reached out and snatched it from him with small, delicate pink fingers.

"Did she see you?"

Roach shook his head. "I don't think so."

The blow came from nowhere, his head pushed to the side, his lip bleeding. He didn't know if she had kicked or punched him. All he knew was the Dark Dragon was not to be underestimated. She might look like a sweet little girl, but she was anything but.

"You don't *think* so?"

Roach narrowed his dark eyes and rubbed his aching jaw. "No, she didn't—I'm sure of it."

"Good."

The Dark Dragon sat back on her throne and unrolled Paisley's scroll. She greedily read the Old Celtic script.

Roach watched as her small shoulders relaxed and her lips curled into a cruel smile.

He knew what the scroll said, and that the Dark Dragon had been worried that it was in Paisley's stars to stop her, but the girl's track did not bend that way, and Roach was glad for many reasons.

"Excellent," the Dark Dragon said. "The stars are in my favor."

3

DRAGON TOUCH

As Paisley pushed open the front door, the comforting smell of warm gingerbread hit her, and she felt her hollowness turn to hunger.

"Ah, there you are, miss." The housekeeper, Mrs. Keen, bustled through the large hallway from the steps under the grand staircase that led from the kitchen. She made straight for the library carrying a tray full of gingerbread cogs, each one iced in yellow.

Paisley stood still for a moment; she wanted to suck up every detail.

The way the house smelled, the way the light from the chandelier spilled over the floor, the curve of the stairs in the hall as they led up to the landing where her father's nightsilver armor stood. And, most important, the way she felt when at home—loved and safe. Who knew how much longer she would have before her track ended? Before she felt nothing.

She dashed her tears with the back of her sleeve and followed Mrs. Keen, removing her coat and unwinding her scarf as she entered the library, dropping them and her satchel onto the nearest armchair.

There were four long windows in the library flanking the fireplace, and two doors, one behind her and one to the right that led to Mother's study.

The rest of the walls were covered in books.

Paisley's brother, Dax, was sitting at a large table, examining an array of maps through a pair of magnifying glasses.

He didn't look up when Mrs. Keen put the tray down or when she left the room, but as the door closed, he shot out a hand and grabbed a cookie.

Paisley smiled as her little brother brushed crumbs from the maps onto the floor, still unaware of her entrance.

She took a step closer, and Dax started as he saw her. "Goodness, Paisley, you almost stopped me in my track," he said with a giggle.

Paisley felt her breath catch as she thought of her stars.

"What's wrong?" He looked at her, his messy golden curls sticking up from his head like faulty springs, his eyes small and distant through the many lenses of his magnifying glasses. "Have you been crying?" he asked softly.

"No, why would I be crying? It's just so cold out there," she lied as she crossed to the fireplace and began rubbing her hands.

"Well, I'm glad you're back. I've been bored."

"I can see that," she said, nodding at the maps.

He had laid the maps out so that they formed one big atlas. The Northern Realms were at the top of the table, their cold lands traced out in icy blue.

The Empires of the George lay below them: Albion, a green jewel nestled in a sea of turquoise. The green continued with the vast landmass of Europa till it gave way to the expansive swath of yellow and brown of the Empires of the East. Away to the west, across the vast ocean, lay the Amerikas; it was these lands that Dax was studying.

"Ah, Amerika," she said.

"Yes, it's fascinating. Did you know that Amerika is where the Great Dragons fled to when the first King George began his purge? And that the King's Knights followed them across the ocean—the Krakens got some of them, but most made it all the way to Amerika—settling in the land as they hunted the dragons?"

Paisley smiled. "Yes, I knew that."

"I thought that you would," he said, smoothing his hand across the sea and over Amerika.

"There's a book about it," he added, hopping off the chair with a clank and grabbing his cane. "Did you know that some of the knights are now outlawed and that they have set up their own forces against the George? They want an Empire where there can be dragons and Dragon Walkers," he told her.

"It's a bit more complex than that," Paisley said as Dax made his way to the bookshelf near the reading chairs, his brass leg brace over the top of his gray trousers shining in the flickering light from the fire. It clinked with every second step he took, his face wincing a little with each strike.

"I thought Mother told you not to wear that old leg brace anymore," Paisley said.

"Well, Mother's too busy in her study to notice, and the new one rubs."

"But that one's too small," Paisley told him.

"It's fine," he said, reaching for a book. "I'll change it before Uncle Hector turns up to take us to Mother's lecture."

Paisley reached for her satchel as she remembered Mother's lecture mentioned in the newspaper article. She smoothed out the front page, then flicked through articles about the ill health of the current King George and worry over his lack of an heir, followed by a larger article on the unrest in the Northern Realms, before arriving at page eight.

The Dragon Lord, the headline said.

Paisley knew what it would say—she knew the prophecy better than almost anyone: *One day a boy will be born with Dragon Touch, and he will call forth the Great Dragon Malgol to destroy the Celestial Mechanism.*

Even though there were no Great Dragons left to be called, all the hatred and fear of the Dragon Touched came from the prophecy. It was what had gathered the crowd to the shop that morning and had made the Men of the Yard so aggressive to the girl.

Paisley remembered every tug on the chain, every harsh word from the crowd. *"At least it ain't a boy,"* one of them had said.

There were no boys with Dragon Touch, and if there ever was to be one, the world at large agreed that it would be best for him to die at birth rather than live to fulfill the destiny of empowering the Dragon Walkers.

Returning with a heavy book, Dax stumbled and then cried out. "Is it your leg?" Paisley asked, moving toward him.

Dax gripped the edge of the armchair and nodded. His jaw was tight with pain.

Paisley eased him into the chair, then kneeled next to him, working fast to undo the buckles and straps of the brace that held Dax's leg out and straightened it.

As soon as the tension was released, his leg rotated outward.

Dax groaned again, clenching his fists.

"Where's your ointment?" Paisley asked.

"Pocket. Blazer," he said through gritted teeth. He motioned back to the table he had been sitting by.

Paisley found the glass tub of translucent ointment in the inside pocket along with a piece of string, a knight token, and a small set of screwdrivers in a dragonhide pouch that she had been hunting for weeks.

"Hurry, Paisley," Dax whimpered.

He had taken off his shoe and sock and pulled his trouser leg right up to the top of his thigh. Paisley went to him. She had long ceased to be startled by the sight that greeted her.

Although the top of Dax's leg was pale and straight, his thigh twisted outward and was covered in blackened green scales all the way down.

His dragon leg spasmed, his clawed foot jumping.

"See, you should have worn your new brace," Paisley said gently as she kneeled again and opened the pot of ointment.

The scent of lavender and patchouli filled the room, accompanied by another scent, deep and powerful, one that Paisley had never been able to identify.

She smeared the cream all over Dax's scaly leg, beginning at his ankle before rubbing up over his shin and calf to a little past his knee, where the skin began to match the rest of his body, covering the scales in a glistening film.

Then she massaged all the way back down again and over his twisted foot. The scales felt like soft velvet under her fingertips.

"You know you can't use this to get out of Mother's lecture," Paisley said with a grin.

Dax wasn't smiling back at her. He was staring down at his leg.

"It really is frightful," he said. Paisley realized he was still wearing the magnifiers and that they must be making every scale on his leg look even bigger and darker.

She softly pushed the magnifiers onto the top of his head and pulled the handkerchief from his waistcoat pocket to wipe away his tears.

"I don't think it's frightful at all," she told him. "I think you and your leg are magnificent."

It was true. Paisley thought of the shopgirl, of her extraordinary ability. She remembered the way she had been treated and hated it—it wasn't fair or right. No one should live in fear of being who they were, especially not her little brother.

"I'm not magnificent, Paisley. I'm cursed."

Paisley cupped his cheeks in her hands and glimpsed her own stars glint out beneath her dragonhide bracelet

"We're all cursed, Dax," she said. "We're all trapped in our tracks. But you know what? I refuse to be ruled by mine or to let you be stuck in yours. I'm going to prove that we can *choose* our own tracks. I don't know how, but I promise you, Dax, if it can be done, then we will do it."

4

THE DAY OF SMALL TURNINGS

Paisley and Dax had almost finished building the Orrery. The replica of the Heavens sat on a low coffee table, its golden tracks showing the path of each of the planets and their moons. In the center was a brass sun, connected to the circular tracks by a network of cogs that lifted the tracks of the Celestial Mechanism off the table, suspended by long metal poles. Paisley sorted through the large wooden box. Only a few small cogs and pieces of rail glinting golden in the electrica light remained at the bottom.

Building the Orrery, along with receiving presents and eating festive food, was one of Dax's favorite parts of the Day of Small Turnings, when the sun turned for a short time in the sky and the long night signaled the start of winter and a new turning.

"Ahh, here it is!" Paisley reached into the box and picked out a little golden cog.

Dax came toward her, wearing his new brace and leaning heavily on his cane, his hand outstretched.

"I'm sure it gets more complicated every turning," he said as Paisley handed him the cog, unconsciously tugging down the cuff of her blouse to hide her bracelet-covered stars.

"I'm sure you're right. Only a few bits left, though we should have it finished before we need to leave for the lecture," she said, scooping the last few items from the box and following him over to the coffee table left of the sitting room windows, where they were building the Orrery.

"I wish we had an Orrery like they have in the Mechanist chapels," Dax said as he took another cog from Paisley and fixed it into place. "I'd love one with all the stars on it as well as the planets. That way we could use it to plot out your stars and see what your track holds, just like the Mechanists do when they forge the disk that prints your stars in the schematica."

Paisley resisted the urge to grab her wrist and looked at Dax, suspicious that he knew something. His face was blank.

"Wouldn't you like to know your fate?" he went on. "I think it's rotten that the Mechanists have kept it from you for so long."

Paisley tried to give an uninterested shrug, although she was sure that her cheeks were red. "It's not their fault," she said. "They can only tell me when the stars are right. But I'm not all that interested anyway. I intend to do what I want along my track."

Dax nodded. "Me too. But it would be nice to *know*, wouldn't it? And an Orrery with stars would help, I'm sure. I'm definitely going to ask Mother if we can get one for the next Day of Small Turnings."

Paisley felt hot inside as she thought about her stars—the idea of Dax knowing what the Chief Designer had in store for her filled her with dread. "Could you imagine how long that would take to put together?" Paisley said as she fixed a piece of the moon's track into place.

"Umm . . . you're right. This Orrery is fine—I guess."

"Besides, we wouldn't have the slightest idea how to read it— that knowledge is part of the most sacred Blueprints. Only the Mechanists know how."

At that moment, the door opened and Uncle Hector came bounding in. "Merry Turnings!" he called as he bumbled into the lounge, a mischievous twinkle in his eye.

Paisley put the cogs on the table and followed Dax, who had abandoned the Orrery and raced to greet Uncle Hector. Uncle Hector lifted Dax high in the air before hugging him close.

"What, you've almost finished the Orrery? I thought we were going to do it together?"

"Dax couldn't wait," Paisley said. She hugged her uncle hello, his beard bristles brushing her forehead as he kissed her.

"Sorry, I was a bit delayed. There's a Dragon Touched on the loose, and the Men of the Yard are stopping everyone to search for her. I got all the details from the Captain in charge of the search: They'd apprehended her after a struggle, but she used her Touch to escape." Uncle Hector gave a little shiver. "Gives me the creeps to think that she might be lurking about."

Paisley slipped her hand around Dax's shoulder and gave it a squeeze. He had gone pale and quiet. Uncle Hector noticed too. "Although nothing to worry about, I'm sure. The Touched can be ... unpredictable—all that hot dragon blood in them, I guess— but I'm sure that the Men of the Yard will find her soon and bring her to justice, nothing to fear."

Paisley thought there *was* much to fear; she knew what the justice of the Men of the Yard looked like for the girl with the red-scaled arms—and Dax, if they were ever to find out. She squeezed Dax again. She was sure that if Uncle Hector had only known about Dax's dragon leg, he would think differently about those who had the Touch.

"Well, it looks as if the two of you have done a fine job so far ... although one of those tracks looks a little wobbly." Uncle Hector moved over to the Orrery. "There. How about you finish it while I look over the evening edition of the *Herald* and then, when it's done, I get to turn the crank first? I think that sounds fair, as you did start without me!"

Dax gave his uncle an incredulous look. "Fine, but I get to put the Fire Diamond in."

"Agreed." Uncle Hector winked at Paisley.

She smiled and shook her head as she and Dax finished putting the last bits of the Orrery together.

"Anything interesting in the paper?" Paisley asked, after listening to Uncle Hector groan over the pages for a while. "Mother was in the morning edition."

"Yes, I saw that; she will be pleased!" he mocked. "Just more on the unrest in the Northern Realms. It seems that they continue to be without electrica power. Their giant Fire Diamond is still missing; you know they've got a special name for it—the Fire Diamond—they call it Soul Fire. The people are becoming quite mutinous, by all accounts. Well, you know how barbaric they are up there in the North. Apparently, they're blaming the George and his Knights, of all things! The King of the Northern Realms has even threatened to send his Krigare to the Empire."

"Really?" Dax asked.

Uncle Hector nodded, eyes still on the newspaper.

"Brilliant!"

"Oh yes, Dax. A flock of trained Luff Krigare on dragonback terrorizing the skies of London is just what we need on top of the Small Turning festivities and your mother's lecture this evening. Chaos and carnage will ensue." Uncle Hector gave a wry smile over the top of the newspaper. "Listen to this interesting bit of gossip.

According to the *Herald*, the Krigare have a new leader," he said as he continued reading. "The Princess Thea has taken over from her brother Hal—I guess he got a bit too old for it. Oh, she's only ten turns, Dax—same age as you!"

"I wish I was a Krigare," said Dax dreamily. "I've always wanted to ride a dragon."

"Me too," Paisley said with a nudge and a smile as she clicked the last cog into place.

"Me three," Uncle Hector said. "Your father and I once ran away to join. We made it as far as Liverpool Aerodoc Station before the butler found us and returned us to our parents." He sighed heavily. "But I'm far too old for it now and, Paisley, in a turn or two you will be too."

Paisley sighed. He was right. Dragons only trusted children, and at thirteen, she was on the eve of adulthood—not that she had the turns in her stars to get there, according to her recently revealed track. She felt a lump rise in her throat and her wrist burn with the weight of what was to come.

"Paisley?" said Dax. "Will you help me with the Fire Diamond?"

She nodded her head and swallowed the lump down. "Sure. Do you have the connector ready?"

Dax carefully adjusted the positive and negative connector plates. Then Paisley passed Dax the tweezers and slid open the lid of the box.

Inside was a tiny black stone, no bigger than a small gemstone.

Once the Fire Diamond was in place and the connecting plates lowered, it would be ready to set the sun and planets of the Orrery into motion.

Paisley held her breath as Dax reached in with the tweezers and pulled out the fire stone, safely securing it, ready to spark electrica through the machine.

"It's done," Dax proclaimed, the tension leaving his shoulders.

Uncle Hector folded his newspaper and came to stand beside them. "Ahh, this is the best bit!" Dax glared at his uncle as he turned the crank that lowered the plates to connect with the fire stone and set the Orrery into motion.

Paisley worried for a moment that they hadn't put all the cogs in the right place, but the universe soon began to spin.

Paisley looked at Uncle Hector's newspaper and gave Dax a nudge. "Imagine how fast it would go if we replaced our small Fire Diamond with Soul Fire!" she said.

Dax smiled, and Paisley knew he was imagining the planets spinning around at dizzying speeds.

"I've always wondered why we don't put the Orrery up for the Day of Long Turnings?" Dax asked as they watched the planets spinning around on their tracks.

"Well, the days are longer then, warmer, pleasant—just like it is in the Australias now. Ah, life is always brighter on the other side of the cog! Besides, there are better things to do on sunny days than sit inside and build," Uncle Hector said.

Dax gave Paisley a look that said, "Is he joking?"

"Well, we don't get presents then either," Paisley added.

"Presents!" Uncle Hector slapped his forehead. "I almost forgot presents!"

He reached inside his jacket and pulled out two small red gift boxes, each one tied with a golden ribbon.

"Thank you, can we open them now?" Dax asked

"Of course, but do it quick. I think I can hear your mother coming, and she will probably have ideas about opening presents before dinner!"

Paisley looked at Dax, both of them breaking into a grin before tugging the ribbons undone.

"Well?" said Uncle Hector. "Do you like them?"

Paisley looked over at Dax's open box; his gift was identical to hers. Inside sat a small mechanical dragon, made out of brass and copper and nightsilver; delicate scales covered the little dragon, and its eye was made from a glistening gemstone.

"It's beautiful," Paisley said, lifting it from the box. Moving its tail up and down made the mechanism within turn and spread the dragon's wings as it reared up on its legs from crouching.

"It's magnificent!" Dax exclaimed as he made his dragon move too.

Mother's voice sang from the door, "Presents already?"

"Look!" Dax rushed over to their mother, showing his dragon. Violetta put down the papers that she was carrying and pulled her glasses down from the top of her head. She shook back her dark chestnut hair, which fell down in loose curls around her shoulders, and took the small dragon in her long fingers, holding it up to the electrica light and examining it as she did everything.

"Gosh, that looks awfully intricate and expensive—and nightsilver! You shouldn't have, Hector!"

"I should have! They are my only niece and nephew, and you are all the family I have. I'm allowed to spoil you. *All* of you." He reached inside his coat and pulled out an identical box for Violetta.

"Hector." She took a step forward, her long skirt sweeping the floor, and kissed his cheek, just above his beard. "That is very kind of you."

"The Alchesmith at the forge makes hundreds of these little things as Small Turning gifts, and I thought, this way, if your comet does turn out to be just a boring lump of space rock, at least you will each have a tiny dragon of your own."

"Really, Hector!" She smiled and Uncle Hector let out a jovial laugh.

"Speaking of Comet Wolstenholme," she said, scooping up her papers and placing Uncle Hector's gift on the top. Violetta then struggled to pull her watch from her pocket, its long nightsilver chain linking her to it. "We had better have dinner now; I need to be at the institute early to set up." She kissed Dax on the head, then turned to Paisley and did the same. Paisley caught a scent of Mother's perfume, soft and mysterious, like the smell of old books and spices from the Eastern Empires.

"I'm counting on you to rally these menfolk for me, Paisley. Ensure they're not late."

"I'll do my best, Mother. But I can't make any promises," Paisley said with a smile as she followed her mother to the dining room.

5

ALL THE STARS IN MOTION

Roach leaned against the wall of the Dark Dragon's war room, listening to the Master of Stars's pen scratch on the parchment.

He'd been in this room a few times before. Like the rest of the Dark Dragon's subterranean lair, it was large and cold—even the addition of a giant fireplace had done nothing to warm the space. Roach wrapped his arms around himself as the light from a wall torch danced on his face. Like the fire, on the other side of the enormous table that dominated the room, its heat was sucked away before it reached him.

Still, Roach liked this room best of all. The walls were painted with a fresco that flickered in the torchlight. The images on the wall told the story of the creation. How the First Dragon Anu had helped the Chief Designer to forge the heavens, giving her breath to the stars and bending the tracks of the Celestial Mechanism all to the Designer's plans. How she worked tirelessly, until one day, exhausted, she fell to Earth and formed a great landmass that over millennia had broken up and traversed the globe. How her children, the Great Dragons, had shared the Earth with its inhabitants, until one man banished them all.

The Dark Dragon had told him the story when they first met. Roach had been younger then, but not too young to believe her at her word.

Unlike the man sitting writing at the table, who in Roach's opinion believed first, then found reason—like all Mechanists.

The Master of Stars was an old man, balding, with wisps of gray hair brushed over the top of his creamy scalp. His gnarled fingers held the pen like twisted tree roots, each one splattered with black ink, blooming like dark mold.

All the Dark Dragon's associates had grand titles. Even Roach had one—she called him the Master of Mischief—but Roach had always felt that knowledge was power and the name of a person or a thing held a special type of authority. He kept his true name to himself and had erased all connections between it and the one he had given to himself. To the world he was now Roach.

He had made sure to discover the true identities of everyone connected to the Dark Dragon.

The Master of Stars's identity had been easy to find. His knowledge of the Mechanism and skill at reading the Heavens could only be attained by a Major Mechanist. It hadn't taken Roach long to track down the Stararrium where he lived, worked, and worshipped. His work meant that he was in close contact with Arch Architect Harman, advising him on many things and whispering secrets back to the Dark Dragon.

Roach still did not know exactly why the Master of Stars had joined the Dark Dragon—he was the only one of the inner circle whose motives were unclear.

But the person that he was always most surprised about was the Dark Dragon herself. She had given her history freely. Even shared her ancient name, Sabra, and secrets of her distant origin. But Roach had not believed that she was who she claimed to be. How could she?

He searched and searched, and yet all he came up with was more and more proof that she was telling the truth. She was as old as the Great Dragons, and, if the Dragon Tales were to be believed, just as fierce.

"Ah . . . the stars are turning in our favor," the Master of Stars proclaimed.

The Dark Dragon sat up in the chair where she had been lounging next to him. "Soon I will have the power to steal the stars from their tracks and place them where I wish," she said, her face full of excitement. "But for now I am governed by them. What do they say of Malgol?"

"They say that the Great Dragon Malgol grows in power and

closeness. That you and he will be united. The professor is the key."

Roach shifted to standing upright as the Dark Dragon flicked her long plaited hair over her shoulder and curled it neatly around her head like a dark halo.

"What do the stars say of the Veil?" she said. "How will I breach it?"

The old man hesitated as he turned the scatter of stars on the chart and consulted a complicated table full of Old Celtic script in one of his many books. The Dark Dragon was just beginning to grow bored when the old man said, "That is unclear. But the way will present itself, eventually."

Not for the first time, Roach wondered if the Mechanist was just telling the Dark Dragon what she wanted to hear.

"Just out of curiosity," Roach interjected, "if you Mechanists can read the stars, and know all that is to come, then your lot must know about our mistress and what she's about to do. So why aren't all the Mechanists looking for us?"

"Who says that they aren't?" The Dark Dragon raised an eyebrow.

"Rest assured," replied the Master of Stars, smiling faintly, "there are very few who have the skill that I possess to tease out the hidden secrets of the stars. Most only have the skill to glimpse a fraction of the track ahead."

"If you say so," Roach said with a shrug. He often wondered if the Dark Dragon only ever showed him a fraction of what was to come, giving him just enough reason to believe that she would deliver on her promises so that he would do her bidding.

As he stood deep in thought, a small mechanical dragon flew in on wings of fine filigree metal and landed on the table in front of the Dark Dragon.

"Speak," she commanded, and the little dragon stood proud on the table and opened his mouth wide.

Roach recognized the voice of the Master of Lies at once. "All is proceeding as planned. I understand that the lecture is of the utmost importance to our course. I will attend and report back."

Roach watched as the Dark Dragon lifted the dragon-spy and placed it on her shoulder, where it draped itself and fell dormant.

"Yes, the lecture is important. I want to know everything the professor has found out about her so-called comet. The stars say, after all, that she is the key to the Veil, the key to unlocking it and restoring the Great Dragons to the world." The Dark Dragon paused, pensively stroking her delicate chin. "I am close, so close, to fulfilling the destiny that the Great Dragon Anu trusted in me, the destiny that she secretly forged into the Mechanism. She saw what the Chief Designer had planned, how the first George would hunt the Great Dragons and force them into the Veil of the Dead. How he and the sons of his sons would persecute the Dragon Touched, strike them from the land, vilify them, and kill them. She saw all this and chose me as her emissary. It is my destiny to control the Celestial Mechanism; I will decide the fates of all. I will not fail; the Great Dragons will be restored along with all those we have lost."

Roach felt his heart leap as she looked at him. *"Those we have lost."* There was the hope; there was the hook that pulled him deeper.

As he glanced at the Master of Stars, he saw the same look.

Maybe that was it. Maybe like him and the Master of Lies, he had someone in the Veil whom he could not live without, or whom he needed forgiveness from, or both.

"Roach, you will secure entry to this lecture," said the Dark Dragon. "You and I will see for ourselves what the professor has to say."

"Shouldn't be too difficult," Roach said. "The place will be busy, by all accounts. This comet has caught the imagination of the people— the *King's Herald* had a big piece on it this morning. Seems that all the fashionable people are excited about it."

"Let them be excited, for they will soon fear it." The Dark Dragon rose from her chair and walked toward Roach, her eyes low and dangerous. "If we are to pass as fashionable people, you had better rustle up some new clothes," she told him as she cast a disapproving eye over his thick woolen coat and dark trousers.

"These here clothes are inconspicuous, but if it's fashionable you want, not to worry. I'll be back in an hour looking the part and with two invitations to the lecture."

6

THE DRAGON IN THE MACHINE

The electrica car stopped outside the Institute of Celestial Mechanics, and Uncle Hector groaned loudly. "Do you think your mother would mind awfully if we gave it a miss?"

Paisley raised her eyebrows at her uncle as he made a face. "Do you want to let Mother down? Besides, you might find it interesting."

"No, no, I don't want to let Violetta down, my petal. But I very much doubt I'll find any of it interesting," Uncle Hector said as he exited the car and held the door open for Paisley. "I only ever understand about twenty percent of what your mother says, and then only if she speaks very, very slowly."

Dax gave a chuckle as he clambered out and stood next to Paisley. "Me too," he agreed. "But I still think it's fascinating, and besides, I want to learn more about that dragon."

"Dax, you know it's a comet, not a dragon," Paisley told him as she led the way up the stone steps to the doors of the Institute, the sky above the tall building a darkening blue. The floating borough of Kensington Above twinkled like a guiding star directly overhead.

"Ah, yes, a Great Dragon—now, that *would* be more interesting than all the science nonsense," Uncle Hector said. "I fully understand why the first George needed to get rid of the Great Dragons, but I always think the current George is missing a trick by banning the little ones from the Empire." He looked around him quickly. "I know it's traitorous to say so— but I think that's one thing that they do right in the Northern Realms."

Dax smiled up at his sister as she pushed open the double doors of the Institute, their heads full of dragons, their ears full of the buzz of chatter from the crowd filling the entrance hall.

Paisley had long since stopped trying to work out where everything was in the Institute of Celestial Mechanics. It was a giant kaleidoscope of a building, with more moving parts than a Mechanist chapel. The rooms, corridors, and lecture halls all moved, growing bigger or smaller with the turn of a cog. One day, there might be a series of connected spaces down a long corridor; the next, these may have been moved to form a large meeting hall. The interior layout of the building constantly changed to reflect the needs of the scientists.

Today the entrance hall was large and looming to accommodate all the people waiting for the lecture. And beyond the crowd,

Paisley could see the doors that would lead to the lecture hall.

"Are they all here for Mother?" Dax asked, surprised.

Paisley looked around at the crowd. "Yes, I think they are," she replied with a tone of shock—none of Mother's other lectures had ever had more than a handful of people viewing them, and most of those were family or colleagues.

There was such a large mix of people: scientists in their white coats and bow ties, newspaper reporters with their eager pens, and elegant, fashionable people enjoying being seen in academic circles. Among the crowd, Paisley spotted a little girl about the same age as Dax. She was petite and pretty and stood out in the sea of adults. Her long hair was as black as a dragon's shadow. She had an open, intelligent face that Paisley liked. The girl smiled at her for a moment, and Paisley smiled back before she saw a young man turn around behind the little girl. He followed the little girl's gaze and locked eyes with Paisley.

He was much taller than Paisley, maybe a turn or two older—fifteen or so, she guessed. He stood close to the girl, protectively, as she did with Dax. Maybe he was the little girl's brother, but his face was full of interesting angles, where hers was round and sweet; his skin was more olive, compared to the girl's paper-white complexion, and his hair was a little lighter than hers. Something about him tugged at the edge of Paisley's memory—she was sure she had seen him before. Then the crowd shifted, and the two of them were gone.

"Miss Fitzwilliam? I'm Corbett Grubbins." Paisley looked up and shook her head a little as she smiled at the boy in front of her. He hadn't been Mother's junior apprentice for long and was still in his first turning of study. Paisley swallowed down the rise of bitterness she felt; it wasn't Corbett's fault that only boys were allowed to start their apprenticeships at thirteen. Girls were allowed to start theirs then too, just not as scientists or explorers or anything that Paisley found interesting and exciting.

Paisley snapped on a smile. She looked at Corbett; he was tall for his age, with light sandy hair, tortoiseshell glasses, and a tartan waistcoat. "It's a pleasure to meet you," she said warmly. "Mother has spoken of you often." That was true; Violetta had nothing but praise for her new apprentice. She reached out a hand, which Corbett heartily shook. "How are you enjoying London?"

"Well, to be honest with you, I'm missing the Highlands a bit. London is busy, isn't it? But I'm too excited about the work we're doing to go back over the wall to Scotland just yet."

"I'm glad to hear it," said Paisley. "Mother is always saying how much of a help you are and what a brilliant scientist you are going to be one day."

Corbett blushed, but Paisley could see he was proud. "Aye, I hope so, miss."

"This is my brother, Dax, and my uncle, Hector," Paisley said. They all shook hands, and then Corbett glanced at the clock.

"It's starting soon. I've come to take you to your seats," he said. "The best ones in the house."

He led the way through the crowd to the doors of the lecture theater and ushered Paisley, Dax, and Uncle Hector toward the front. The seats filled up noisily behind them, and Corbett left through a door at the back of the presentation space.

"It's just like being at the theater, isn't it?" Dax said to Paisley as he looked at the audience in their seats and the large space in front of them.

He even gave a little "Ooh" when the electrica lights turned off, plunging the lecture hall into twilight and silence.

At the front, Corbett wheeled out an Orrery—it was far grander than the one they had at home.

Dax elbowed Paisley and leaned toward her. "Mother's been holding out on us!" he said.

Paisley grinned and rolled her eyes as she hushed him. But she had to admit, it was the most beautiful Orrery that she had ever seen, the Heavens depicted in brass and silver and copper. All looping tracks and glittering orbs.

In the center of the Orrery was a golden-filigreed sun covered with cut glass, behind which an electrica light shone. Around it, on brass tracks, sat all the planets and moons of the solar Mechanism.

Corbett turned a crank on the side of the Orrery, and the Heavens began to spin.

Some excited aahs escaped from where the fashionable people had seated themselves, and Dax poked Paisley in the ribs.

"It's even better than the ones in the chapels," he whispered. Paisley nodded in agreement.

She watched as the metal planets turned along their tracks, each one following the motion that the Chief Designer had set for it.

She hadn't noticed that her mother was standing at a lectern close to the machine until she started to speak.

The crowd hushed.

"My fellow scientists and distinguished seekers of the truth, welcome."

Violetta's voice was strong and clear. The light from the Orrery lit half her face, her chestnut curls neatly pinned in place, her long plum-colored taffeta skirt iridescent in the half-light. Paisley smiled as she watched her mother tug on the chain of her nightsilver watch, checking the time before placing it back in the pocket of her high-necked white shirt. Her mother was as calm as the sea before a storm.

Violetta cleared her throat, and Paisley felt a turn in the tide as her mother's look changed to one as unyielding as nightsilver.

"Today I wish to share with you a most wondrous and amazing finding. As you all know, a few weeks ago I discovered a comet traveling through our solar Mechanism from the Heavens beyond.

"What many of you do not know is that I was able to detect this comet long before the astronomers of the Empire could see it in their telescopes, by measuring the effect that it had on the tracks of the celestial bodies it passed."

As Mother said this, there was a murmur from the scientists and an uncomfortable stirring from the audience.

Mother continued unperturbed. "Some of my colleagues have suggested an explanation for this. They argue that, as the comet is very large and very fast, it has warped and melted the unseen tracks of the Mechanism, causing the objects traveling on the tracks to wobble and move. I think there is some interaction taking place—an influencing, if you will. But as for the warping of tracks, my fellow scientists are quite wrong."

Another murmur rippled throughout the audience. Paisley shifted slightly awkwardly in her seat; she looked behind her at the audience of socialites, scientists, and reporters.

She wasn't quite sure what her mother had said that was making people whisper, but the reporters looked perplexed, the scientists angry. As she turned back around, Paisley caught sight of the young girl from the entrance hall, and the boy, who Paisley assumed was her brother, sat next to her. He looked over at Paisley, his dark eyes narrowing slightly, his jaw set. Paisley felt an awkward thrill travel through her as he examined her. She met him look for look, taking in his smart bottle-green coat and black waistcoat and tie. His white shirt shining against his dusky skin. He looked away first, turning to face his sister.

The girl swiped her hand up, to stop him from speaking, and he balked. She was looking at Violetta with a sense of awe, the same awe that Corbett was looking at Violetta with.

Paisley tried to see what they saw in her mother, what was inspiring such looks of devotion.

She had always thought of her mother as different from other people, other parents. In the half darkness, Violetta's shadowy eyes flashed, and her light skin looked pale, like a spirit of the Veil, Paisley decided. Something otherworldly, and as if, just by talking, Violetta could shift the whole room, the entire world even, into her realm.

"Astronomers of the Empire have been compiling photographs of the comet." Violetta nodded at Corbett, who stood by the projector; he shone an image of the comet onto a large blank screen behind Violetta.

"These images have been collected by the Great Observatory of Gujarat. You will see how, over time, the comet follows its track across the sky."

Corbett clicked image after image on top of the original one. It was easy to join the dots of greenish light as the comet traveled along against the unmoving background of stars.

The lecture hall was silent, and Paisley had the impression that some of the scientists were holding their breath. She struggled to see what this demonstration of rudimentary Celestial Physics meant.

"Three nights ago," her mother went on calmly, "I performed an experiment unlike any before. I influenced Comet Wolstenholme as it had influenced those around it. With the aid of a machine of my own devising, I moved the comet and set it on a new track."

As Violetta said this, Corbett clicked three more images into place, showing the comet not continuing its smooth arc, but taking a steep upward turn and following a new trajectory.

For a moment, it felt like the universe stopped as Paisley took in the change and its implications. It was as if a new cog had suddenly been forged and was spinning the track of the world in an unknown direction—just like the track of the comet.

The room around her was eerily silent for a tick or two before it erupted. Shouts of the impossible rang out.

"Nonsense!" someone called. "Lies!"

"Fraud," someone else yelled. "This is a hoax."

"Blasphemer," a louder voice called. "Agent of the Dragon. Deceiver of the Mechanism. You speak lies. You can no more bend the tracks of the Mechanism than you can steal the stars. *All is fixed and moving to the Designer's will.* The Blueprints declare it as so."

Paisley craned her neck to see who was talking and saw a tall man wearing the white robes of a Mechanist Bishop. Paisley recognized him as Arch Architect Harman, head of the Albion Mechanists.

Violetta looked at the Bishop with a calm resolve. "I assure you, sir, this is the truth. The data has been verified by three independent sources. This is real. My experiment proves that we can forge new tracks for objects to follow out in the universe of the Celestial Mechanism or, I believe, anywhere else within it for that matter."

Paisley noticed that Mother was now looking straight at her and Dax.

If there was a way of moving the tracks, if Mother was right, then she was free to live ungoverned by her stars. She didn't have to die, she didn't have to fulfill her destiny, and neither did Dax.

They could make their own.

Paisley felt a giddiness descend upon her, rising from an unspeakable fear and into unwavering hope.

7

THE MEN OF THE YARD

As she lay in bed that night, Paisley could feel the cogs of the world spinning, or maybe it was just those in her head. She kept replaying what Mother had said, the photographs of the comet; the way that it struck out on a new course after the experiment.

"I set it on a new track."

Paisley pulled her hand out from under the covers and unclicked the dragonhide bracelet. The golden stars on her wrist glinted in the soft light from the streetlamps as it pushed through the curtains.

If Mother could change the course of the comet, then surely Paisley could change the course of her own track? If she could, she wouldn't be held to the fate of her stars; she wouldn't die.

But how would one even go about doing such a thing? Would she need to build a machine just like Mother had?

She had so many questions and wished that Mother was home. But she would be in her observatory on the floating borough of Greenwich Overhead now.

+ + ✳ + +

After the presentation, there had been no time for them to speak; Mother had to talk to reporters, scientists, and Arch Architect Harman.

Uncle Hector had been uncharacteristically quiet as he had brought them home. He kept turning the brim of his hat through his hands. "If only she had told me what she had found, and was plotting," he said at one point, "I could have warned her."

"Warned her of what?" Paisley had asked.

Uncle Hector seemed to shake himself a little. "Why, I would have warned her about the press. They're not going to leave her alone now, and neither will the Mechanists. Changing tracks isn't in their interest at all."

After Mrs. Keen had served them supper, Paisley and Dax were alone; they talked between mouthfuls of beef Wellington.

"Don't you see, Dax? *Tracks can be changed.* This means that we don't have to worry about the stars or stupid prophecies anymore. You're safe."

Dax shrugged as he pushed his food around his plate. "My stars never said anything about"—he lowered his voice and instinctively looked around—"my Dragon Touch. My stars say that I'm going to live *a long life full of fearless service to the Mechanism and that I will lead a great many cogs into action.* Whatever that means."

"It means that you'll probably end up being a Mechanist priest or Prime Minister."

"Urgh, I don't want to be either of those things—especially not Prime Minister."

"That's why you'll make a good one—I don't think anybody who wants to be Prime Minister ever should be," Paisley said. "Don't you think it's strange that your stars never mention *it*? Your Touch, I mean."

"Yes, but maybe the Chief Designer doesn't know everything." He looked up at Paisley. "And I guess, sometimes, things just don't go to plan."

Paisley thought hard about that as she lay in the darkness of her bedroom looking at her stars, wondering again if the Mechanism applied to the Dragon Touched. Dax had received his track when he was a baby, but the schematica made no mention of his Dragon Touch or of the prophecy. Maybe the Dragon Touched were special and the Chief Designer couldn't tell their fates as clearly as everyone else's.

A loud knock on the front door jolted her upright.

Who could be calling at this time? Paisley thought about what Uncle Hector had said about newspaper reporters and the Mechanists. She swung herself out of bed and crossed toward the window, half expecting to see Arch Architect Harman standing at the front door, his robes billowing, calling Mother a blasphemer.

The electrica streetlights shone in hazy rainbows in the freezing air. There was no Harman, but Paisley could make out the dark shapes of three men, and beyond the gates to the house was a vehicle covered in the crest of the Men of the Yard.

Paisley's heart skipped a beat.

She remembered the last time she'd seen the Men of the Yard. The shopgirl's frightened face filled her head, the way the Yardmen had pulled so roughly on the chain around her neck, the way she had writhed and cried.

Mother had told them what to do if the Yardmen ever turned up uninvited.

Paisley grabbed her dressing gown and ran at full speed to Dax's room as the knock on the door came again.

Visions of Dax chained up and being dragged from the house flooded her imagination.

"Dax, wake up!"

He sat up, looking groggy and frightened. "What . . . what is it?"

"The Men of the Yard are here. You've got to hide, Dax." Paisley crossed to the fireplace and pulled a secret latch on the wall next to it. A hidden door in the wood paneling sprang open to reveal a small, dark passageway.

The knocking came again, and this time Paisley could hear Mrs. Keen's keys jangling loudly as she moved through the hallway.

Paisley grabbed a blanket from the bed and wrapped it around her brother's shoulders. "I'll come get you as soon as they've gone, okay?"

Dax looked up at her and nodded. She kissed the top of his head, then led him to the passage, taking the electrica lamp from its hook on the wall and turning it on.

"Straight to the safe room. I'll be there soon."

Dax looked up at her, his face pale, his eyes wide and scared. Paisley smiled at him.

"I'm sure it's nothing. I'll be quick, I promise." He nodded again, and Paisley pulled the secret door shut, clicking it into place. She could feel her heart pounding as she put her ear against the wall and listened to the sound of Dax walking away.

She took a deep breath. *If my track ends because I am protecting Dax, then I'm okay with that*, she thought to herself. As long as he was safe, she could face the Veil and what lay beyond it.

Her breathing was back to normal as she quickly made his bed, throwing the leg brace under it. If the Men of the Yard asked where Dax was, she would tell them that he'd stayed the night at a friend's house.

Paisley raced down the stairs. The lights were on in the sitting room, and as she neared the door, she heard Mrs. Keen cry out.

Paisley stopped. She'd heard a cry like that once before, when the Principal of the League of Explorers had come to tell Mother that Father had perished.

Paisley's breath was fast as she burst into the room to find

Mrs. Keen was crying, and Uncle Hector was there too, comforting her, his face pale and jaw set. The two Yardmen looked at Paisley with somber expressions.

"Miss Fitzwilliam?" the taller of the two men asked. He was not dressed in the same red-and-black uniform as the younger Yardman; instead, he wore a quiet gray suit that matched his bleak expression.

Paisley looked from them to Uncle Hector.

Uncle Hector avoided her gaze. The Yardman carried on speaking, but Paisley's ears were full of a buzzing that made his voice muffled. "I'm Detective Bell. I'm sorry, miss, but . . ."

"It's all right," Uncle Hector said to the Yardmen. "I'll tell her." He gently released Mrs. Keen, and she crumpled onto the sofa, sobbing into her dressing gown uncontrollably.

Uncle Hector looked at Paisley for the first time, and she felt as if her cogs were spinning fast and slow all at once.

"Paisley, my flower." He took a step toward her, and Paisley held up both of her hands, her heart pounding, her throat tense, and tears already gathering.

"No, don't tell me. I don't want to know." Paisley felt a trembling rise inside her, as if two cogs were grinding painfully together.

"I'm so sorry. There was an accident at the observatory that your mother was working in. It would seem that her experiment failed. It caused an explosion and—"

"She's gone!" Mrs. Keen wailed. "The mistress is dead. The

explosion killed her and blew a great hole in the floating borough. Oh, to think of her body being sucked out of the borough and dashed in the frozen Thames."

Paisley didn't want to think of it, but it was all that filled her mind. Her legs trembled; she flung her arms around herself and moved away from Uncle Hector as he reached out to her.

She turned toward the Yardmen, the tears flowing freely now.

"Is that true? Is she dead?"

"I'm afraid so, miss—no one can survive a fall from that height."

Paisley nodded. "The Thames . . . did she land in the river?"

"No, miss. We haven't . . . er, that is to say . . . It's just a matter of time before we find her body. I'm sorry, miss."

Paisley thought of the last time she had seen her mother, just a few short hours ago. She remembered the way that the light had shone on her, making her look like a spirit of the Veil, and Paisley wondered now if it might have been a premonition. Grandmama Fiona was always said to have had the gift to see into the Veil; Paisley had often wondered, hoped even, that she might have a tiny spark of it.

She turned to Uncle Hector. "Are you sure it was an accident? I mean, even you yourself said that there were many people at the lecture last night who were not happy with what Mother had to say, not happy at all." She remembered the look on the Mechanists' faces: angry and hateful.

"The Men of the Yard are quite sure, Paisley," Uncle Hector said softly.

"We have no reason to suspect that this was anything other than a tragic accident, but rest assured, we will be conducting a thorough investigation, miss," Detective Bell said.

"I understand." Paisley wiped her tears.

The detective continued to look at Paisley. "We are authorized to search the study and if necessary remove any relevant paperwork— just temporarily, you understand. To help with the investigation." He shifted his gaze to Uncle Hector.

"Yes, yes, of course . . . let me show you where the study is." Uncle Hector got up and escorted the men to the library, squeezing Paisley's shoulder as he passed her.

The room felt big and hollow. Mrs. Keen continued to cry on the sofa. Paisley wiped her eyes on the cuff of her dressing gown, then shook back her hair and crossed to the brandy bottle. She poured a drink and handed it to Mrs. Keen. "Sit here for as long as you need to," she said. "I'll tell Dax."

8

THE DARKNESS OF DREAMS

Roach walked through the back alleys, descending lower and lower with each step. Soon he passed through an arch and entered a little-known door. Beyond it were steep steps cut into the ground that led down into the sewers beneath the great city.

He scuttled along the midnight-black passages, dodging unpleasant puddles as his eyes adjusted to the darkness. He looked for the tiny flicker of fiery movement that was his guide.

He listened to the dark, picking up the faint beating of the dragon-spy's wings as he followed it obediently.

Even as a small child, Roach had felt comfortable in the dark, never scared of what it held. But down here, he shivered. Down here there be dragons.

A rush of water swept past him; it was a grumble when it first met his ears, but now it was a roar as a torrent of dirty water filled the sewer, its spittle spraying the stones of the narrow walkway. Roach trod with care.

The last time he had been summoned in the middle of the night by the Dark Dragon, he had ended up accompanying her on a trip to the North. He gave a little shiver, remembering how cold it had been, colder still after he had stolen the Fire Diamond.

The dragon-spy flitted ahead, beckoning him on with every flash of fire.

Roach felt his unease grow as he caught each flare.

After the lecture, he had arrived back at the modest rooms he called home in the small hours of the night to find the dragon-spy waiting for him, perched on the photogram that sat next to his bed, its metal wings folded neatly, its mechanical head turning from side to side as its pixelated eyes recorded every deed it saw.

Roach had fought the urge to tip the dragon-spy from the photogram. It lay lazily on the frame, its tail curling around the face of the little girl in the picture.

Roach kept his eyes on the picture, remembering exactly why he was in league with the Dark Dragon and what he wanted to get out of their partnership.

As the dragon-spy opened its mouth, the Dark Dragon's voice filled the room. He could hear both excitement and rage in her voice as she summoned him back to her.

He'd followed the tiny dragon halfway across London, sticking to the back alleys and cut-throughs.

The dragon-spy had stayed in the shadows, always ahead, signaling via the small red bulb in its mechanical mouth that Roach was to follow it down into the sewers.

Now, deep in the belly of the city, it flashed again, beckoning him on, past the roar of the water dying in the darkness. Roach found his feet slipping as he moved uphill along a narrow passage.

As the darkness lessened, an unease spread inside him. It was always the same when he met her, the shock of seeing someone so young hold so much power. At first, he had felt slightly cheated. But he soon came to realize how wrong he was to make assumptions about the tiny girl. Now the Dark Dragon filled him with a deep dread that no grown man ever could.

The passage continued. A glow came from a small room full of copper pipes and pressure gauges with large turning wheels to open and close the valves of the underground sewers.

The orange electrica lighting reminded Roach of dragon's breath, and the dark silhouette of the young girl in the middle of the room seemed to twist and flicker like a black flame.

The hood of her taffeta cloak covered her head, pulled down over her face. The cloak itself was short, falling to just above her knee, her tall boots and dragonhide trousers showing. Her long black hair was plaited in the style of the North and pulled around to the front, snaking over her chest.

Roach bowed his head, keeping his eyes on her.

The Dark Dragon spoke. Her voice was smooth as nightsilver and just as strong.

"Something is missing," she told him straight.

Roach paused and looked around him, trying to work out what she might be getting at, but he was at a complete loss.

The Dark Dragon thrust a small dragonhide journal at him; the page was open, and it was covered in elegant Old Celtic handwriting and a hand-drawn diagram of a shaded black rock. Roach recognized it at once.

"It would seem that we have underestimated the professor," the Dark Dragon said as she pulled the journal back toward her and flipped the page. "Her maternal family line—the Daxons—are in possession of a Heart Stone." She ripped a photogram from the pages of the journal and handed it to Roach.

The photogram was old, forty turnings or more, Roach guessed by the fashion of the time, the way the smiling woman wore her hair, and her long, layered dress that fanned out as she was captured mid-dance. On her neck, she wore a large dark gemstone, so black it almost shone. It was set in a golden mount on a long chain.

"Violetta's mother, Fiona. She had the Heart Stone made into a necklace." The Dark Dragon did not hide her feelings on that. "The fool never knew what she had, but Violetta did. In her journal, she said that she discovered it among her mother's things on

Kensington Above, and as soon as she saw it, she realized its Fire Diamond—like properties. It was what made her experiment possible. The power of the Heart Stone pushed the Dragon onto a new track. And now I need it to pull the Dragon onto one that leads to me."

"Do you need it?" Roach asked, raising a dark eyebrow.

The Dark Dragon reached into her pocket and pulled out her prize from the North—Soul Fire. "Yes, soon I will have all four stones; then I will wield so much power that not even the Chief Designer will be able to stop my track," she told him with an intensity that made Roach feel uncomfortable.

Roach nodded. "Where would you like me to search?" he asked.

"The Fitzwilliam house. The Master of Lies has already checked the study while the family was unaware, but she may have it in her dressing room. If not, it may be in the Daxon family's Dragon Vault."

"The Dragon Vault." Roach gave a little snort. "Shouldn't be too difficult, then."

"I can get you inside, but you'll need one of the Fitzwilliam children to open the vault."

Roach instantly thought of Paisley.

"Very well. Consider it done."

9

NIGHTSILVER PROMISES

A freezing fog had settled over London during the night, scattering the weak winter dawn into an eerie glow.

Paisley woke in Dax's room. He was curled up asleep next to her in his bed, a welcome warmth in the cold room.

She sat up and listened to the world quietly waking beyond the window. She gave a shiver; there was no fire in the grate. Paisley was about to get up and call for Mrs. Keen when she remembered the last time she had seen her: the sitting room, the Men of the Yard, Mother.

Paisley closed her eyes tight.

The world felt as if it was turning too fast.

The pain of loss sat heavy in her chest like a breath she couldn't quite get out. The feeling stung in her lungs and made her body rigid and full of a dull ache. The last time Paisley remembered feeling like this was when her mother had told her about her father's track ending.

Paisley looked down at Dax as he slept, his unruly curls falling down over his eyes. Surely he was feeling this pain too. Paisley had held him tight as they had both cried into the night. She was determined that Dax wouldn't feel this way again. Not now. Not for her.

Paisley needed her mother now more than ever. She needed her help to find a way to move her own track, just as Mother had that of the comet.

There had to be a way to cheat fate. To steal back her stars and reclaim her destiny. But, she realized, without Mother's help and knowledge, her track would soon end and Dax would be left *all* alone.

Who would help him? Who would keep him safe? Besides her, Mrs. Keen was the only other person in the world who knew the truth of Dax's *condition*. And although Mrs. Keen was kind and loving, she wasn't brave or strong or clever, not in the same way Mother had been. She wore her heart and feelings on her sleeve, and even though she'd never betray Dax, she'd also never be able to fight for him, not in the same way Father could have, not in the way that Paisley would.

Paisley's mind whirled; she could always tell Uncle Hector. Yes, that was it. Uncle Hector would help. He loved Paisley and Dax as if they were his own children; he would never see them in danger or trouble.

But then Paisley hesitated; Mother had always said the knowledge of Dax's true nature was not something to be shared without extreme caution.

Paisley slipped from the bed and began to make the fire.

There must be a reason why Uncle Hector had never been told.

Paisley thought this through as she stacked and lit the kindling. Uncle Hector was funny and gentle and loved to gossip and . . . yes, that was it. She wasn't sure her uncle could be entirely trusted with a secret.

As the flames glowed in the hearth, she felt a little sob rise in her chest.

If she couldn't tell anyone, then Dax would soon be all alone. Her stars played heavily on her mind. She remembered what the scroll had said:

Before the end of your fourteenth turning, your cog will cease, your track will end, and you will die.

She thought hard about what the rest of the scroll had contained and berated herself for losing it. When she had returned home that day, she had searched her satchel for it, wanting to read it again, wanting to see if it still rang true, but the scroll was missing. She remembered taking it from the schematica—she was sure that she had put it in her satchel—but it wasn't there or in her coat pockets when she had checked them too. She must have lost it while she had wandered the streets of Lower London feeling sorry for her stars, or perhaps it fell from her pocket when the Dragon Touched shopgirl's roar had made her faint.

Paisley stared into the flames, feeling the searing pain of her loss, until the flames remained when she closed her eyes, her tears drying in the heat.

Mother couldn't be gone; she just couldn't. Mother was always there, always. She would never leave Paisley and Dax. Mother could move the Mechanism; why would the Chief Designer stop her track now? Maybe someone had stopped it intentionally? Was such a thing possible? Just yesterday Paisley would have said no—but so much had changed. Mother had moved the Mechanism; anything was possible.

Paisley glanced behind, worried that dark forces were moving around her.

She got up and crossed to the window, peering up and down the street.

She let out a sigh and looked up into the pale dawn light, the dark silhouette of Camden Beyond floating across the sky, the snow clouds behind it. This was silly; there was no one out there; no one had done this. It was an accident, just as the Men of the Yard had said.

Paisley was about to drop the curtain when she saw movement in the garden. Someone was out there, moving toward the back of the house, a tall, thin someone in a long dark coat.

Paisley slipped from the room as a small point of concentrated fear rose inside her.

At the top of the stairs was her father's suit of nightsilver armor. A monument to him. As Paisley passed, she silently released his sword and swung it deftly in her right hand, ready to attack whoever had come for her and her family.

Fear sharpens the mind, Father used to tell her.

She moved swiftly down the stairs and across the hall toward the alcove that led down to the kitchen and the garden beyond.

Once at the bottom, she took a stealthy look into the kitchen; there was a shadow at the back door. As she swiftly turned back to change her course, she heard the handle on the door rattle.

Paisley crossed the hall to the sitting room quickly and silently; she ran across the room, the Orrery moving smoothly to her left as she leaped over the nearest couch and pulled up one of the sash windows. It squealed sharply, and Paisley inhaled rapidly before climbing onto the sill and swinging herself out of the window.

She landed in a dull thudding crouch, her nightgown billowing in the cold, her father's sword held straight out to her side. It had snowed in the night, and Paisley could easily see the footprints that had been left by the shadow.

She took care to step only in the marks already made, moving at a swift pace, the cold snow pushing between her tiptoes, the sword up, ready to strike.

As she turned the corner of the house, she could see that the intruder had his back to her and his face pressed up against the glass of the kitchen door, hands shielding his eyes as he peered in.

Paisley slowed her steps and steadied her breath, just as Father had taught her. She had the element of surprise and wasn't about to give it away.

She took a step closer, twisting the sword in her hand, then jumping to bring the hilt down and strike the intruder on the head.

It worked. He went down hard, falling into a large drift of snow.

Paisley held the sword at his neck as she crouched and pulled him onto his back, revealing his face.

"Corbett?" Paisley recognized her mother's apprentice from the evening before; he was even wearing the same tartan waistcoat.

"Oh no." She quickly pressed her ear to Corbett's chest; she could hear his heart pumping.

Then she looked at him and whispered a quick "sorry" as she straightened his glasses.

The snow had started again; small wispy flecks of white landed on Corbett's sandy-colored hair.

He'd catch his death if he stayed out here; so would she, Paisley realized as the adrenaline faded from her and cold seeped in.

She tried the kitchen door as Corbett had, but of course it was locked. She'd have to go back the way she had come and drag Corbett into the kitchen.

She ran to the sitting room window, thinking how any other day

Mrs. Keen would have already been in the kitchen getting breakfast ready.

The windowsill to the sitting room was at chest height. She took it at a run, stepping one foot up onto the wall of the house, then pushing up for the window ledge. She heaved herself through the window, landing with a somersaulting thud on the other side. The sword clanged to the ground.

She scooped it up and closed the window before running to the kitchen.

After opening the back door, Paisley stepped out into the snow and looked around in amazement. Corbett was gone.

"Hello?" she called, following the footsteps that continued around the house in the fresh snow.

She called out again, and he turned the corner of the house, looking dazed and holding the back of his head.

"I think I slipped over," he told her as he stumbled toward her on punch-drunk legs. "Careful, it's icy under the snow," he warned as his legs gave. Paisley rushed to his side and propped him up. Guilt made her cheeks glow.

"Come on, let's get you inside."

"Can't," Corbett mumbled. "I've got important work to do." His eyes focused on somewhere just left of Paisley.

"The comet can wait, Mr. Grubbins," Paisley said, dragging him toward the kitchen.

"It's not the comet. It's your mother."

Paisley settled Corbett down at the table in the center of the kitchen.

"My mother?"

"Yes, there's something you need to know."

She looked him straight in the eyes. "The Men of the Yard came last night; I know about the accident. I know that her track has ended."

She bit her lip to stop the tears and Corbett grabbed her wrist.

"No, no, it's not. She's not dead."

Paisley felt sorry for the poor lad—the hit to his head had made him confused in his grief.

"I know, it feels like her cog is still turning, but . . ."

Corbett looked earnestly at Paisley, his focus clearing. "No, you don't understand. She's still alive, and I can prove it to you."

Corbett dug his fist in his pocket and pulled out a small object that he thrust into Paisley's hand.

He let go of her wrist as she looked down at it.

"Mother's pocket watch!" She turned the black metal watch over in her hands before flipping open the front to reveal the elegant face and slim, ticking hands.

"Why do you have it? She always kept it with her; it was a gift from Father."

"She left it in her office and had me fetch it before she did the experiment; I was on my way back to the observatory when . . . but that's not important. What is key is that it's made from nightsilver."

"Yes, I can see that, Mr. Grubbins." She really must have hit his head hard.

"And," Corbett added, "it's warm."

Paisley's eyes widened. Corbett was right; the watch was warm. She held it to her cheek and felt the soft glow that came from the metal.

"Mother always used to say that she knew Father was dead because his armor was made of nightsilver and the silver was cold, therefore so was he, but how can that be?"

"My family are Alchesmiths," Corbett said. "It's a little-known Silver Law that when they make nightsilver, they unite the metal with the blood of the person that the object is for."

Paisley blinked as she looked at him, unsure of what he had just said. She knew that nightsilver was mysterious, a combination of silversmithing and alchemy. It was only made by a few forges, and the practices of the Alchesmiths were shrouded in secrecy.

"Blood?" she asked, looking down at the watch in her hand.

"Blood. Alchesmiths call it *marrying*; we marry the consort with the metal through the blood. But as a scientist, your mother called it something else—*entanglement*. She said it was a way of bonding the atoms in her to the atoms in her machine and the metal of the watch."

"And that's why it's warm?"

Corbett nodded. "The nightsilver was made with her blood and is warm because she is, because she is alive. If her track was ended, then the nightsilver would be dull and cold and brittle, but until then, it's warm and strong. In fact, it is virtually unbreakable, like your mother's will."

Paisley wrapped her fingers around the watch. "She's alive," she whispered.

Corbett nodded. "She is."

Paisley dashed the tears away as she allowed herself to hope.

"Tell me more about nightsilver and Mother's machine; how did it push the comet to a new track? Is it like a magnet? Could I use the watch to find Mother—like a compass finds magnetic north?" Paisley asked, her mind reeling with possibilities.

Corbett began to pace the room, pushing back his glasses and digging both his hands into his trouser pockets. "Not magnetism— nightsilver isn't magnetic; it's neutral—but it does have force.

"It's not just about the sharing of blood and heat when night-silver is bonded to a person—there is something else too. The metal takes on some of the characteristics of the consort." Corbett stopped pacing and stood next to Paisley. "Can I see your mother's watch?"

Paisley lifted the watch by the chain and lowered it into Corbett's hand.

He turned it in the light. "There are subtleties at play." He unbuttoned his shirt cuff and pulled it back to reveal a nightsilver bangle. He held the watch next to the bangle.

"Look. You may think that the two are made of the same metal, but they are as different from each other as you and I."

Paisley leaned closer, examining the two shining black surfaces.

"They look the same to me," she said, her brow furrowing.

Corbett moved the objects around in the light, and Paisley thought she caught a hint of what he was talking about. Mother's watch was a deeper, darker black, whereas Corbett's bangle reflected just a tiny bit more light.

"Here." He passed the watch to her and then his bangle; she held one in each hand and weighed them.

"Close your eyes. What do you feel?"

Mother's watch was heavier, but they also felt different from each other in a way that she couldn't explain. As though each one had a different taste that her skin could detect.

Corbett smiled. "You see what I mean?"

Paisley nodded. "So, this difference is what forced the comet to change course?"

"I don't know, a little. This might sound strange, but I think if the machine was made with anyone else's blood, it would not have been able to move the comet. Your mother's special, Paisley."

Paisley looked up at Corbett, giving him back his bangle and clenching her mother's watch in her hand. "You're right, and she's alive. The only questions are where she is and how we get her back."

10

DARK ACTS

Roach had arrived at the Fitzwilliam house shortly before dawn. He huddled in the large evergreen bushes at the side of the house, his collar turned up against the wind. Every now and again he would stomp his boots on the frozen ground around the roots of the bush and wiggle his toes, pulling his thick black coat farther around him.

The electrica streetlights went out and plunged the world into a fresh darkness. Roach had found that dark acts were always best done at night.

The snow started to fall thickly, and Roach allowed himself a small smile as a memory flitted across his mind, a memory of snow and laughter, and his little sister, her long plaits flowing as she ran through the falling flakes, squealing in delight. He caught the memory and quickly wiped it away, his customary stony look back in a blink.

He focused his mind on the task at hand. He was waiting, waiting for just the right moment. Roach had entered many houses uninvited; he had found from experience that if you are patient enough, then an opportunity will present itself.

This time opportunity presented itself in the shape of Corbett Grubbins. Roach knew everything about the young lad from Inverness, who had grown up in a silversmith's forge and whose stars had been aligned with those he so wanted to study. This boy had never had to worry or work hard. His stars had lit his track and smoothed the turning of his cogs.

Roach watched as the apprentice scientist made his way up the path toward the front of the house. He heard a knock on the door; then a moment later Corbett appeared again, making his way around to the opposite side of the house that Roach was on.

He waited for a little while, then followed, moving slowly and stiffly as the cold pushed its way out of his body.

As Roach turned the corner of the house, a front window opened. He snapped up against the brickwork of the building and slid back around the corner, watching from cover as Paisley fell out of the window, landing lightly in the snow, a nightsilver sword in hand. The black metal sang amid the white of the snow.

He watched as Paisley made her way in pursuit of Corbett. As soon as she was out of sight, he leaped up the side of the house, reaching for the window and pulling himself in.

He stopped and gazed at the sitting room—the lavish blue sofas and armchairs, the large gold-edged mirror above the fireplace, the thick, large rug in the center of the room that he was sure had come from the lands to the east of the Empire.

He gravitated toward the Orrery and reached out a finger, stroking the golden track. They had never been able to afford an Orrery when he was little. One Small Turning, he had made one from wood and presented it to his mother on the Day of Small Turnings. It didn't turn and the sizes were all wrong, but he'd been so proud of the look on his mother's face, and the giggling of his sister, Clara, when he'd presented it to her.

Roach looked down and realized that the snow from his shoes was dripping water all over the wooden flooring.

He stepped onto the rug, softly wiping his feet on the thick fibers of the carpet.

A gust of cold wind blew in through the window, and Roach followed it through the open door, into the hallway, and up the stairs.

He had just reached the top when he heard a noise and looked back to see Paisley rushing through the hall toward the kitchen stairs.

He paused for a heartbeat and listened to the stillness that returned to the house.

The Dark Dragon had given him a map of the Fitzwilliams' home and strict instructions not to be seen.

He had snickered as she'd said that and had half expected to be punished for it. Roach had never been caught thieving—not once. Not even the Krigare of the North, with all their dragon guard, had been able to catch him when he had stolen Soul Fire. A house of two children was not a challenge. He was as silent as a dragon's shadow and twice as cunning.

The nightsilver armor on the landing caught his attention. He saw where Paisley had pulled the sword from and caught his own reflection in the dark black metal.

The Dark Dragon had first become interested in the Fitzwilliam family when Sir Edmund had died. It had been Roach's job to find out all he could about the family, to gather facts and lies and find the truth that hid in both.

He ran a finger over the nightsilver and looked deep into his own dark eyes in its reflection. His olive skin looked almost ghostly in the metal, and he shivered, feeling that the Veil had brushed past close to his track and that those he loved in it had reached out to touch him.

Roach pulled his mind back to the plan of the house that was scribbled on the paper in his coat pocket, and made his way to Violetta's bedroom. Before he could get there, though, he heard Paisley coming up the stairs. He darted into the nearest room and pushed the door behind him, watching as she moved away from the armor and into her bedroom.

Roach was about to leave when he heard a shifting behind him. In the large bed, he saw Dax sprawled out and dreaming. The heat from the fire had warmed the room, and the boy had kicked his covers back.

Roach narrowed his eyes and took a step closer to the bed. The green-black scales on Dax's dragon leg danced in the light from the fire.

Roach knew that if he were to touch the scales they would be as soft as velvet and hard as nightsilver all at once, just like Clara's scales had been. Hers had not been on her leg, though. Hers had covered her back and from them had sprung two small wings of the brightest sapphire blue.

His breath caught in his chest as he thought of his little sister. She would have been about the same age as Dax now if the Men of the Yard hadn't found her.

Dax stirred in his sleep.

A Dragon Touched boy. It was a Dragon Touched boy who would fulfill the prophecy of the Dragon Lord, who would call forth the Great Dragon Malgol, and together they would avenge Anu and punish the George.

Roach froze to the spot as a realization hit him. Dax was a *Dragon Touched boy*. Dax was the Dragon Lord.

Roach moved a hand inside his coat and pulled out a short sharp dagger. He could kill him now. That way no one would be able to hurt him—not the Men of the Yard, not the George, not the Dark Dragon. Roach had no doubt that if she knew about Dax, she would use him to fulfill the prophecy of the Dragon Lord, the boy destined to return and rule with the Great Dragons of old.

Roach's thoughts raced through the Dark Dragon's plan. If it worked, if she succeeded, then Dax and all the other Dragon Touched never had to live in fear again. But if she didn't and the Men of the Yard found him . . . Roach shook his head, his dark hair fanning out. He didn't want to think of Dax's fate, but he knew it would be worse than Clara's.

Roach held the dagger tight while trying to decide which way his track leaned.

Moments later, he slipped from Dax's bedroom and made his way to Violetta's. If the Heart Stone was there, he would find it.

11

A DISCOVERY OF DRAGONS

Paisley hurried from her bedroom and passed her mother's room, unaware that Roach was inside, silently seeking treasure.

She had shed her nightdress and now rushed down the stairs dressed in a topaz-colored skirt and white shirt, over the top of which she wore a nut-brown waistcoat. In the pocket sat her mother's watch, warm and solid and reassuring.

As she got closer to the kitchen, she could smell fresh coffee and the first whiff of bacon. Corbett was sitting at the table where she had left him a short time ago, but now he was joined by Mrs. Keen, who was busy fussing around the stove.

"Morning, miss." Mrs. Keen's eyes were puffy, and her face was white.

Paisley walked over to her and gave her a quick hug. She couldn't tell her about the watch, not yet. She didn't want to get anyone's hopes up.

Mrs. Keen started to cry a little and wiped her face with her apron as she pulled back from Paisley.

"I didn't introduce Mr. Grubbins to you," Paisley added.

"Not to worry, my lovely. Me and young Corbett have long since made our acquaintances. Your mother would often send him to the house to pick up papers and such that she'd left in her study," she said, bustling about the breakfast, cutting two muffins and putting them to cook on the griddle. "I expect your uncle will be around soon too, Paisley."

"I'm surprised he isn't here already," Paisley said as she helped herself to coffee with cream and sugar and sat next to Corbett.

"Well, I need to get out—a bit of chill air will do me good, and now that it's started snowing in earnest, I need to make some arrangements with the butcher and the coal merchant. After all, the Mechanism still turns and your mother—well, she always did like things done proper."

She dished up three plates of buttered muffins, eggs, and crisp bacon and placed a plate each in front of Paisley and Corbett, adding the third to the warming oven. "That's for Dax when he wakes," she said. She reached for her coat and hat, pulling on both followed by her sturdy winter boots.

"I'll be back just after lunchtime—I've left some cold cuts and bread for you. There's enough for you too, Corbett, if you want," she said as she picked up her basket and headed out the back door, giving them both a wave.

Paisley knew that Mrs. Keen was being strong, that she didn't want anyone seeing her cry, and she felt a twist of guilt as her fingers strayed to the watch, warm in her pocket.

"You were right not to tell her," Corbett said, reading her mind between forks full of scrambled eggs.

"It doesn't feel right," Paisley said as she scooped up her own eggs. "If I told her, she wouldn't suffer; she'd have hope, like I do."

"I understand. And you *will* tell her, but I think you were right not to do it yet."

Paisley took a long time to chew before saying, "When we know more, I'll tell her, and Dax too. I hate the idea of keeping things from him. But if it turns out that she is . . . or that I can't save her, then giving him that hope and snatching it away would be far worse."

Corbett nodded, then swallowed down his breakfast with a swig of coffee. "I've been thinking about who would want to take your mother. I think we can work out the why—they wanted to stop her from performing her experiment anymore."

"Surely Mother's experiment is for the good of all, the progress of knowledge, the advancement of science—"

"And the destruction of everything we believe about the universe, the Celestial Mechanism, and the Chief Designer," Corbett interrupted. "It's a brilliant discovery; I can't fault the logic or the science, but still … it scares me, and I think others feel the same way too."

Corbett put his hand in the breast pocket of his jacket and pulled out a small notebook. He pushed his plate away, and Paisley leaned closer as he opened the book and smoothed down a page.

"I've made a list of the people who I think would have wanted to stop your mother."

Paisley looked at Corbett's list. His handwriting was just like him, she realized: careful, considered, and regular. She read the list out loud.

"Arch Architect Harman—Head of the Imperial Mechanists. Guy Tennyson—Master of Greenwich Overhead. Dr. Derek Langley—Dragonologist. Hector Fitzwilliam—"

She looked up. "Why is Uncle Hector on this list?"

Corbett ran his hand over the page, then looked straight at Paisley. "They had words. Last night, your mother and I returned to her laboratory on Greenwich Overhead to perform her experiment again, and your uncle followed her there.

"I wasn't eavesdropping. Your mother had sent me to fetch her watch; she'd left it in her office two floors below when she'd got changed into her work clothes and lab coat. When I got to her office, I realized that she hadn't given me the key, so I went back to retrieve it and that's when I heard them. They were both very angry with each other. He wanted to know why she hadn't told him about the ramifications of the experiment."

Paisley nodded. "That makes sense. He said something about that when he dropped me and Dax back here after the lecture; he was worried about her. He must have gone to Greenwich Overhead instead of heading home."

"Maybe, I guess so. He asked her to give him something, and she refused. He told her that for all her learning she knew nothing. Then he stormed out of the room and almost knocked me over. Your mother was . . . emotional when I went in to get the key. I left to fetch the watch, and that was the last time I saw her."

"Oh no, poor Uncle Hector," said Paisley softly. "I bet he feels terrible. He's quite a sensitive person, really, for all his pomp. And since Father died, he's become very important to us all, Dax especially; he is his heir, after all."

Paisley shifted in her seat before she continued. "To think that they had words, and that the Men of the Yard had gone to him and told him before they came here. No wonder Uncle Hector left so soon after the Men of the Yard. He probably blames himself in some way and felt that he couldn't stay in this house."

Paisley gave a little cough to clear the tightness that had gathered in her throat. She ran a finger down the page of Corbett's book, pausing at Harman's name.

"I agree with you on the Arch Architect—I think he would have stopped Mother's cog at the lecture if he could have. Why do you suspect Master Tennyson? He's the head of the Institute, isn't he?"

"Aye, and he was never that welcoming of your mother. I think he was secretly a little jealous that she found this comet too. Her findings change absolutely everything. Not just for the Mechanists but for the foundations of Celestial Mechanics and the way we see the world, the universe even. The implications are ... huge. If they could remove your mother and denounce her work, then nothing would change."

Paisley nodded. She could see the headlines in the *King's Herald* already. *Lady Scientist is a fraud!*

"What about this Dr. Langley, the Dragonologist?" Paisley gave a little smirk. "I don't think Mother ever cared too much about dragons, not the Great Dragons of myth anyway, though she told us all the Dragon Tales. My grandmama Fiona had brought her up on them, although Mother had firmly placed them all in the realms of make-believe. Actual dragons are a different matter, however, but since Dragonologists insist that there is a direct lineage from the Great Dragons, Mother always had a little disdain for the science and all who practice it."

Corbett was smiling. "Really? That's interesting," he said before draining his cup of coffee. "Come with me."

Paisley followed Corbett up the stairs from the kitchen and into the library. It was strange following someone who she had never known was so familiar with her house. She kept expecting him to get lost, but he ended up right where he wanted to be, in Mother's study. He even knew which bookcase and book he wanted.

He pulled a small, thick volume from the shelf and began to flick through it.

"Here. Do you know this man?" he asked Paisley, turning the open book toward her and showing a photogram of an elderly gentleman with white hair and a jovial smile.

"No, should I?" She took the book from Corbett and closed it, reading the title: *A Discovery of Dragons: A Modern and Comprehensive Guide to the Study of Dragons Great and Small. By D. T. Langley.*

She flicked back to the picture. "Dragonologist Dr. Derek 'Doc' Langley is the world's foremost expert on dragons. He graduated summa cum laude from the Massachusetts Institute of Trackology and is the current Head Curator of the Dragonian Wing at the Natural History Museum in London."

"This man"—Corbett pointed at the picture—"used to visit the professor a lot. He started coming not long after I started my apprenticeship; they would meet once a week and discuss something called OORT. I think it was a project they were both working on.

"When your mother first detected the comet, she told him about her intentions. He didn't want her to build the machine. He told her it wasn't safe. Just like with your uncle, they had words. I think he stopped coming after that. A few times your mother's progress stalled and each time she found a way around the issues that were stopping her, but she blamed Doc Langley. She said he was trying to thwart her."

Paisley looked down at the picture again, then flicked through the pages, scouring anatomical diagrams of dragons, timelines and histories, theories and facts, amazed that Mother had this book in her study at all. As she flicked through the pages, she suddenly stopped and felt as if the cogs of her track had jammed.

A photogram showed a slightly younger Doc Langley standing amid some rocky terrain alongside a young man in his late teens, his hair swept back, his hat in his hands, as he smiled for the camera. Paisley's heart leaped.

The young man was her father.

The caption underneath read, *Doc Langley on a fact-gathering expedition to India, with Dragonology scholar and explorer Edmund Fitzwilliam.*

Paisley looked at the image again; her father had known Doc Langley. He had known Doc Langley before he had become a knight, before he had married Mother, and when he was studying . . . dragons!

12

A COGLESS FOOL

Whilst Paisley had been discovering her father's dragon-studying past, a thief was searching through her mother's room, leaving no corner unexamined, yet left no trace of his search.

Roach had been meticulous. Well-versed in hiding places, he ran his fingers along the underside of every drawer and searched for false bottoms in the cupboards and trunks, as well as Violetta's jewelry box. He examined the floorboards for any loose places; he checked the walls for secret rooms and hidey-holes.

When he found a safe, he thought he might be in luck. He pulled a pair of dark green glasses and a glove from one of the many inside pockets of his heavy woolen coat. He slipped on the glasses, turning the whole world forest green, then pulled on the glove.

He flexed his fingers, the metal tips touching one another as he closed his fist. He hit the button on the back of his gloves, and when he stretched his fingers again, he could see a thin blue-green flicker of electrica spreading between each digit. He placed his gloved hand palm down on the safe, and with his un-gloved hand turned the dial slowly. When the light between his fingers leaped, he stopped and turned the dial the other way.

Moments later, he had the safe open.

Inside, he found letters, mostly legal documents, some personal— but no sign of the Heart Stone.

As he put the papers back, though, something caught his attention: a deposit slip dated for the day before from the Dragon Vault in Kensington Above.

Roach read the deposit slip again. By the designation on the vault, he could tell it was for one of the deeper, larger vaults protected by the Dragon Walkers.

Roach folded the slip, crisping the edge as his mind raced. The Dark Dragon had promised help, inside help, but that didn't fill him with hope.

Thieves like him had been trying to work out how to break into the Dragon Vaults for turnings with no success. The women who protected the treasure vaults were well trained—too well trained. All but the most cogless fool had long since realized that there was no way of stealing anything without being caught and killed.

Roach crisped the edge of the slip again. "Call me a cogless fool," he whispered as he made his way out of Violetta's room, off to catch a Fitzwilliam.

As he opened the door, he started for a second. Standing in front of him, his hand outstretched for the door handle, was Dax. He was dressed in a light blue shirt, navy-blue waistcoat, and gray trousers. Over the top of his right trouser leg, his brace glinted silver.

Roach grunted in pain and surprise as Dax swung his cane up to smack him in the ribs, then back down to connect with his shins. Roach reached out for the cane, missing and stumbling forward as Dax turned and fled to the safety of his room, clicking the lock into place.

Roach reached into his coat and pulled out an electrica lock pick and stuffed it into the lock. The door clicked open, and he pushed his way into the room to see Dax disappearing through a secret panel in the wall. Roach leaped onto the bed, then dived at the door. Hitting the floor, he reached out his hand and jammed the electrica lock pick into the gap just as Dax pulled the door shut.

The lock pick made a crunching sound as it stopped the door from closing. Roach pushed himself forward, and as Dax made to slam the door again, Roach grabbed it with his free hand and wrenched it open.

Roach dropped the broken lock pick and reached into the secret passage, his fingers latching onto the cold metal of Dax's leg brace.

Roach, still lying on the floor, tugged hard. He felt Dax fall to the floor with a thud and yell. Roach reached into the darkness of the secret entrance with his other hand, gripping both sides of Dax's leg brace.

He pulled the boy toward him. Dax struck Roach's hands with his cane.

Knuckles smarting, Roach gave another mighty pull, only for the brace to fly toward him, buckles undone, and hit him in the face. Blood ran from his nose, the pain making him see red. He reached into the folds of his coat and pulled out a tobacco tin. Dax's footsteps receded into the secret passage.

Something inside the tin hissed, like the sound of many tiny pistons moving. When Roach pulled off the lid, out scurried an army of metal cogroaches, each one with long antennas and mechanized jaws. They set off in search of Dax, some opening their glistening wing cases to deploy small wings that whirled, making a sound like the propeller on an aerocopter.

Roach sat up, his head swimming as he wiped the worst of the blood onto the back of his coat sleeve.

From the passage, he could hear Dax struggling against the cogroaches, yelping as they tried to climb up him, scratching with their metal legs, biting with their serrated, sawlike little jaws.

Inside the tin was an electrica display; like the lenses of the glasses, it showed small green dots, each one a cogroach and where they were swarming to. Roach turned away from the secret entrance and, looking at the display, made his way out of Dax's room to surprise him when he ultimately exited the secret passage.

But Roach was too slow. He looked up as he entered the hallway to see Dax coming out of Paisley's room, slamming the door shut on the cogroaches that weren't clinging to him.

Roach spread his arms and stood at the top of the stairs, blocking Dax's exit.

Dax stepped backward, Roach following, as he edged closer to Edmund's armor.

"You're coming with me," Roach said.

"No, never!" Dax yelled, lifting his cane like a sword.

Roach took a step closer to Dax, but before he could lunge for him, Dax moved swiftly behind the suit of armor and pushed it at him.

Roach jumped out of the way as it crashed to the ground, and Dax ran swiftly up a small narrow staircase that led to the attic. He was much faster than Roach was expecting.

The cogroaches had made their way under the door, and they flew in the air around Roach as he made his way up the stairs in pursuit. He barged into the door at the top with his shoulder, and the door splinted it in a terrific crack. The time for stealth had passed.

Roach took a moment to gaze around the attic and saw the small window that led to the roof swinging gently back and forth.

Roach wiped his bloody nose again and smiled as he slowly walked to the window.

He was as good at cornering his prey as he was at delivering his promises.

Soon he would have the boy, then he would have the Heart, and once the Dark Dragon had fulfilled her path, he would have his sister too.

13

THE FALL OF ROACH

An almighty crash rang out from upstairs.

Paisley dropped the Dragonology book on the desk and ran from the study through the library into the hall and up the stairs, Corbett trailing her.

When she reached the top, she saw Father's armor littering the floor in brittle pieces. Corbett picked up the helmet and held it aloft in appreciation. "This really is fine work," he said. Paisley shushed him.

A moment later, the sound of the attic door splintering filled the house, and Paisley set off up the stairs.

The small window that led to the roof banged shut as she entered the attic. She dashed for it, Corbett following. She heard him groan as she stepped up onto the large wooden storage trunk, pushed the window open, and scampered out onto the rooftop.

"Dax!" The bitter cold of the wintry wind came as a shock as it whipped around and snatched at her breath and muffled her shout.

Dax's cane lay on the rooftop; she picked it up and looked around for him.

There was a short expanse of flat roof to the left of the window that rose to meet the raised roof on the other side, forming an L shape around the flat roof with the pitch of the attic. Paisley scanned the raised slopes of tiles as she slowly walked over the flat roof covered in melting pools of snow around the chimneys.

Beyond the chimney, Paisley saw Dax, being held by a boy a little older than her. She recognized him from the lecture.

"Paisley! No!" Dax yelled, and struggled.

The boy pulled Dax roughly, pinning him in front of his body, a small knife to his throat.

Paisley took a step closer. "You. I saw you at Mother's lecture, with your sister."

"She's not my sister," the boy said. His hair was disheveled, his eyes wide. He took a step back, toward the edge of the roof, dragging Dax with him.

"Easy, now," Paisley said, looking the boy straight in the eyes. He had the look of someone at the edge of their track. She knew that look; she had seen it on her own face in the mirror the day she had received her stars. Loss and uncertainty.

"Give me my brother; whatever it is that you want, whatever it is that you need, we will help you get it. Just let go of Dax."

The boy took a step back, looking from Paisley to Dax.

"Please, he's just a child," said Paisley.

The boy looked at her. Something had shifted; he stood taller, his jaw set, his knife held firmer, and he took another step backward.

"I need him; she needs him," the boy said. Paisley could hear the bitterness in his voice. "It has to be like this. I'm sorry."

"Please!" Paisley yelled, and Dax began to say something, but the knife moved closer to his throat. "I won't let you take him."

Paisley raised Dax's cane in a swift movement, pulling it apart to reveal a thin, sharp-tipped nightsilver sword.

"You don't have any choice," the boy said. "It's in my track to give her what she wants."

"Who? Give *who* what she wants?"

The boy looked at Paisley, his dark eyes low. "The Dark Dragon," he said.

Paisley looked puzzled and was about to ask him what he meant when Dax called out, "Watch out, the cogroaches!"

Paisley looked down to see a wave of mechanical bugs quietly clicking their way toward her.

Her eyes flitted up to Dax and the young man, then back to the mechanical assailants.

Paisley watched as the bugs formed a tight ring around her before jumping up on her, scratching and chomping through the fabric of her dress and tights.

Paisley tried to bat the creatures from her, moving her head from side to side as she felt them claw their way up her hair, their tiny metal barbs pulling with each step toward her scalp.

The window to the roof banged shut. Paisley caught a glimpse of Corbett as he righted himself and took in the scene before him.

The boy began to pull Dax back, but Dax dug his dragon leg into the roof, scrabbling for purchase and slowing their progress.

Paisley lunged toward Dax, the cogroaches still attacking her as she grabbed her brother's outstretched hand.

Corbett was rummaging around in his pocket; he pulled out a small metal box. He rushed forward and turned a winding key on the side, placing it next to Paisley, then reached out for Dax's hand too.

Paisley locked eyes with the boy, and raising the sword in Dax's cane, she swiped him across the face.

He was tipped off balance, and his grip on Dax relaxed.

Dax took advantage, kicking out with his dragon leg and knocking the boy away.

His eyes grew wide and his arms flailed as he flew toward the back of the house.

Dax propelled straight into Paisley, knocking her down onto the flat roof, the cogroaches scattering and regrouping before charging toward them all.

Just then, the small tin Corbett had placed on the floor began to whirl, the sound growing in strength and pitch until Paisley thought that she would have to cover her ears. It reminded her a little of the

Dragon Touched shopgirl and her mighty roar, but this sound was much higher in pitch. Paisley hugged Dax close, covering his head and shutting her eyes. Then the sound stopped, dead, and so did the bugs.

"Wow, what was that?" Dax asked as Paisley pulled him to his feet. Paisley looked to where she had last seen the young man as Dax began examining the dead bugs.

"What is it?" Dax asked, lifting the box.

"It's just a thing I made," Corbett said with a shrug. "It gives out a burst of electrica energy that can disrupt the energy field of other small electrica-powered objects. I use it in the lab; you'd be surprised at how much it comes in handy for shutting things down."

"That's amazing," Dax said.

"I didn't think it would work. It doesn't reach very far."

Paisley made her way to the edge of the roof, crunching bugs as she walked slowly, fearing what she might see. Whatever the young man had done, she had no wish to see him dead on the ground below her.

It all happened in a split second.

One moment she was looking over the edge of the house, and the next she was falling.

The boy had hung on to the drainpipe when he fell, and now he pulled at her ankle, tugging her off the edge. Paisley grasped at the metal gutter as she fell.

The boy was a little below her; he had slipped down the drainpipe, and she realized in an instant that when he had reached for her ankle, he was trying to pull himself up, not pull her off the edge.

Dax and Corbett were yelling from above as she took one hand off the gutter and reached it down to the boy.

"Take my hand," she told him.

He locked eyes with her. Paisley could see the hesitation; then he reached out for her. But before their fingers touched, he lost his grip on the drainpipe and fell to the ground, like a marionette puppet whose strings had been cut.

14

THE TREASURE OF KNOWING

"Is he dead?" Corbett asked, his eyes wide as he looked over the edge of the roof at the boy lying on the ground, pushing his glasses up as he did.

"I don't know," Paisley said with a grunt as she reached back up to grab the gutter. She hoped not. He had something to do with Mother's disappearance; she was sure of it. Maybe he could tell her where she was.

"Go back to the attic and see if you can find anything to help pull Paisley up," she heard Dax say.

"Right, yes, of course, something helpful."

Dax's head poked over the top of the roof. "He's gone. I'm going to pull you up with my dragon leg."

"No, Dax. It's too dangerous," Paisley said.

Dax's feet came into view. "Please, Paisley, I can do it. I know I can."

Paisley felt her fingers slipping as the cold of the metal gutter made them numb.

"Hold on to something so that you don't slip," she called to Dax as she reached up with one hand, keeping the other on the gutter, ready to let go of Dax at the first hint of strain on him. She grabbed his ankle.

The moment her grip was tight, Dax bent his knee, lifting Paisley smoothly into the air; she let go of the gutter and grabbed the top of the roof lining. Dax, keeping his leg bent, crawled forward, dragging Paisley to safety.

"Wow," Dax said as he looked at his leg.

"You saved me," Paisley said, reaching out and hugging her brother.

"You saved me first," he said.

"I will always be here to save you, Dax." Paisley hugged her brother tight there on the roof of their house, with the borough of Towering Hamlets casting a shadow down on them. In that moment, she swore to herself that this was a promise she would keep forever.

Corbett called out, "Don't worry, Paisley. I've got some rope; I'll save you." The window to the attic slammed shut. "Oh. You're all right!"

Paisley sat up, then stood, pulling Dax with her.

She tentatively took another look over the edge of the roof. The north wind whipped at her warm cheeks. She gave a shiver as the adrenaline faded and the cold took root.

He wasn't moving; the boy's dark eyes were closed, his square jaw set. He was flat on his back in a drift of snow that had piled up at the side of the house, his coat open, a line of blood on his cheek where she had caught him with Dax's cane. A scant line of leftover cogroaches were making their way over the parapet and flying down to land on his chest.

"Those metallic beetles—are they made from nightsilver?" Paisley asked.

"I don't know." Paisley watched Corbett as he stomped on one of the fallen cogroaches before kneeling down and scooping it into his handkerchief. With the edge of his pen, Corbett rummaged in the bits of shattered metal.

"Aye, there's a wee bit of nightsilver in here, but there's an awful lot that isn't." He lifted up a tendril of copper-colored metal that seemed to wrap itself around the rest, once holding the many parts of the cogroach in place. Corbett squinted at it. "I have no idea what this is, but it isn't just copper, that's for sure."

Paisley grabbed the rope from Corbett. "Come on, he's still alive," she called over her shoulder as she ran for the window.

Dax was straight after her.

"Paisley, he fell all that way; he's dead!" Corbett told her as he ran down the attic stairs, trying to keep up with her and Dax.

"No, there's nightsilver in the cogroaches—if they're alive, then so is he. That's how it works, right?"

"Right, of course," Corbett called from behind.

Paisley took the stairs two at a time and rushed for the kitchen door as Dax asked questions about nightsilver and Corbett tried to answer while keeping pace.

Paisley burst out of the back door and around to the place where the young man lay, only to find a dent in the snowdrift and a fresh set of footprints leading off around the side of the house.

Hitching the rope onto her shoulder, Paisley followed the trail, but it disappeared into the blackening sludge on the road.

She looked up and down. There was no sign of the young man.

Dax met her in the middle of the road.

"He's gone," she said, flinging the rope to the ground in frustration. "He knew something about Mother, I'm sure he did, and now he's gone."

Dax took a step closer to her and put a hand on her arm. "It's all right, Paisley. It's good that we didn't, you know, kill him. And besides, I know where he's going."

Paisley snapped her head toward her little brother. "You do? Where? How?"

An electrica car was making its way down the street. Dax tugged on Paisley's arm, and she stooped to pick up the now soggy rope, then allowed Dax to lead her to the path and up to the front door. Corbett followed, puffing out great clouds of air.

Dax looked around and lowered his voice. "He said his name was Roach; he was taking me to the Dragon Vault. He had this."

Dax held out a deposit receipt from their family's treasure trove in the Dragon Vault on the floating borough of Kensington Above.

Paisley took it and saw that it had her mother's signature and was timed and dated for yesterday morning.

"The Dragon Vaults?"

"Yes," Dax said.

Paisley folded the slip of paper. "And he's after whatever Mother put in our vault?"

"I think so, only it's not him that wants it; it's the Dark Dragon."

Corbett gave a little scoff. "The Dark Dragon? I was never told Dragon Tales as a child, but even I know that she's make-believe."

Dax looked at him hard. "There are more things in Earth and the Veil, Corbett, than are dreamed of in your science. Mother used to say that all the time."

Dax looked at Paisley, and a level of understanding fell between them.

"Dax is right," she said. "I don't think Mother would have discounted anything until she had evidence, even the old Dragon Tales. If she had, she would never have moved the comet."

Corbett's cheeks reddened, and it had nothing to do with the wintry weather or his fitness levels.

"Shall we go inside before we catch a cold, or someone sees us?" Paisley suggested. "We can come up with a plan, to get Mother back."

"Back?" Dax stood rooted to the spot. Paisley felt her heart quiver at the hope in his voice.

"Dax," she said, holding the door open for him and Corbett to enter. "I want you to hold this." She pulled the watch, still comfortingly warm with the promise that Mother was still alive, out of her pocket and gave it to Dax.

She put an arm around his shoulders and directed him to the sitting room, where the fire was blazing.

"Come on. Corbett has a thing or two to tell you about nightsilver."

✦ ✦ ✳ ✦ ✦

The ringing in Roach's ears continued as he stumbled away from the Fitzwilliam house and headed first down the middle of the road, then away toward the hiding place he had earlier occupied.

He slumped against the wall, then trickled down to the ground, hiding in the foliage, holding his ribs and taking short, shallow breaths.

He groaned as he moved his right arm, his shoulder bursting into pain.

He sat perfectly still as he saw Paisley run out into the middle of the road, her flame-red hair twisting around her as she looked from left to right before throwing the rope down onto the slush-covered street.

With his left hand, Roach reached into his coat and pulled out two cogroaches.

His head swam for a moment; then his intention formed and one of the cogroaches flew off toward Paisley and Dax as they moved toward the house, and the other climbed up to Roach's ear, the tiny barbs hardly hurting as his other pains outshone the sharp scratches.

Moments later, the cogroach, entwined in Paisley's hair, accompanied the Fitzwilliam siblings into the house, and Roach listened as Corbett told Dax all about nightsilver and Dax told Corbett and Paisley all that Roach had said to him on the roof.

"He said that the Dark Dragon believes all our tracks are connected. His, hers, ours ... Mother's. I don't think he wanted to hurt me," Dax said. "I think he was ... a sad boy, really, behind it all."

Roach felt his throat catch. He had been sad for so long that it felt normal. Sadness had become his existence, and happiness the thing he searched for in the darkness.

In his mind, he saw his sister—her mischievous smile, her bright eyes, her dark hair, and her horns, the same blue as the small wings that ran down her back like the peaks of waves on a sandy beach of olive skin. She was bright and beautiful.

Roach wiped the tears from his eyes, turning his attention back to eavesdropping.

"This thing that he wanted—that the Dark Dragon wanted—this Heart Stone, he was sure that it was in our vault?" Paisley's voice was smooth and inquisitive. He had seen that about her; he had seen it in her mother too.

Roach thought of the star scroll he had stolen from Paisley. He knew that soon her track would end; soon she would slip from the world just as Clara had.

He felt a coldness drift over him as he thought of it.

"I think we should go to the vault, try to find this Heart Stone—and use it to barter for Mother's life," Paisley said, lingering on the words *Mother's life*.

"I took this." Roach heard something crumple. "He showed it to me as you arrived and I swiped it and put it in my pocket along with the deposit receipt when he held me with the knife."

Roach cursed as he realized Dax had the photogram that the Dark Dragon had given him.

"Is that Grandmama Fiona?" Paisley asked.

"Yes, and that is the Heart Stone around her neck."

"All of this is for a necklace?" Paisley's voice sounded disappointed.

"I don't think so; maybe it's just one part of why they took your mother," Corbett said. "Let's say we find this necklace in the vault; how will you get it to this so-called Dark Dragon, or this Roach character?"

Roach could hear the disbelief in Corbett's voice. If only he knew how wrong he was. Roach rolled his eyes as Paisley answered.

"I very much think that they will find us," she said. "I think this Roach is right and all our tracks are crossed."

There was silence for a few moments. Then Paisley said, "Come on, we need to get going. One thing I know for sure is if they've let the world think that Mother's dead, then they have no intention of delivering her back to us safely."

Silence again as Corbett and Dax took this in. Across the street, Roach also reflected and realized that the Dark Dragon had no intention of delivering on the promises that she was making to the professor. He didn't like to think about what that meant for the promises she had made to him.

"Paisley, you've something in your hair," Dax's voice came through Roach's ear.

Roach managed to knock the cogroach from his ear a moment before Corbett snatched the one in Paisley's hair and crushed it. The screech from its expired comrade was high enough to pierce the Veil.

15

CORBETT'S MISTAKE

Paisley led the way up the staircase. "We need to leave before Mrs. Keen returns; I'll write her a note, but if she's here, we'll have to explain and—"

"She'd never believe us or let us go to Kensington Above," Dax said.

"Quite. Corbett, here's Father's dressing room." Paisley opened a door next to her mother's bedroom. "His things are still all in there. I'm sure you'll be able to find something to fit you."

"It's okay, really. I can just wear this."

Paisley looked at him and raised an eyebrow. His clothes were wet from the snow and filthy from the dirt on the roof.

"They won't let you into Kensington Above looking like a street urchin, and that goes for all of us." She looked at Dax, his trousers stained, his shirt covered in tiny shreds thanks to the cogroaches.

"We've got to be stealthy now, and that means fitting in." She raised a hand to her wayward hair and tried to smooth it down. "Quick as you can; we'll meet in the library in ten minutes."

She pretended not to see the look that Dax and Corbett exchanged as she made her way to her bedroom.

Once the door was closed, she slouched against it for a second and took a deep breath.

Her legs suddenly went to jelly, and she dashed the tears from her eyes. She had almost lost Dax. She didn't think she could bear it if anything were to happen to him, especially not now when it was just the two of them, and Mother was depending on her to keep him safe.

It felt like so long ago that Uncle Hector and the Men of the Yard had arrived to tell her of the accident.

So much had changed in that moment and even more since.

Paisley plunged her hand into her waistcoat pocket and pulled out Mother's watch. She held it tight in her palm and felt the warmth of the nightsilver. Mother was alive; the knowledge flooded through her, making her feel stronger, giving her the resolve to get moving, to start doing, to never stop trying.

That was what Mother would do, and it was what Paisley intended to do too.

She tenderly placed the watch on the bed before attacking the buttons of her waistcoat and shirt. Paisley crossed to the wardrobe and wrenched open the door. Reaching in and taking out a green taffeta pinafore dress and a high-necked white shirt, she flung them on the bed.

She thought about the Dark Dragon. Could an ancient Dragon Walker really have taken her mother? Corbett didn't think so. It was easy to see why. The legend of the Dark Dragon was just that—a story. The ageless warrior obsessed with restoring the Great Dragons to the world and overthrowing the Chief Designer's will and all who followed his tracks. No sensible person believed in it.

But, she thought, it *was* logical that someone was masquerading as the Dark Dragon. Someone who followed those beliefs, someone who wanted to bring about an end to the Mechanists and bring back the Great Dragons that the First George had banished so long ago.

And there were plenty of dragon whispers out there. Even she would have been intrigued to have dragons in the Empire—but maybe not the return of the Great Dragons. If the history books were to be believed, the Great Dragons of old were as fierce as wildfire and twice as vengeful.

She shuddered at the thought of the destruction that they might cause in retaliation for their exile.

Paisley lifted the photogram of Grandmama Fiona and felt a little disappointed; had her mother been captured for nothing more than a necklace? If so, she doubted that this Dark Dragon was the one feared and famed in legend! She was obviously nothing more than a thief.

Paisley picked up the watch and secured it in her pocket before grabbing her satchel and placing the photogram of Grandmama Fiona in it.

Sitting in the satchel was her summons to the Mechanist chapel.

She smoothed the letter out before flopping onto the bed. If only she hadn't lost her star scroll, it might have told her something useful, something else that could have helped. She unclipped the dragonhide bracelet and watched as the metallic points hit the light and danced on her wrist.

There they were, her stars, all crammed into one half of a circle. If only she could steal a few of them over to the other side, spread them out, give them room for her to *be*.

There was a knock on the door. She stuffed the summons under her pillow and fastened the bracelet as she called out, "Come in."

It was Dax. He had on fresh clothes and had tried to control his halo of curls.

Dax sat next to her on the bed, his leg stretched out, his new brace pinning it in place and holding it tight.

He rubbed at the place where the straps crossed his navy trousers.

"It still hurts," he said.

"You've strapped it too tight. Here, let me look at it." He sat on the bed, and she kneeled down on the floor in front of him so that she could lift Dax's leg up and loosen the brace.

"Do you think we'll find her?" Dax asked.

"I hope so."

"Me too." His voice had an edge of fear to it that Paisley had never heard before; the sadness of it tugged at her.

She slipped the brace from Dax's leg. He gave a sigh of relief.

"I wish I didn't have to hide it," he said. "I pulled you up on the roof with my leg. I could do so much more..."

Paisley could hear the longing in his voice; it brought a lump to her throat.

"I wish you didn't have to wear it too," Paisley said as she pushed up her brother's trouser leg and pulled down the long cream stocking that reached up past his knee. She ran her hands over his dark green scaled skin; it was warm and soft and sticky. The brace had already started to rub. Glistening patches of secreted oil coated Dax's ankle, and above and below his knee. His dragon scales were trying to protect themselves, reacting to the pinching by excreting a soft thin oil to lubricate the area.

"You need a thicker stocking," Paisley said. "Wait here." She hurried to Dax's room and searched his drawers for a thick woolen sock. She also grabbed the small bottle of ointment and his coat, before hurrying back to him.

As Paisley opened her bedroom door, she stopped dead.

Corbett was standing in front of Dax; he was wearing one of Father's old suits. He'd rolled up the legs of the nut-brown trousers, and the pale green wing-collared shirt that sat underneath a bottle-green waistcoat was a little baggy. The pin-striped tie of brown and gold fit perfectly. On top, he wore a heavy woolen coat, the same nut-brown as the trousers. Corbett was tall for his age, and like the rest of the clothes, the coat almost fit him.

He should have looked very smart, but something about the look on his face made Paisley scowl.

Corbett was looking down at Dax, down at his outstretched leg, bare and green, shimmering black. His mouth hung open in shock, his eyes wide in horror.

Paisley moved forward with a spurt, brushing past Corbett.

"I . . ." he began but stopped, nervously pushing his glasses up his nose.

Paisley fixed him with a stare like burning torches in the night. Corbett instinctively stepped back and looked away, the glow of her gaze burned heavy on his cheeks.

Paisley ignored him. She tenderly lifted Dax's leg onto her bent knee and began to rub it with ointment, the small scales deepening in color as the lavender in the salve filled the air with a bitter sweetness.

"I'm sorry, Paisley," Dax said in a small whisper.

"You have nothing to be sorry about," Paisley said as she untied Dax's shoelaces and slipped off his shoe and sock. She rubbed his twisted talons with more of the soothing balm.

"I'm sorry," Corbett said, his voice low. "I shouldn't have come in."

"No, you shouldn't have. I told you we would meet in the library." Paisley could feel her barely concealed rage mounting. She shot him a warning look.

Corbett hesitated, keeping his eyes locked with Paisley's, as if she were a wild dragon; he took a tentative step closer, then looked away.

"I shouldn't have ... I didn't know. 'Twas a shock. I thought he was just ..."

"A cripple!" Paisley spat like a spark from a burning log.

Corbett reddened. "I've never seen Dragon Touch before, not in real life anyway. In books, aye, but not in the flesh, so to say." His voice was almost awed as he watched Paisley's long fingers slide over the scales.

"And now you have," Paisley said curtly as she looked away from Corbett and gently pulled the thick woolen sock over Dax's scaled skin, leaving it smooth and white.

The room was silent as Paisley laced up Dax's shoe. She watched Corbett as she tried to process what he must be thinking. Dax was Dragon Touched. He was a *boy* who was Dragon Touched, like the prophesized Dragon Lord. And meanwhile in the sky burned a bright green comet that looked like a dragon's eye. Someone claiming to be the Dark Dragon had captured the only person capable of changing the course of the Mechanism. Suddenly, the Dragon Tales didn't seem so far-fetched.

"You won't tell anyone, will you?" Dax asked, his voice shaky and his face pale. He looked very young sitting on the bed while his sister tied his shoelace, much younger than ten.

"Why would I tell anyone?" Corbett asked.

Dax shifted his shoulders in a shrug, and Paisley's fingers held the laces still as she waited for Corbett to continue.

He looked at her; she kept her eyes low.

"I won't tell anyone, I promise. I swear it on the Celestial Mechanism, and may my cog stop turning if I break my word," Corbett said, looking from Paisley to Dax and then back to Paisley.

Her eyes were on him now—the glow was not as bright and terrifying as it had been, but a low smolder sat just beneath the crisp blue iris, waiting to flare at a moment's notice.

She nodded at him. If he did break his promise, she would be the one to stop his cog.

Paisley pulled Dax's trouser leg down over the sock and began attaching the brace with its series of leather buckles, cogs, and clips.

Dax winced as she tightened the buckle below his knee.

"Does it hurt? The brace, that is, not the . . . you know," Corbett asked him.

Paisley gave a sigh but controlled herself; keeping her scorn inside, she stuffed the spare sock into her pocket.

"All the time," Dax said. "Sometimes it's not too bad—if I leave the brace off for a day or two, then the pain slowly drifts away. Once I was ill with the mumps and had to stay in bed for a whole week. I kept faking it even after I felt better because my leg didn't hurt at all not having to wear this darn thing."

When the last buckle was secure, Dax thanked Paisley and made to stand up.

"Is it time to go?" he asked, motioning to the pile of their coats next to him on the bed.

"You don't have to come, Dax. You can stay here. Mrs. Keen will look after you, and I'm sure Uncle Hector will be around sometime soon."

"No." He slipped from the bed and landed with a dull metallic thump. "I want to come with you. I want to help, and besides, I feel safer with you than anyone else in the world."

Paisley stood and smiled. She kissed the top of his head. "I think we should take Father's sword with us, just in case."

"Good idea." She scooped up his coat and helped him into it as he shifted his cane from hand to hand.

Dax made his way out of her room and toward Father's fallen armor.

Paisley caught Corbett's arm as he made to follow. Her long fingers grasped the top, half circling the brown coat.

"If you ever betray my brother . . ."

"I won't. I swear I won't. I would never do anything to harm him, or you."

Paisley studied Corbett. His face was full of blind sincerity. She nodded solemnly and let go of Corbett's arm, following Dax.

As she walked down the curving staircase, her boots clunking on the stairs, she worried that a time might come when she would have to protect Dax from Corbett, and if that were the case, how far would she go?

Paisley gave a little shiver; she didn't want to think about that, but she knew the answer.

As she reached the bottom of the stairs, Dax passed her their father's sword and the scabbard he'd retrieved. She threaded it through the belt of her pinafore, then covered it with her coat, swinging her dragonhide satchel across her body.

Paisley quickly wrote a note for Mrs. Keen and left it on the hall table before turning to Dax.

"Are you ready?"

He nodded and lifted his cane and made for the door.

Paisley signaled for Corbett. "After you, Mr. Grubbins."

16

THE MASTER OF LIES

Roach grimaced as he lowered himself into the chair. His limbs were stiff from his fall. If it hadn't been for Paisley, he was sure his cog would have stopped. She had put him closer to the ground. The break in his descent had seen him land with the air knocked out of him and a few bruises to more than just his body.

"Are you sure they are going to the Dragon Vault?" the Dark Dragon asked as she paced up and down the room. Her shadow loomed larger than her tiny frame, flickering over the mural on the wall as the cold fire danced.

"Yes, I'm sure."

"How will they know what to look for?"

"I gave the boy the photogram of his grandmother wearing the stone," Roach lied.

The Dark Dragon nodded, her small lips relaxing as she continued to pace up and down with strong, sure steps. "That was wise of you," she said. "And he knows that his mother is alive?"

"Yes, he knows."

"I wonder if his sister believed him."

Roach didn't tell her that it was Paisley who had told Dax or what he had overheard Corbett saying about the nightsilver; he wouldn't have gotten a chance even if he had wanted to, as the Master of Lies cut in.

"Everyone knows that Paisley Fitzwilliam dotes on her brother. Even if she doesn't believe what he tells her, she will go along with what he says. She is easily led."

Roach said nothing but raised an eyebrow. That was not his understanding of Paisley's character: the fierce girl who carried a sword, jumped out of windows in her nightdress, and did battle on rooftops to save her brother. Roach stroked a finger over the line of dried blood on his cheek—he was sure it was going to leave a scar.

"Roach, you will travel to Kensington Above, immediately. The Master of Lies will take you in his aerocopter if needed."

"Not necessary. There's a public copter leaving soon," Roach said with a grimace as he shifted his weight in the chair, the bruises from his fall smarting.

"Very well. You will persuade the Fitzwilliam children to give you the Heart Stone; once it is in your possession, bring them to me. There is one final cog in my plan that requires oiling."

"Is she still refusing to work?" the Master of Lies asked.

"Yes, but maybe you could help with that?"

The Master of Lies blinked. "Me?"

"Yes. I think she might be more responsive to you."

Roach had been about to leave for the aerodoc station, but he couldn't miss seeing this.

Violetta had raged like a mother dragon when he and the Master of Lies had taken her from her observatory on Greenwich Overhead, and stolen her machine and research too.

Now he followed the Dark Dragon and the Master of Lies through the tunnels and up out into the snowy afternoon air of Lower London, emerging in the disused buildings of the old Greenwich Observatory.

He thought there was something poetic about making Violetta recreate her experiment there.

As they neared one of the old observation domes, the Dark Dragon fell back and nodded to the Master of Lies. She smiled sweetly, her childlike face angelic.

"After you," she said, stretching out her small hand and giving him a key.

His fingers trembled as he took it.

Roach sneered as he made his way up the steps and into the observatory dome.

Violetta was sitting defiantly on the floor in front of her machine. Her hair was wild and her lip was bleeding, her clothes disheveled and dirty.

"How dare you," she spat as she locked eyes with the Master of Lies. "I trusted you."

Roach watched as the Master of Lies looked away, shamefaced. The Dark Dragon walked toward him, and he rallied.

"No, Violetta, how dare *you*. How dare you refuse to help the Dark Dragon bring about our rightful future. How dare you put Paisley and Dax in danger."

"*I* put them in danger? You are the one who is in league with this . . . child and her preposterous ideas."

The Master of Lies straightened, his eyes glinting with the same reverence that Roach had often seen in the sworn disciples of the Dark Dragon. "She is going to reset all the tracks. She is going to call forth the Great Dragons and break the Veil. Don't you see, Violetta? All those we have lost will be restored; do you not want to see your husband again? And when the Great Dragons are restored, they will shape our tracks once more, but this time under the guidance of the Dark Dragon. The Master of Stars has seen your track— you are destined to help them return."

Violetta shook her head.

"Do you doubt it?" the Dark Dragon asked.

"Completely," Violetta replied flatly. "Only a few days ago, *I* moved the Mechanism. Not a Great Dragon, not the Chief Designer. Me! I can stop you if I wish."

"Really." The Dark Dragon walked toward Violetta and reached out a hand to stroke her cheek. Violetta flinched away, and the

Dark Dragon grabbed her chin in her hand, her sharp little nails biting into Violetta's skin. She tried to pull away, but the grip was too strong.

"You will do it for me. You will perform the experiment and bring me my dragon. Let me tell you why." She leaned close to Violetta's ear. "See that young man standing on the stairs?" Roach held perfectly still as Violetta's imploring eyes sought out his. "He is going to bring your children to me, and when he does, I am going to hurt them until you do what I want."

Violetta's eyes widened. Roach felt that he couldn't bear the way she looked at him; it was the same way his mother had looked on that day, as the Men of the Yard had held her back, forcing her to watch as they dragged Clara away.

The Dark Dragon let go of Violetta's chin, and her bottom lip trembled.

As she took her eyes off Roach and concentrated all her vengeance on the Dark Dragon, Roach felt a wave of uncertainty pass over him. Violetta only wanted to protect those whom she loved. But so did he.

"Roach, don't you have somewhere to be?" the Dark Dragon said. He nodded and turned to leave as the Dark Dragon instructed.

"If you prove your loyalty and do as I say, I might not need to hurt both of your children," Roach heard her tell Violetta. As he left the observation dome and headed to the nearest aerodoc, Roach wondered which of the Fitzwilliam children he would choose to spare if the task fell to him.

17

LONDON ABOVE

London boasted seven floating boroughs, two less than Paris. But Kensington Above was more splendid than any in the Empire or beyond, only rivaled by Manhattan Skyward, with its smaller Upper-Upper East Side and Upper-Upper West Side satellite cities orbiting it like twin moons.

Kensington Above sat in the sky like a giant snow globe. The lights of the borough twinkled under its glass dome, and bright blue skies shone above a thick gray blanket of soft, wintry clouds.

Paisley led the way out of the aerodoc station and into the splendor of Kensington Above.

"I've never been here before," Corbett said, straightening his glasses as he looked about in awe.

Paisley watched him look around openmouthed at the marbled

walkways and lampposts gilded with gold leaf, each with a colorful stained-glass shade protecting an electrica bulb.

His eyes danced over the tall, elegant buildings, each one grander than the one before. The air was warm, and it felt as if they had left the winter of London Below and arrived in spring. Trees and hedges were bursting with green, adding a sweet smell to the late-afternoon air.

Paisley took in a deep breath and sighed, a calm settling over her. Everything felt better on Kensington Above.

She led the way toward a small row of electrica cabs, waiting to whisk passengers across the borough. They passed the small newsagents' stall just outside the station. Its billboard proclaimed: *Turmoil in the North could lead to war, the George in talks with his knights.*

"Which way to the Dragon Vault?" Corbett asked.

"It's close; we could walk," Dax said.

"What about your brace? Is it still rubbing?" Paisley asked, her eyes darting toward Corbett.

Dax shrugged. "A little, but I've been sitting still for too long and need a walk."

"Only if you're sure," Paisley said, pulling out her mother's watch. "The Vault closes at nightfall; that only gives us a couple of hours."

"We can cut through the park," Dax suggested.

"Sure, that would be quicker." Paisley followed Dax as he led the way across the road through the gates to the pleasure gardens.

Kensington Above was the only floating London borough with outside space. It was so unlike the other boroughs. They all looked like massive floating buildings, while Kensington Above looked exactly as a floating city should, in Paisley's opinion and, it would seem, Corbett's too.

"This is more like it," he said as he walked alongside Paisley. He was looking at everything in the early twilight as they followed the snaking path between the grassy lawns and flowering borders; every now and again an electrica lamppost flickered into light, illuminating their way.

"I read that in Old Berlin, all the floating boroughs are like this," Corbett said.

"Yes, Mother's been there a few times, although I don't understand why they have floating boroughs at all; it's not like dragons or the Dragon Touched are banned from the Prussian Empire. I mean, I understand why the Dragon Walkers built floating boroughs in the Albion Empire. Having Dragon Touch, they'd be killed if they were found on the ground. But up here, they can live their lives; they're safe." She looked over at Dax and for the first time realized why he loved visiting the floating boroughs so much and why she felt more relaxed there too. No Men of the Yard, no King George and his guiding stars' obsession with eradicating anyone with Dragon Touch.

She picked up her pace as she looked down the path at Dax, who had gotten a little ahead of them.

"Not so fast, Dax. Anyone would think you ran on electrica energy."

"Just plain old-fashioned clockwork," he said as he tapped his leg brace with his cane. Paisley gave a small chuckle. Corbett smiled.

They reached the fountain in the middle of the garden. Three Great Dragons stood in the pool, one made of greened bronze, one of gray steel, and one of gold, although despite all the opulence Paisley doubted that it was actual gold. From their mouths splashed water rather than fire. They were huge, three times bigger than the average Northern Dragon, almost as large as the skeleton of Ealdorgedāl, which resided in the throne room at the George's palace in Westminster. An eternal monument of the last Great Dragon, slayed by the First George.

At the feet of the three dragons in the fountain lay a fourth made of nightsilver. It looked like a single black shadow of the three. Paisley's thoughts turned to the Dark Dragon: Surely she was just a myth, a Dragon Tale?

"Paisley, can I have a penny to make a wish?" Dax asked.

Paisley snapped out of her thoughts and plunged a hand into her satchel, searching for her purse, but before she could find it, Corbett had reached into his pocket and pulled out two big bronze coins. "Here, make a wish for your sister too," he said as he handed over the coins. Dax dashed off.

"Wish for cake for me!" Paisley called after him. "That was very kind of you."

Corbett shrugged and pushed his glasses back up his nose. "He's a great kid, your brother; I like him," Corbett said.

"He's all right, as brothers go," she said with a shrug. "I'm glad you like him, Corbett, and I'm glad that you'll keep his secret," she added in a small, serious whisper.

"I will, and not just because I think you might seriously hurt me if I didn't," he said with a smile. "I saw what you did to that Roach character."

"It's true, as true as I am to my word. And I sincerely mean it; if you betray him, or me for that matter, I will hunt you down, Corbett Grubbins, and when I find you, it will be slow and painful. A Fitzwilliam always fulfills their oaths."

Corbett looked a little pale, and Paisley didn't think it had anything to do with the electrica lighting.

They continued on in silence as Dax rushed back.

"Are you all wished out?" Paisley asked.

"I think I've done the best I could with them," he said with a thoughtful look on his face as they walked away from the fountain and out of the gardens toward the Vault.

"Paisley, who do you think grants wishes? In the Dragon Tales, Great Dragons answered the wishes of men, bending their tracks with their fiery breaths and whatnot, but now there are no Great Dragons, who does it?" Dax asked.

"I think maybe wishing died when they did, Dax," Paisley said.

"Oh, don't say that," Corbett said. "I think that we answer our own wishes—you understand—through hard work and the like."

"Yeah, me too," said Dax.

"Ah, but what about the Chief Designer?" Paisley asked.

"What do you mean?" Dax said as he kicked a stone off the path and into the grass.

"Surely, if we all follow the paths that have been laid out for us, then the Chief Designer grants your wishes before you've even had them, because your course was cast when the Mechanism was made. So, I guess, the Chief Designer gave you the wishes to wish for."

Dax looked at Paisley incredulously and lowered his voice a notch. "No one's that clever, Paisley, no one, not even Mother! Besides, they're *my* wishes, all mine; I feel it here," he said, pointing to his heart.

"So, what did you wish for?" Corbett asked as they walked through the gates that exited out of the park and onto a road full of tall, elegant houses.

Dax raised an eyebrow and glared at Corbett.

"He's not going to tell you," Paisley said. "He doesn't want to jinx it," she added in a carrying whisper.

"It's just not worth the risk," Dax protested as they turned away from the park with its audience of stylish houses and onto a road that led straight to the Vault. "Even Mother says that..."

But whatever it was that Violetta had to say about jinxes was forgotten as they caught their first glimpse of the Dragon Vault and Corbett let out a gasp.

"What is it?" he exclaimed. "It looks like a mountain forged into a castle."

"More of a fortress, I think," Paisley said as she too stared up at the rough stone and twisted metal of the Vault. Its many turrets looked like talons reaching up to the Heavens, almost piercing the glass dome of the great borough.

"It's the Dragon Vault," Dax proclaimed. "Although it doesn't have any dragons inside, only Dragon Walkers. I think it's a very misleading name."

"I've seen a few photograms of it, but I didn't realize it was quite so big...and monstrous-looking," Corbett said.

"It's just because it's getting dark," Paisley told him as she strode down the pavement toward the imposing building. "With the electrica lights shining up at it from below like that, it casts deep shadows, and all that darkness makes it look..."

"Creepy?" Corbett offered.

Dax nodded. "Definitely creepy."

"In the daylight, it's softer, more Dragon Tale than nightmare," Paisley said, gazing up at the twisting turrets and metal dragons that looked as if they were scurrying over the Vault. She pointed up at them. "They're all colored: moss green, flame red, sunshine gold, and the sandstone of the brickwork is soft against the nightsilver railings; it's magnificent." She sighed. "I think it's beautiful even now, in the dark. A kind of savage beauty, like the Great Dragons themselves, beautiful but dangerous."

Paisley smiled, her face half-bathed in shadows, her fiery red hair gleaming in the electrica streetlights, her eyes full of an intense wonder as she gazed up at the Dragon Vault.

"Come on," Dax said as he impatiently strode ahead, his cane tapping on the pavement. "It'll close soon."

Paisley turned her head and looked at Corbett.

"Shall we, Mr. Grubbins?" she said with a nod; he gave a half smile before they both lengthened their strides to catch up with Dax.

18

THE DRAGON VAULT

The railings on either side of the stone steps were twisted intricately into a pattern of dragons and cogs, hearts and airships, floating boroughs and stars.

"I always struggle," Dax grumbled as he navigated the oversized stone steps, his brace not allowing him to bend his leg enough to get up.

Paisley moved down onto the step below him. "Come on, I'll give you a piggyback."

"Don't be silly," he said, shaking his head.

"I'm not. Come on, it will be fun. Think of it as a dragonback ride if you want."

"All right." A cheeky grin crept across his face; he shifted his cane and leaped onto Paisley's back.

She walked up the dragon-sized steps, Dax hugging her tightly, his arms around her neck, Corbett beside her mesmerized by the scale of the design and the intricacy of the workmanship.

As they neared the top of the steep stairs, they saw two guards—Dragon Walkers—flanking a huge metal door. The door was at least twice the height of Uncle Hector and wide enough for an electrical car to drive through. Around the door, ornately wrought in metal, was a dragon's head, openmouthed so that the door gave entry into its throat.

Its glaring eyes looked down and made Paisley feel seen. Neither of the women guarding the entrance looked at them, but Paisley felt that they had all been fully scrutinized.

Corbett shifted uncomfortably. He was still staring at the Dragon Walkers, taking in their weaponry. Each guard had a lethal-looking spear in their hands and a glistening sword at their hips. They wore matching uniforms: long brightly colored robes of loose, flowing material over trousers that tapered around the ankles. On the left of the robes was pinned a golden dragon brooch.

"Close your mouth, Corbett. You're gawking," Dax said in a whisper, and Paisley grinned as Corbett shook himself, closed his mouth, and fumbled with his glasses, looking anywhere but at the guards.

The trio stopped a few steps away from the door as the Dragon Walkers sprang into action, their long plaited hair whipping out like lassos, startling Corbett. He let out a little scream as the

Dragon Walker guards crossed their spears and barred their way.

Dax slid from Paisley's back and smiled mischievously at Corbett, who was composing himself.

Paisley stepped forward. Usually, Mother did the announcing, but she guessed it fell to her now.

"I am Paisley Fiona Marie Fitzwilliam, and I come with perfect trust in my heart to visit the Daxon Trove. I pledge responsibility for the actions of myself and my companions, Daxon Ezra Silas Fitzwilliam, and..." Paisley hesitated and quickly stepped toward Corbett; she whispered in his ear, and he whispered back. She hastened forward to the guards. "And Corbett Montgomery Grubbins. If any error or devious doings are committed, I promise to pay the Dragon's Price."

The guards sprang back to their stations as if they had never moved, and the large metal doors opened soundlessly inward.

Paisley crossed the threshold with sure steps. Dax followed her, his cane tapping on the marbled floor. Corbett lagged behind, gawping at the inside of the Vault.

It was grander than the inside of the largest Mechanist's chapel but richer, smoother, lighter, and without a cog in sight.

The vaulted ceiling was held up with what looked like white bone pillars. Paisley had always felt as if she had stepped through the mouth and into the dragon's sprawling rib cage.

Electrica light glowed from the walls themselves, illuminating the space. Everything seemed to glint like treasure.

The small desks and counters of the Vault were made of a deep, dark, highly polished wood. The chairs were sumptuous and grand with jewel-colored cushions. It smelled expensive: like spices from the Empires to the East, mixed with musk and fruity zests.

The Dragon Walkers in the room looked as if they were performing a graceful and complicated dance. They went about their work in flashes of colors, their tunics as light and fluid as their bodies, moving with purpose and dignity.

Paisley's eyes swept the hall again. This time she noticed several stationary guards, just as brightly colored. Each one held a lethal weapon like the guards outside, but unlike those guards, their heads were completely bald. The mark of the initiate, the Dragon Walkers in training.

Paisley looked behind her and saw Corbett had stopped, his face turned upward as he took in the Vault.

She cleared her throat, and Corbett looked at her before rushing to her side.

"What was all that about out there, the Dragon's Price business?" Corbett asked, nodding back toward the doors that were now shut tight against the outside world.

Dax looked up at him, then back at the entrance too. "You have to pledge an oath to the Great Dragons before you're allowed to enter, and if you're not truthful, then when you cross the threshold of the Vault, the dragon's jaws descend upon you and, *bam*, you're dead."

Corbett guffawed and looked at Paisley with disbelief. Paisley gave him a wry smile and pointed up at the ceiling of the entrance. The color drained from Corbett as he looked up and saw terrifyingly sharp spikes glinting in the blackness. He took a deep, steadying breath.

"But how can it know if you're being truthful or not?"

"Dragons always know about stuff like that. And if you steal anything while in the Vault, the same will happen to you on the way out. If you get that far. Usually, the Dragon Walkers kill you before you can even get to the entrance hall," Dax said.

"Oh." Corbett gulped. "I'll be sure not to steal anything, then."

"Good," Dax said. "Because Paisley vouched for you, and if you die, she dies too."

A tall Dragon Walker in soft brown robes decorated with a deep orange pattern glided toward them. On her shoulder sat an intricate clockwork dragon.

She stopped in front of Paisley and nodded her head in greeting. With the palms of her hands and fingertips touching, she shook them in two short, sharp motions toward Paisley.

Paisley repeated the gesture.

"I am Mistress Lorena. How may I be of assistance to you?"

Mistress Lorena had long blond hair, plaited in a series of intricate knots that fell down her back to her waist. Her gray-blue eyes were clear as ice. Something about her reminded Paisley of a bird, large and majestic, like an eagle.

"That is most gracious of you, Mistress Lorena. We have come to visit our mother's family vault," Paisley said. "The Daxon Trove."

Lorena gave a quick incline of the head, her sharp features shifting. "I know which trove it is, thank you, Miss Fitzwilliam."

Paisley turned her head and looked at Dax; Mistress Lorena was not the friendliest of Dragon Walkers.

"Oh, look, Mistress Io is coming," Dax whispered.

Paisley looked toward the back of the hall; Mistress Lorena followed her gaze.

"We shall wait for her," Lorena said calmly.

"Who's Mistress Io?" Corbett murmured to Dax.

"Actually, it's Grand Mistress Io. She's in charge of . . . everything, basically. She's amazing." Dax leaned in and whispered to Corbett, "She *knows* stuff, Grand Mistress Io does, in the same way the Great Dragons knew it."

The Dragon Walker approached. "Miss Paisley, Master Dax, I'm sorry I am a little late. I was just preparing for your visit."

"See what I mean!" Dax whispered.

"What a pleasure to see you both again, and you have brought a friend, I see; I thought that you might." Grand Mistress Io tilted her head to one side, so that her dragon-slit eyes could get a better look at Corbett. "Ah yes, I'm afraid you'll do nicely." She nodded.

Paisley watched as Corbett took in Grand Mistress Io.

Her eyes were purple, with very little white around them. In the middle, instead of a round pupil, there were two infinitely black vertical slits. She was older than she sounded, and her gray hair was cast up in soft sweeping braids. Her eyes glittered when she smiled, lines gathering around them like the trails of shooting stars. She had a face that looked as if it preferred to smile; the deep lines around her mouth hung disappointed as soon as she stopped.

"Allow me to present Mr. Corbett Grubbins," said Paisley. "He's a colleague of Mother's."

"It's a pleasure to meet you, Grand Mistress Io," Corbett said, stepping forward to shake her hand.

The old lady raised both of hers and touched them palm to palm, then shook them twice as she nodded a small bow to Corbett, just as Mistress Lorena had done to Paisley.

Corbett paused, pulled his hand back, and then, glancing at Paisley, who nodded encouragingly, he repeated the Grand Mistress's gesture.

"I was just about to escort our guests to the Daxon Trove, Grand Mistress." Lorena bowed to her superior.

"Were you? Oh yes, I can see that was a possibility now given that I was a little detained—the possibilities do tend to shift so much lately. But, Mistress Lorena, I feel that it is best if I attend to the needs of our honored guests."

There was no disagreeing with Grand Mistress Io.

Mistress Lorena nodded and smoothly swirled away.

"I was sorry to hear about your mother's accident," the old Dragon Walker said as she began to walk off, her soft pink-and-silver robes sweeping the floor as she gestured for them to follow her toward the back of the hall.

"We will be more comfortable in here," she said, opening the door to a small private antechamber decorated in rich fabrics that hung from the walls and ceilings.

A low table was surrounded by bright, colorful cushions. A stern-looking young Dragon Walker stood at the back of the room, her bright blue tunic with red embroidered dragons fighting all over it under a pale blue cloak, her head completely shaved. Her brown skin glistened against her blue tunic. She bowed deeply to Mistress Io.

Dax stared at her as he walked across the room and sat down on a low emerald-green cushion, stretching out his leg.

Paisley gently nudged him as she sat down next to him on a soft amethyst cushion.

Corbett hung back, unsure if he was included in whatever private communication would be taking place in the chamber. "You too, Mr. Grubbins; you're mixed up in this whether you like it or not now," Mistress Io said, with a knowing look.

Corbett tentatively stepped into the room, and Io closed the door firmly.

Grand Mistress Io swept past Corbett and took her place opposite Paisley and Dax. She sat perfectly straight and still. You could have balanced a dragon egg on her head, and it wouldn't have trembled.

Corbett sat on the other side of Paisley, plonking himself down on the cushion and wiggling about till he was comfortable. The Dragon Walker waited until he was done fidgeting before she smiled deeply and said, "We do not have long. There are things in action that are moving just out of my seeing. But this much I know. Soon you will be betrayed, and one of you will enter the Veil."

Paisley felt the stars on her wrist tighten. She was going to die, and soon. She looked over at Dax, her heart rising in her throat.

He locked eyes with her, his gaze as steady as a ticking cog.

19

DRAGON TALES

"Is this to do with the Dark Dragon?" Paisley asked.

Mistress Io nodded. "She is one of the cogs that move against you."

"I've heard stories of the Dark Dragon, of course. But I always thought she was a myth," said Paisley. "Something we were told as little kids to get us to behave. You know, like, *You best go to bed now, or the Dark Dragon will steal you away.*"

Mistress Io smiled. "There is some truth in that. You must have heard of the story of the Soul Sisters?"

"Of course!" Dax said.

"The what sisters?" Corbett asked as he shot a look at Paisley.

"It's an old Dragon Tale," she answered.

"Mother used to read it to us when we were little. Do you remember, Paisley? There were four Dragon Walker Sisters; their names were Ayn, Sabra, Estrella, and..."

"Viola," Paisley said.

"Ah, of course, Viola, a little like Mother's name. Anyway, the four of them were not real sisters, but sisters in the way that all the Dragon Touched are said to be, through the Touch that came from the Great Dragon Anu."

"Aye, I know what you mean. But I've never heard of *these* 'sisters' before. I wasn't exactly brought up to believe in Dragon Tales," Corbett said; Paisley watched as he gave Grand Mistress Io an apologetic look.

"Not everyone is," she said with a smile. "Do continue, Dax."

Dax frowned, thinking, leaning toward Corbett. "Well, you see, turnings and turnings and turnings ago, before the King's Men began the Purge that got rid of all the Great Dragons, the Soul Sisters were entrusted with looking after the most sacred of all the gifts that the first and greatest of all the dragons, Anu, had bestowed on the Dragon Walkers. They had to look after her Soul! Cool, right? Except, the sisters had a massive argument."

"Like siblings sometimes do," Paisley said with a wry smile.

"Yeah, well, we don't argue that much," Dax said. "Anyway, the eldest of them, Sabra, decided that she should be the one to look after Anu's Soul.

"She wanted to use the power of the Soul to dominate the hearts and minds of everyone in the world so that they would do the Great Dragons' bidding.

"The other sisters didn't really like that idea and accused Sabra of being power-hungry and selfish, which it turns out she was.

"She tried to steal the Soul, and her sisters had to fight her. Three against one, they beat her and cast her out, leaving her to wander in the darkness of the world.

"Over time, the three remaining Soul Sisters began to have their own ideas about what they should do with the soul. And when the Great Dragons had all been banished in the Purge, they felt lost and confused about what to do.

"The next eldest, Estrella, wanted to use the power of the Soul to unlock the secrets of the Mechanism and give the Dragon Walkers dominion over the Earth as the Great Dragons had once had.

"The middle sister, Viola, thought that the Soul should be buried deep in the earth and never used again, for good or evil.

"The youngest sister, Ayn, was bright and good—the youngest ones usually are. She could see that this wasn't going to turn out well, that one of the others was bound to steal the Soul at some point and do their own thing with it, like Sabra had tried to. So she took it and smashed it into four parts."

"Wait a minute. Exactly how can you smash a soul?" Corbett asked.

"Well, the Soul was more of a big black diamond. It was the dried and shriveled heart of Anu, you see."

"Gross," Corbett said, and he gave a little shudder.

"Anyway," Dax said impatiently. "Each sister was to take a part and travel in a different direction. One toward the point where the sun rose, one to where it set, and one to where the star was constant.

"They pledged to keep their parts of the Soul safe and never to unite them until the Great Dragons returned."

"What about the fourth part?" Corbett asked.

Mistress Io spoke in her soft and soothing tone. "That was kept in our most sacred trove. Even today it is prized and protected by our Supreme Mistress Hypatia, in the Dragon Walker mountain hold, in the free lands east of the Empire."

"So, do you mean that the Dark Dragon is one of the sisters?" Paisley looked to Grand Mistress Io. "Sabra."

"She was the Dragon of Darkness—the dragon who was cast from her sisters, Sabra. She was not entrusted with a piece of Anu's Soul."

"But—but that cannot be. She'd be thousands of turnings old."

"Yes, she is," Mistress Io said with a smile. "Her Touch allows it, a rare gift of eternal youth; she will never age past the time her Touch developed."

Paisley considered that as Corbett opened his mouth to protest, and Mistress Io started talking again. "Of the remaining three sisters, Estrella, the Dragon of Smoke, traveled east. Ayn, the Dragon of Shadows, traveled north. And Viola, the Dragon of Fire, went to the West. Only the line of the youngest Dragon, Ayn, is known to us.

"It would seem that, for all her wisdom, she never managed to pass on her gift. One of her descendants gave up the ways of the Dragon Walkers when she fell in love with a man." Mistress Io said this as if it was the most abominable thing she had ever heard. "The man happened to be a powerful lord of the North, and with her and the piece of Anu's Soul at his side, he soon became king of his lands, the first King of the Northern Realms, Håkan the Unifier.

"The new king Håkan soon discovered that the Soul had other properties. Soul Fire, they called it."

"I know about the stone; it's the biggest Fire Diamond ever found." Paisley said. "It's the purest source of electrica energy in the world. The Northern Realms use it to keep their cities running. I remember Mother explaining that, until we recently learned to generate electrica energy through scientific methods, only the North had the ability."

"Yes, except it isn't a Fire Diamond; it is part of the heart and soul of Anu—that is why the electrica energy is so pure and constant. It is connected to everything."

"Wait a minute. Soul Fire," Paisley said. "In the paper, there was an article about a disturbance in the Northern Realms. The stone has been taken; they were blaming the George and his men."

Grand Mistress Io sighed. "This is true, and I think we can work out who is really behind its disappearance."

"Sabra, the Dark Dragon," Paisley said, her eyes wide as she began to pull all the threads she had collected together.

From the main hall beyond, a clock began to chime.

"Goodness, is that the time? I've kept you too long." Mistress Io rose elegantly from her seat and turned to the young Dragon Walker in the bright blue tunic, who was still standing at the back of the antechamber.

"Odelia, I want you to take Miss Fitzwilliam, her brother, and their friend down to the Daxon family trove." Mistress Io pulled a key from within the folds of her robes.

Odelia bowed, taking the key and slipping it into a concealed pocket of her tunic.

When she turned to face them, Paisley realized that the Dragon Walker was about the same age as she was and felt a twist of admiration followed by a bite of jealousy.

She was beautiful and powerful, with large, intelligent, almond-shaped eyes and full lips. She was tall, and although her tunic was loose, Paisley could tell that she was strong, much stronger than she was. Paisley wished that she could have been an equal to this warrior girl.

Paisley got up from the low table and placed both of her hands together. "Thank you, Grand Mistress, for your valuable assistance and teachings."

"I hope you find all that you are looking for," Mistress Io said. "But remember; sometimes we find that which we *need* rather than that which we *want*."

20

THE WEALTH OF THE WORLD

The elevator descended into the Vault, plummeting deeper down into the floating borough. Odelia stood ramrod straight, operating the lever on the elevator.

Something in Paisley's understanding had shifted since speaking to the Grand Mistress. She was sure that she was beginning to understand it all. The Dark Dragon had stolen Soul Fire from the North, just like she had stolen Mother. She was convinced that Comet Wolstenholme was a Great Dragon and she needed Mother to perform her experiment again, but she was missing something...

Next to her, Dax began to chatter away in a low whisper. "I do enjoy our chats with Mistress Io; she always has important things to say, and it was fun to tell Corbett the story of the Soul Sisters and everything, but it doesn't leave us much time to look for..."

Paisley's eyes widened, and she shot a look at Dax at the same time he looked up at her in disbelief. "The Heart Stone!" they whispered in unison.

Paisley instantly questioned it and then shook her head. How could it be anything else? The Heart Stone, the dark diamond that made up Grandmama Fiona's necklace, had to be part of Anu's Soul.

Paisley shot a look over at Corbett; he looked at her, puzzled. She darted a look at the Dragon Walker—neither of them seemed to have made the connection. She looked back at Dax, who was biting his lip in a state of agitated excitement.

The elevator came to a smooth stop, and the doors slid open.

"Not a word," she whispered to Dax as Odelia stepped out of the elevator.

Beyond them was darkness, and who knew what lay in it, what the Dark Dragon was capable of? Sweat collected on the back of Paisley's neck as she thought of the darkness of the Veil, of the golden points on her wrists. She took Dax's hand and squeezed it, and he squeezed hers back.

Small red lights dotted on the wall grew in intensity as Odelia stepped toward them. They burned like small electrica fires, flickering and twisting, each one sparking into life as Odelia moved farther into the darkness.

Soon the stone-like walls were littered with small electrica bonfires, illuminating a vast, cave-like hall.

If she hadn't known for certain that they were still on the floating borough, Paisley would have thought that they were under the Earth. The walls of the hall looked as if they had been hewn from rock, rough and strong and cold. She gave a little shiver as they moved forward. Her eyes adjusted to the light; her flesh pimpled with cold and wariness. The air smelled of charcoal and tasted earthy.

The torches gave off no warmth or cheer. Paisley wanted to wrap her brown woolen coat around her but instead undid it, allowing it to flow open and giving her quick access to her father's sword and free movement, should she need both; the threat of the Dark Dragon suddenly felt more real.

She followed Odelia out of the elevator, in front of Dax, and cast her eyes around.

The floor was solid and covered with a thick layer of dirt and dust that crunched lightly underfoot.

Odelia lit a torch from the nearest burning briar; she held it aloft and turned to face Paisley.

"There is no threat here, Miss Paisley. As long as you are within the Vault, the only thing you have to fear are your own promises."

Paisley watched the flickering flames reflecting off the initiate's smooth head. She reached up and ran a hand through her own hair, thick and coarse, as she wondered what Odelia's hair would look like if it had been allowed to grow: dark like the shadow of an oak tree, and long, with a tight curl.

Dax stepped out of the elevator; Corbett was close by him. Odelia led the way, snaking through the warren of dimly lit passages. Paisley brought up the rear, listening intently for anyone who might be following them.

"This is fun, right?" Dax asked Corbett.

"Oh yeah. It's . . . interesting," he replied.

"*Interesting* is a nothing word," Paisley said coolly. "It's like *nice*; it's something that people say when they don't know what to say. Or feel that they can't say what they really think." She smiled at Corbett, but it was a tense smile. It stopped long before it reached her eyes.

"Fine, if you must know, I think it's a bit . . . unnerving. You understand, being under the ground, but actually floating above the ground, all the darkness and torches and twisting passages. You could easily get lost in here."

Odelia gave a small snort. "Of course, that is the idea," she said as she made another sharp turn. "Although no one has ever been foolish enough to try and steal from us, we still use the passages as a deterrent."

Her voice had a cutting edge to it that sliced through the dark much farther than the light from the torch did, which barely licked the rough walls of the wide passage.

"I would have thought that the skills of the Dragon Walkers would be enough of a deterrent," Paisley said.

Odelia turned her head toward Paisley and gave a small nod. "It is true, but it is not our only means of protection."

"I think I remember reading somewhere that Dragon Vaults are booby-trapped," Dax said.

Paisley smiled as Corbett looked around and gave a little shudder, then he started paying attention to where Odelia walked, matching his footfalls with hers.

"This too is true," Odelia confirmed. "But as long as you stick to the rules, there will be no need for you to die."

"Die? Hey, wait a minute, I don't know the rules. What if I accidentally break one?" Corbett said.

Odelia turned her head to glance behind her, and Paisley was sure she saw Odelia smirk into the shadows. "There are six rules: three for Dragon Walkers, three for guests to the Vault.

"Here are your three rules. The guests are only allowed to enter the Vault under supervision. They are only permitted to enter their own trove. And they must declare all that they take from their troves when returning to the main reception chamber, collecting their deposit or withdrawal slip."

"Okay, they sound pretty straightforward," Corbett said.

"What about your rules?" Dax inquired, looking up at Odelia, the light flickering mysteriously on her face.

"We Dragon Walkers are not permitted to enter a trove. We are not permitted to touch any item in a trove. And we must protect the treasure with our lives."

"But what if someone is in trouble? What if they have a heart attack while in their trove?" Dax asked.

"Then they die," Odelia replied. "It has happened."

"But you can go in and help, right?" Corbett asked.

"No."

"*No*? What about the body; do you not go in and collect it?"

"It stays, and becomes part of the treasure until someone who owns the vault comes to claim it."

"Couldn't you just pop in and do it or, even better, help them before they die?" Dax asked. "It is an emergency, after all."

"If we did that, then we would be trading our lives for theirs. It is not permitted for us to enter, and punishment for all those who break the rules is death."

"Death! That seems a bit extreme, especially if all you're doing is helping," Corbett said. At that moment, Odelia stopped next to a large dark door. The light of her torch caught the metal of the curved swords that hung at her waist.

"It is the way. It has always been the way. The Great Dragons killed anyone who tried to steal their hoard, and we Dragon Walkers do the same, in their name. It is why we are trusted with the wealth of the world."

Paisley moved close to the entrance of her family trove. Like the other doors they had passed, it was perfectly smooth; unlike the others, it was double the size.

Odelia took the key from her robes. It was no longer than her little finger.

"You use that wee thing to open these giant doors?" Corbett didn't sound convinced.

Paisley nodded. "Mother says that you can move the world with a toothpick—if you know where in the Mechanism to place it."

"Which one of you will pay the price?" Odelia asked, looking from Paisley to Dax.

"I will." Paisley stepped forward, and Odelia pulled a small knife from her belt and gave it to Paisley. She reached out her left hand and without hesitation made a cut in her palm, then smeared her blood on the door.

Where Paisley's blood had touched it, the metal of the door became darker and then a keyhole formed.

Corbett pushed his glasses up his nose. "How? It's like liquid silver," he said, examining the door; as it fluidly moved, the keyhole appeared as it transformed.

Dax whispered to him, "It's a kind of illusion; Dragon Walkers are full of brilliant tricks."

"Aye, this impossible underground lair, the labyrinth of tunnels, and now this. I can't wait to see what's next," Corbett muttered.

A series of clunks issued from behind the doors. A soft whirling accompanied the thuds as cogs rotated, opening the double doors and folding them back as they swung into the trove.

Paisley stepped forward. Bright white electrica light illuminated a small antechamber, its floor covered in smooth, clean gray stones, each cut into octagons and linked together perfectly to form a sleek surface.

The walls of the antechamber were created from brass bars that ran from the high ceiling to the floor. The gaps between the bars were just wide enough to fit an arm through, but nothing more.

Corbett was fixed to the spot, looking at the enormous space beyond the bars.

It seemed to go on forever, and every inch of it was covered in treasures.

Antique furniture, Persian carpets, reels of richly embroidered silk, marble statues, works of art in gilded frames, and jewels. Jewelry hung from open drawers and boxes, just as ivy would trail on a ruin. Necklaces with large precious stones dripped from the edges of picture frames; tiaras sat on marble busts.

Corbett let out a long, low whistle.

The others turned to look at him. Paisley blushed as she took in his awed expression; for her these things had always been part of her mother's family, but she could see how this might look extravagant to Corbett. Or to anybody.

"We won't be in here long," Paisley said.

"Right, the rules! I'm not allowed in, or Odelia here will have to kill me," Corbett chuckled, and Odelia rested her hands on the hilt of her swords.

"Right. I guess I'll just stay here, and the two of us can get to know each other a wee bit better." He cast a look back at Odelia, who crossed her arms over her chest and gave him a steely look.

"The Vault is closing in thirty minutes. If you do not conduct your business before we seal it for the night, then you will have to stay here until we unseal the doors tomorrow," Odelia told Paisley.

Dax looked at his sister as she pulled out her mother's watch. "Come on, Dax. We can do it," she said, feeling the warmth of the watch and thinking of Mother alive and in need of help. She considered the vast trove before her. Paisley threw her shoulders back, grasped Dax's hand, and made her way into the warren of treasure.

21

THE DAXON TROVE

"Slow down, Dax! Where are you going?"

Dax darted left, and Paisley followed him. He'd stopped behind a large painting that obscured them both from Corbett and Odelia.

"Do you think it's true?" Dax said breathlessly as he plowed on through the trove, avoiding toppling piles of treasure. "That the stone in Grandmama Fiona's necklace is a part of Anu's soul?"

"I don't know, Dax," Paisley said. "Maybe, but it seems a bit far-fetched."

Dax paused, looking around to get his bearings.

Paisley took her brother's hand and pulled him away to the left.

"All Grandmama Fiona's things are over here. I remember find-ing them when I was little and Mother showing me a necklace with a black stone in it. It was in a box full of letters, or papers; Mother read them all and then stuffed them away..."

The memory was coming back to Paisley as she spoke; she remembered that her mother had cried as she'd read the letters.

"Paisley, if Grandmama had a piece of Anu's soul, does that mean that we're related to the Soul Sisters?"

"I've been thinking about that, and I think it might. It would certainly explain a few things." She gazed down at Dax's leg, encased in his metal brace.

"You know what this means," Dax said with a smile as they hurried past treasures and priceless antiques. "It means that we're both dragons."

Paisley stopped and smiled at him. "I guess it does, but we're both other things too. People are made up of many parts, Dax, and knowing that part of you comes from a certain place doesn't define the whole of who you are. The things that you *do*—that's what defines who you are."

She looked up. They had reached an oil painting of their grandparents on their wedding day. "There she is, Grandmama Fiona and Grandpa Ezra. We're made up of parts from both of them, and Mother and Father, and all our ancestors like Great-Grandpa Piter, who Mother named Comet Wolstenholme after, but we get to choose what we do with all of that."

Dax nodded as they both gazed up at the enormous canvas. Paisley got the same impression that she always had when she saw pictures of her grandparents—she wished she had known them better.

Mother had always told her that Grandpa Ezra had been a great thinker. It was he who had introduced her to the wonders of astronomy. Whereas Grandmama Fiona had been more preoccupied with being a star than studying them.

Paisley reached out a hand and gently stroked the canvas. "She was a socialite, a beautiful dazzling jewel."

"Look, Paisley," whispered Dax. "She's wearing the necklace." Paisley's eyes widened. She dug in her satchel and pulled out the photogram. The necklace in the photogram matched the painting exactly.

"Yes, that's it." Paisley looked around. "I think this is where Mother and Father must have stored all Grandmama's belongings. Quickly, help me look."

Paisley pulled open the nearest hatbox, then crossed to a chest of drawers as Dax plowed through a chest full of furs.

"Where do you think it is?"

"If I knew that, Dax, I wouldn't be searching," Paisley said as she found a photogram of her mother and father. They were both very young and looked so very happy.

Dax squealed with excitement.

Paisley replaced the photogram. "Have you found it?" she asked.

"No, but look," Dax said in awe as he lifted what looked like a nightsilver filigree-covered dragon's egg. The base of the black egg sat neatly in Dax's cupped hands as he examined the intricate pattern of silver that ran over it, encasing it in the same way his brace did his leg.

"It's amazing," he said, clutching it to him. "Do you think it's real?"

"No, no, I don't. Now, come on; we don't have much time." Paisley pushed her hand into her pocket and pulled out her mother's watch.

"Can I keep it?" Dax asked as he held the egg up to catch the light, the shell beyond the filigree pattern shimmering with a rainbow of colors, like oil in a muddy puddle.

Paisley nodded as she opened a large wooden blanket box. "Technically all of this stuff belongs to us now, so I guess we can take what we want."

Paisley watched with a smile as Dax took the egg and pushed it into his coat pocket, point down with the larger bottom end sticking out. He checked that it was safe; the pocket stretched to its limit, holding the egg snugly.

Paisley moved to a chest of drawers full of boxes. She opened the first few: Inside was jewelry, a pair of gold-and-jade bangles, some dangly onyx earrings, and . . .

"Oh no." The color had drained from Paisley's face when she looked up from the slim box she was holding; the pink ribbon that had tied the lid in place lay limp in her hands.

"It's gone," Paisley said. She lifted out a length of gold chain, the setting hung from the end like an empty picture frame; the black stone was missing.

"What do you mean?"

"Look." Paisley held the necklace up to the painting—the setting was exactly the same, the flourish of gold and silver that had once held the Heart Stone.

Paisley lowered the chain back into its box, onto the letters below it, and closed the lid. She could feel tears pricking at the corners of her eyes.

"What do we do now? How can we get Mother back?" Dax asked.

"I . . . I'll think of something." Paisley shook away her tears, her red hair waving. "We'll just show Roach that we don't have it anymore." She stood up and gently placed the slim pink box into her satchel, knowing, though, that it wouldn't be enough.

"Maybe I could give him the egg," Dax suggested. "There might be a Great Dragon in it? You never know; I reckon the Dark Dragon would be interested in that!" Dax touched the egg. Paisley knew that if there were a dragon in there, he would be sad to give it up, but this was for Mother, after all.

Just then, they heard a scream.

"What was that?" Dax looked over his shoulder, back toward the antechamber.

"I don't know . . ." Paisley swallowed. "But it doesn't sound good."

22

THE MISTRESS OF WAR

The cogroach scurried back under the jaw-like doors of the Vault. With a whirl of cogs and a flap of flimsy nightsilver, the mechanical bug took to the air and headed straight for its master.

In the shadows of the building opposite, Roach held out his hand for the cogroach to land on. Cupping his hand to his ear, Roach heard the voice of the Dark Dragon's Mistress of War.

Her voice was clipped and cold as steel. Roach looked up at the entrance to the Vault, at the two Dragon Walkers stationed outside, and worried that the Mistress of War might be leading him into a trap. He wouldn't put it past her. She was more than just fiercely loyal to the Dark Dragon, he had noticed.

The Dragon Walker would look at Sabra with the same intensity that the Mechanists observed the turning of the Mechanism, or the Blueprints of the Chief Designer, reverent and completely devoted.

Roach held on to that knowledge as he walked up the steps toward the mighty jaws of the entrance to the Dragon Vault.

The Dragon Walkers on either side paid him little heed until he reached the top.

The two guards uncoiled from their stations to block his way, expanding as they reached with every fiber of their bodies, their spears crossing in the center.

Roach came to a halt, as did the Dragon Walker on the left, but the one on the right continued moving. She thrust her spear at her sister, catching her off guard and hitting her on the chin. As the guard staggered backward, the attacking guard did not stop. She swung her spear up, then brought it crashing down on the top of the sister's head.

Roach looked down at the crumpled Dragon Walker on the ground, then up at the victorious guard.

"The Mistress of War sends her greetings. I am Prime Mayme, sworn Dark Dragon Walker, loyal to the Dark Dragon and charged with your safe passage into the Vault," the Dragon Walker said with a slight bow of the head.

Roach nodded back. He hadn't had much contact with Dragon Walkers but had found that a rigid formality and power of righteousness flowed through them all. He wondered if it was something to do with the Touch or the training.

"The Dark Dragon wants us to bring the stone from the Dragon Vault and the Fitzwilliam children to her. Their mother has been ... uncooperative," Roach told her.

"Ah, leverage. Just like the Great Dragons of old, a mother will do anything to protect her young." Mayme gave a cruel smile that even Roach found uncomfortable.

Roach glanced from Mayme to the Vault entrance. "I know the stories about that door, that it has the ability to sense intentions. I guess this place has a hidden back entrance."

Mayme regarded Roach. "There is no other way into the Vault; it is part of our security measures. But do not worry, Master of Mischief. My Dragon Touch will see you through."

"Really? And what exactly is your Touch?"

"I can shield the minds of men, manipulate them if I want to, make them see and hear and feel whatever I want them to. I can shield your mind from the door just as easily as I could trick it into seeing what isn't there. Observe."

Mayme gestured down to where the Dragon Walker had been lying unconscious at her feet. There was nothing there; instead, the fallen Dragon Walker was standing in her position to the left of the entrance, as if nothing had happened.

"How?" he asked.

"It is all an illusion." Mayme pointed down again, and Roach saw the fallen Dragon Walker reappear, as if someone had pulled back the veil covering her.

Roach wished he hadn't asked. Suddenly, he doubted everything around him.

"Take my hand, and I will shield you from the door." Roach tentatively took the Dragon Walker's hand and immediately he felt as if his thoughts had been placed in a jar, each one bouncing about in his head, reverberating inside his skull, like angry bees. "Come, I will take you to see the Mistress of War," Mayme said as she walked toward the door with purpose.

Roach swallowed. The gaping jaws of the door awaited him.

+ + ✳ + +

Paisley's stride lengthened to a run as she made her way back toward the door of the trove. Something was wrong, very, very wrong. The door was open.

As they neared it, an enormous fireball filled the space in front of them, the heat radiating through the trove. Paisley skidded to a halt and shielded her eyes. She heard Corbett scream again.

"Dax, stay in the trove!" Paisley shouted behind her as she opened her coat and pulled her father's sword from its scabbard.

Odelia stood in front of the door to the trove; Corbett huddled on the ground behind her, crawling toward the safety of the wall. "Stay down," she shouted to him as she slashed in swift arcs with the curved swords from her belt. As she attacked, parrying to one side, Paisley caught a glimpse of her opponent. Lorena.

The birdlike Dragon Walker swooped her spear toward Odelia, grazing her bicep and spinning her slightly off balance, before pulling upright and opening her mouth wide.

Flames spilled out of Lorena's mouth toward Odelia.

Paisley screamed. Odelia turned her back to Lorena, and giant wings unfurled from Odelia's back as she crouched protectively over Corbett.

Odelia's wings were covered in midnight scales, smooth and gracefully curving, ending in two razor-sharp peaks.

When the blast of fire halted, so did Paisley.

Before Odelia's wings were fully extended, Lorena leaped forward, thrusting the spear at her.

Paisley watched as Odelia rose into the air in a graceful arc, slicing at Lorena, who jumped back. Again, Lorena opened her mouth, letting out a great blast of fire, just like a Great Dragon.

Odelia whipped a wing in front of the flames, deflecting them from her soft human flesh.

Corbett made it to the safety of the wall, moving along it and still screaming for help.

Odelia twisted her head around and gave him a look and rolled her eyes, before swiping her smoldering wing out at Lorena as she stopped to pull in a breath.

The tip of the wing sliced across the Dragon Mistress's upper arm, and Lorena gasped as blood darkened the sleeve of her soft brown tunic.

Her eyes narrowed at Odelia as she released a rally of blows with the spear, interspersed with shots of flame.

As Corbett slipped slowly down the wall, squealing with every lick of fire or flash of blade, Paisley moved closer to him, keeping one eye on the speed and grace of the Dragon Walkers.

Lorena was relentless in her assault. If it weren't for Odelia's remarkable wings, and the way that they staved off the fire attacks, Paisley doubted that any of them would still be standing.

"What's going on?" Paisley shouted to Corbett.

"I haven't a clue," Corbett said. "She just came along, and they both started fighting."

"Cool," Dax said in a low whisper as he stood just inside the trove, watching the battling Dragon Walkers. Paisley shot him a look. "I told you to stay back." He sheepishly took a step to safety beyond the bars of the trove.

Lorena let out a roar of fire. Odelia lifted her wing but was too slow; the flames hit her right shoulder, licking her face and sending her to the floor, writhing in pain.

Paisley didn't think; she reacted.

She lifted her sword and launched toward Lorena, who stood over the crumpled Odelia, preparing to blast her with her fiery breath.

The air hung heavy with the singed smell of Odelia's burning flesh. Paisley lashed out with the sword, striking Lorena in the side with a glancing blow. As the sword made contact with Lorena, slicing her skin and tunic, a crunching sound filled the vault and the nightsilver broke into pieces, just as the armor had.

Paisley remembered what Corbett had told her of nightsilver. Mother's watch was strong and warm because she was alive; Father was dead, so his nightsilver was cold, weak, and brittle.

The Dragon Walker turned her attention toward Paisley, and under her glare, Paisley suddenly felt weak and foolish.

She took a step back, dropping the hilt of the sword to the ground.

Lorena opened her mouth and let out a fireball. Paisley dropped and rolled to the side, shielding herself with her arms from the heat of the fireball as it roared over her, heading straight for Dax, who was standing in the open doorway, watching. The fireball hit him on his braced leg.

"Dax," Paisley yelled as she scrambled to her feet and stood in front of her brother, arms outstretched.

Lorena advanced. "The Dark Dragon has a need for you both, but I will kill you if you vex me."

Paisley glanced backward at Dax. He was standing in the opening to the trove, his trouser leg smoldering as he hit it with the edge of a Persian rug rolled near the entrance of the vault.

"Shut the door, Dax," she told him. He stayed where he was.

"Dax, please," Paisley begged, her voice quivering as she glanced at her brother while keeping her attention on Lorena.

Lorena laughed. "You think that the rules of the Vault would stop me from entering the trove to get what I want, what I need for the Dark Dragon? You are wrong. My devotion to her is greater than any loyalty I feel toward the Dragon Walkers."

"The Dark Dragon," Paisley whispered. She reached into her satchel and opened the box, tightening her fingers around the empty jewel casing of the necklace. "She wants this."

Paisley held her clenched fist up, the chain dripping down her hand and hanging like an empty noose.

"The Heart Stone." Lorena's voice was breathless with excitement. "Give it to me. My mistress said that your foolish family had turned it into a trinket, that they never knew what it was they had. A treasure far greater than all the wealth in every trove within the Vault. And with it, my mistress will correct the course of time, restore the Great Dragons, and save the world."

Paisley kept her eyes straight ahead, but she was aware of many movements around her: Odelia stirring on the floor, Corbett inching his way toward her, and Dax shuffling on the spot in the doorway.

"Great Dragons won't save our world. Besides, what exactly about it needs saving? If you ask me," Paisley continued, "the world is better off when people just let it be, rather than try to change it back to something it once was. All you do is stifle it and stop it from growing. Things can never be as they *were*; they can only be as they *are*."

"Well, it's a good job that nobody asked you, isn't it?" Lorena said. "Now, give me the Heart Stone."

Paisley clutched the necklace's chain to her, bringing her hand to her chest. She looked away from the Dragon Mistress, casting her eyes to where Odelia had lain crumpled on the floor. She was now standing behind Lorena, her wings extended, her charred face full of vengeance, and her arms outstretched, ready to pounce.

Lorena began to turn her head, to see what Paisley was looking at. Realizing that the element of surprise would be lost, Paisley thought quickly.

"If you want it, then fetch!" she yelled as she threw the empty necklace setting high above Lorena.

Paisley watched the glint of gold rise into the air. Lorena leaped after it, extending her hand. Her fingers tightened on the chain. Her face twisted into a smile of triumph, which switched to bewilderment as Odelia grasped her, folding her wings around her, dragging her to the ground.

Lorena was smothered by the dragon wings encasing her.

She writhed and thrashed like a caterpillar trying to break out of its cocoon.

Paisley watched as the pounding on the midnight-blue wings got less frequent and more feeble, before stopping completely.

Dax was suddenly at his sister's side. "Here, I found this in the vault." He passed her a sword, made of steel, not nightsilver. The blade was sharp and the hilt plain. Paisley felt the balance of it as Dax looked in awe at Odelia and the trapped Lorena. "Is she dead?" he asked.

Odelia opened her wings, and Lorena fell to the floor.

"She is dead," Corbett said. "You killed her!"

Paisley looked over at Corbett, his face white, his eyes and mouth wide. "She would have killed us," she told him, feeling uneasy but knowing it was true.

"She's not dead," Odelia said. "But she will wish that she was when Grand Mistress Io finds out."

Odelia turned Lorena onto her back and rubbed her hand in the blood from the cut Paisley had made on her torso. She then rubbed the blood over her burned skin.

"Gross, I guess that'll be some kind of Dragon Walker ritual?" Corbett asked. "Washing in the blood of your enemies and all that?"

Odelia sighed as she smoothed the blood down her neck onto her shoulder. "No, because that would be ridiculous. Lorena's Touch makes her able to heal rapidly from any burn. The Touch is always in the blood; I can use it to heal the burns on my human flesh," Odelia explained, and extended her wings. They filled the space glinting blue like the deep sea. "Dragon scales never burn."

The redness on her face and shoulder was already fading, her soft brown skin growing smooth instead of charred and blistered.

"I see you've been burned too, Master Dax," Odelia said.

She kneeled quickly, reaching her blood-smeared hand out toward Dax's braced leg, where the rogue fireball had hit and burned through his clothes; then she paused and moved her hand away.

Paisley watched as Odelia's eyes danced over the scales on Dax's leg.

"The Dragon Lord," Odelia gasped, and bowed her head to the ground.

Dax sighed and shook his head.

23

FLIGHT OF THE FITZWILLIAMS

Paisley shivered as they hurried down the stone corridor away from the Daxon family trove. She held the sword from the vault in her right hand, and in her left she held Dax's hand. Odelia and Corbett led the way.

She half dragged him to catch up with the others, his cane tapping rhythmically on the stone floor.

"Come on, Dax. We have to move fast. We don't know how many other Dragon Walkers are with the Dark Dragon."

"What about Odelia?" Dax asked quietly as he bumped along beside her, the dragon egg in his pocket bouncing between the two of them.

"I think we can trust her. She fought Lorena, and Mistress Io trusts her, so we should too."

The passageway felt much colder than it had before and looked darker and more confusing too. Paisley couldn't remember which way Odelia had led them and she couldn't tell which way was out.

Father had always said that an escape route was essential in all situations, that it was one of the first things that both a warrior and an explorer made herself aware of.

Paisley felt that there was very little that she was aware of, and it frightened her more than all the things that she now knew to be true.

A little ahead of her and Dax, Corbett was keeping pace with Odelia.

"Why are we going deeper into the Vault?" he asked, loud enough for Paisley to hear.

"What makes you think that?" Odelia asked.

"I've spent a lot of time in Greenwich Overhead—it's given me a strong internal compass. Besides, I can feel the sloping and twisting of the floor toward the lower levels. Toward the center of the borough."

Odelia gave him a look of mild surprise. "Sometimes to go forward, you must go back. Besides, Lorena would not have acted alone; she is a coward." Odelia's voice was so flat and damp, it did not travel farther than Paisley's ear.

"If we go any deeper, we'll surely reach the drive level of the borough," Corbett said.

"You know a lot about the anatomy of the floating citadels." Paisley registered a hint of surprise in Odelia's voice.

Corbett gave a shrug. "Aye, they're interesting."

Paisley had to agree with that. Mother would often sing the praises of the Dragon Walkers and their engineering secrets. She said that the scientists from the Celestial Engineering department spoke in sharp tones about the floating boroughs and how they could not get their calculations to mimic the Dragon Walkers' flying boroughs. "Hidden Knowledge," that was what they claimed the Dragon Walkers possessed. They would rave about how unfair it was that the Dragon Walkers wouldn't share their understanding; how many advancements were being held back by their greed? Mother reported this with a glint in her eye and a raise of her eyebrows.

Paisley often wondered about that; she knew that knowledge was treasure and in the end concluded that if the Dragon Walkers wanted to guard their treasure, it was best not to attempt to take it, no matter how many advancements could be made. She knew, however, that her mother didn't feel the same way.

They turned a corner as the noise of a siren filled the air.

Odelia paused, raising her curved sword and flinging a protective arm out to cover Corbett. Paisley pulled Dax in front of her and then turned to look behind them, her own raised sword glinting in the dull light from the flickering torch on the wall.

"What does it mean?" Paisley asked.

"Trouble," Odelia said. "Follow me, quickly."

Odelia slipped around the corner like a shadow, leaving the others to follow in her wake. Dax stumbled as Paisley tried to make him move faster.

"Here," Corbett said. "Jump on my back." He squatted low, and Paisley helped Dax climb onto Corbett's back. His cane smacked Corbett in the face before Paisley took it from him and held it like a second weapon.

Odelia's shadow was a solid mass at the end of the tunnel as Paisley and Corbett ran to catch her.

They found her running her fingers over the rough stone of the wall as she searched the surface.

"Secret doorways, just like home," Dax whispered.

Paisley had her back to the others, flicking her attention between the tunnel they had just traveled down and the long corridor that it had opened onto.

She squinted as she looked between all three directions. The passage they had just traveled down was getting lighter, the darkness racing toward them as a warm glow pressed upon it from the end.

"Someone's coming," Paisley said. "I can see torchlight."

Corbett spun around. "We have to run."

"There is nowhere to run to," Odelia told him, her voice calm and steady. Her fingertips danced over the stone wall as if she had all the time in the world.

"They're getting closer," Paisley said, the light growing brighter.

She tightened her grip on the sword, widening her stance and shielding the others with her body.

"Paisley!" Dax whimpered.

The flickering torchlight of the tunnel shone onto her face. "Don't worry, Dax. I will not let them hurt you."

A low click sounded behind her and the soft whirl of cogs as Odelia's fingers found the release mechanism and a small opening formed as the rock face retracted.

"Quickly," Odelia said, entering the gap swiftly, followed by Corbett, who ducked so that Dax didn't hit his head on the low doorway.

Paisley glanced over her shoulder, making sure they were safely through before she too backed into the secret passage.

Paisley kept her eyes on the steadily growing amber light as beside her, Odelia struggled to turn a mighty brass wheel on the back of the door.

"It's jammed," she grunted as she tried to twist the wheel.

Paisley dropped the sword and cane, sidestepping to Odelia. Together they tugged on the wheel, but the cogs refused to budge.

"Dax, do you have the tool pouch for your brace?"

"Yes, yes, of course." Corbett let go of Dax. He slid to the ground, reaching into his coat pocket for the small wrap.

"The oil, Dax, quickly," Paisley said.

Dax pulled out the small bottle of oil and handed it toward his sister.

"Um...they're coming. I can see them. Pretty sure they can see me too," Corbett said.

Paisley chanced a look as she reached out for the bottle of oil.

Heavy footsteps reverberated in the hall now, and muffled cries announced that they had been found.

Paisley pulled the top off the bottle with her teeth, and she splurged the oil over the exposed cogs of the door. She and Odelia pulled with all their might as Corbett reached forward and picked up Paisley's dropped sword and Dax's cane.

Paisley could feel the wheel turning, the cogs moving into place and the door sliding shut. As it did, she caught sight of the approaching figures through the gap, the torchlight licking their faces into sharp relief.

"Roach and Lorena," she gasped.

The door rolled smoothly into place, shutting with a thud in Mistress Lorena's and Roach's faces.

Odelia pulled a lever on the side of the door, locking it into place and making it impossible to enter from the outside.

They could hear dull thuds on the door and a muffled roar.

Dax shuddered and moved closer to his sister. "You shouldn't make a dragon angry," he told her.

"I think you're right," she said, looking at the door as the pounding came again.

"We need to leave," Odelia said, holding the torch high and sending light into the small room.

A little way in front was a round opening in the floor. She walked toward the hole and jumped straight into it, the light falling away into the gap with her.

They all stared. Corbett let out a little scream, and Paisley clutched Dax as he jumped back.

"Odelia!" Paisley called as she stood completely still. "Odelia!"

A soft glow was coming from the hole in the floor.

"Jump down." Odelia's voice echoed up to them.

"I'm not jumping down there," Corbett said, eyeing the glowing gap in the floor.

"We don't have much time. There are other ways Lorena can get in. If you want to stay up there, fine. But she will find you eventually," Odelia called.

Paisley stepped in front of her brother. "Dax, I'll go first. I'll call up and tell you when to jump—okay?"

Dax nodded, but she could tell that he was unsure about the whole thing. Truth be known, she was a little apprehensive herself, but she shuffled forward to the edge of the soft glowing void, closed her eyes, and forced herself to jump. The fall was over in a second, not even long enough for Paisley to release the scream, which came out as a little gasp as she landed on a large soft pad, like the envelope of an airship. She lay there for a moment, bouncing slightly.

"Are you dead?" Corbett yelled down.

"Not yet," she called back, and scrambled off. "Dax, jump. There's a huge air-filled pocket, like on the copters—it's fun."

She heard a "Pah!" from Corbett. And a cry of excitement from Dax, followed by a loud thud as the air-filled pocket rippled, bouncing Dax back into the air before he flopped back down.

"That was fantastic; can we do it again?" he asked as he rolled off the air pocket and landed heavily on the ground. Paisley helped to pull him up to standing.

"Next time we're being chased for our lives," Paisley said with a grin before calling out, "All clear, Corbett."

Paisley turned back to see that Dax was walking away from her; her feet automatically followed him as she tried to assess what she was seeing.

They were inside a huge chamber, lit with electrica light from above, and filled with small strange airships, but they were unlike any she had ever seen. Completely round and made of metal, they looked like huge cricket balls, dotted with glass porthole windows scattered around the middle like a dotted ribbon.

The nearest one was glowing from within. A curving door was open on the side, and Odelia stepped out of it before crossing to the edge of the room and pulling a large bag from a hook, where other similar bags hung.

"What is it?" Dax asked.

"It's an escape pod," Odelia told him.

"Amazing. What does it do?"

Odelia threw the bag into the open pod, then turned and looked at Dax. "You escape in it, my Lord," she said, raising one eyebrow.

"Oh."

Just then a yell ripped through the air, and Corbett landed on the air pocket. He immediately bounced straight off, landing on his bottom, his glasses askew.

"Are you all right?" Paisley asked as she made to help him up.

Corbett shot to his feet, straightened his glasses and smoothed down his jacket, and brushed the dust from the seat of his trousers. "Fine, fine, never better. Not a very comfortable landing, is it," he said.

Paisley grinned and caught Dax's eye as he stifled a giggle.

"We don't have much time," Odelia said, looking at Corbett before she entered the pod, Dax following her.

Corbett looked from the pod to Paisley. "What's that?"

"That's our way out."

Paisley could tell that Corbett didn't like the look of it at all.

24

THE DRAGON IN THE DARK

Roach lowered his hand from his face. The heat from Mistress Lorena's fireball still hung in the air of the tunnel, sizzling off the blackened, scorched wall.

"Did you expect that to work?" he asked, looking at the wall through which Paisley and the others had fled.

He watched as she set her jaw. "There is another way to our quarry; hurry." The Dragon Mistress turned abruptly, her tattered tunic flying out behind her like broken wings.

She breathed a small ball of fire into her palm and held it out to guide the way. Her hand didn't burn, but Roach could smell something sweet and alkaline, like honeycomb.

He kept his distance as Lorena stalked down the corridor in front of him.

Roach was followed by the four Dark Dragon Walkers, Mayme and three others who had also betrayed their sisters for the Dark Dragon.

Roach's back felt itchy, as if the dark Dragon Walkers were lightly stroking the edges of their blades down his spine.

Lorena led them through the dark, twisting stone passages, past the doors to many great troves, each one full of priceless treasures and even more valuable secrets. Roach ground his teeth at the injustice of being so close to all that wealth and yet so far. Maybe he could gain access to the vaults after his deal with the Dark Dragon was fulfilled, after his world was restored to him and all was as it should be. Then he would become rich and powerful. He'd have been able to protect Clara if he had been wealthy, he was sure of it, just as the Fitzwilliam family had been able to protect Dax.

Lorena halted and placed the orb of fire on the floor, where it began to grow dim.

In the dying light, Roach watched as she took her spear and scratched at the ground. She pushed the dirt away from the stone floor with the sharp nightsilver tip of the weapon, tracing an unseen line, before pushing the blade of the weapon into the ground.

Just as the flame guttered and died, Roach heard a soft click and the whirl of cogs.

Lorena breathed out fire once more, flames lighting the darkness of the passage, revealing a set of stone steps that descended into darkness.

"Ladies first," Roach said, taking a step to the side so that Lorena and the dark Dragon Walkers could descend.

"I don't think so," Lorena replied, cocking her head toward the stairs. "Get on with it."

"Just trying to be gentlemanly like," Roach replied with a shrug.

The steps were steep. The glowing light from Lorena's hands slipped over the tip of each one like a cascading waterfall.

Roach lazily rested his hand on the hilt of the knife at his side, listening to the darkness below him and the light above. The Dragon Walkers moved soundlessly, like smoke pulled along in his descent.

At the end of the steps, a short passageway opened abruptly into a huge room containing lines of round metal escape pods.

Roach pulled his knife from his belt and began to walk slowly among the pods. He noticed that each one sat on top of a large, round plate, sliced in the middle to create a trapdoor.

Lorena and the initiates fanned out on either side of him, forming a line, each one of them with a weapon drawn, all listening to the silence of the pod hangar and stepping lightly on the smooth floor.

As they neared the opposite wall, Roach let out a breath and stowed his knife. He took sure strides that echoed around the room, clanging as he shifted from the stone of the floor to the metal of an empty hatch devoid of its pod. He bent his knees and pressed his hand to the trapdoor.

"They've gone. The Dark Dragon won't be impressed. If you'd only waited for me," he told Lorena as he gazed up at her from the floor.

"What has passed has passed; it cannot be undone. The cogs have spun; the track has been traveled," Lorena said. "But fear not; we will find them."

She walked over to the wall and took a small box from a shelf. Inside was a large, compass-like device.

She brought it back to the empty trapdoor and looked down at the brass plate affixed to it. The number 042 was engraved on the plate. Lorena twisted three dials on the right of the compass; each one glowed as she turned it to display the number of the pod. She then flipped the switch on the opposite side of the apparatus, and electrica energy lit up the glass surface of the device, showing a glowing blue dot over the top of the cardinal lines of North-South, East-West.

"There they are," Lorena said, pointing to the dot.

25

GERONIMO

Inside the pod, Paisley's hands clenched the armrests of the chair as the straps cut into her shoulders and across her lap. She felt as if a huge weight was pushing down on her body, pressing her into the very fabric of the pod, squashing her breath deep into her lungs.

She didn't know how Corbett, who was seated next to her, was able to scream, but that didn't last long before his head drooped to one side.

"Corbett!" Paisley managed in a stifled croak. "Corbett, Corbett, can you hear me?"

"It happens sometimes; don't worry, he'll be fine," Odelia assured Paisley as she flicked a few switches on the chair.

Dax was sitting directly opposite Paisley, smiling from excitement or fear, she couldn't tell. Odelia was sitting at what Paisley guessed were the controls; the arms of her chair had a series of buttons and small brass toggled levers running all over them.

In the soft green glow from the instrument displays, Paisley could see that Odelia was wearing a pair of dark round goggles.

She followed Odelia's gaze to a series of moving dials on the wall opposite her, close to the hatch of the door. Its large porthole showed nothing but an inky black sky full of stars that looked as if they were streaking upward. Paisley felt herself being foolish as she made a wish.

Odelia reached out and pulled the nearest brass toggle back.

Paisley's stomach flipped as the pressure lifted; the pod slowed dramatically as a huge parachute opened above them.

"Dax, are you all right?"

"That was even better than jumping through the hole!" Dax said as he smiled broadly at Paisley. "Odelia, can I have a go at driving the pod?"

"I was not aware that you had a pilot's license, my Lord of Dragons," Odelia said with a slight incline of her head as she monitored the dials on the wall.

"Well, I haven't exactly got a license. But I did once go up in my uncle Hector's airship, and he let me sit in the copilot's chair."

"Then you are in luck," Odelia said. "Because that very chair that you are sitting in is reserved for the copilot, and when it is time, I have a very important task for you; do you feel you are up to it, Dragon Lord?"

Dax nodded enthusiastically.

Paisley scowled. "Don't call him that."

"Why not?" she said. "It is who he is, after all. He is a boy, born with the Touch of the Dragon, heralded by the Heavens."

"No, he's not," snapped Paisley.

"Then, tell me, sister of the Dragon Lord, who is he?"

Paisley didn't like the way that Odelia looked at Dax or that she was so certain of who he was. "He's my brother," Paisley said. "He is ten turnings old. He is a little boy—"

"I'm not that little!" Dax interrupted.

Paisley ignored him, still looking at Odelia. "I won't allow any harm to come to him." Paisley stared at Odelia, who solemnly locked eyes with her.

Odelia nodded. "And neither shall I. He is my master now, and I will give my life for his."

Paisley knew immediately that what Odelia said was true and didn't know whether to feel reassured or afraid.

"You don't have to do that," Dax whispered. "I don't want to be the master of anyone."

"That may be so, but we all have a track to follow, and your track, forged by the Chief Designer in the breath of the Great Dragon Anu, is to be the Dragon Lord. *He who will return to us the days of triumph.* I and many others will give our lives to see that day, to be able to walk the lands of the Empire freely once more. You must remember, my Lord, that my life is my own to give. You cannot stop me. It is my track in the world, not yours."

"But I don't want it," Dax said. "And you can't *make* me be the Dragon Lord."

Odelia smiled. "I am not making you do anything. It is already forged, my Lord."

Paisley took a deep breath, her fingers gripping the arms of her seat in frustration. "That's not true," said Paisley. "We don't have to follow any track but the one of our own making. Our mother believed that; she was always telling us to forge our own lives."

"This is impossible. Only a Great Dragon can forge the metal of the Celestial Mechanism, and only the Chief Designer has the ability to plan the course of the tracks."

Paisley stared openmouthed. Everything she said, Odelia had an answer to, and one that made total sense to the world at large, but Paisley knew that it was not so. She knew deep in her being that her mother had been right, and the thrill of that deep, dark knowledge burned like dragon fire within her.

"What I don't understand is that if you want the return of the Great Dragons, then why don't you help the Dark Dragon? She wants the same thing too, right?" Dax asked.

"Not quite. We Dragon Walkers are striving for unity, recognition, and the freedom to be who we are, where and when we want to be it. We want the same rights as all the other citizens of the Mechanism. We believe that the Great Dragon Malgol will help us to do that, and that he will be delivered unto us and aided by a Dragon Touched boy.

"But we do not believe in tracing a track backward. What is done cannot be undone; what has entered the Veil cannot be retrieved. The Great Dragons are gone. What the Dark Dragon seeks to do goes against everything we Dragon Walkers believe in. She wants revenge. She wants to punish the George and the Mechanists and all who follow them, and rule over all who don't."

"I see," Dax said quietly as Paisley wished that some tracks could be traveled backward and changed.

"What . . . what happened?" Corbett asked groggily as he opened his eyes and raised his hand to his head.

"You passed out," Odelia told him.

"Oh." He looked from Paisley to Dax, the soft light of the instrument display outlining their features. "Did anybody else pass out?"

"No," Odelia answered.

"Oh, right."

"Don't worry," Paisley said, with an edge in her voice and a piercing look at Odelia. "It happens sometimes."

Corbett nodded and brightened a little.

"Brace yourselves for landing," Odelia commanded.

"Are we landing at one of the aerodocs?" Paisley asked.

"No, pods aren't designed to be maneuvered so accurately; we'll be landing in the Thames."

"The Thames! But it's frozen!" Paisley said.

"Only by a few inches," Odelia replied. "We'll be going fast enough to smash right through to the icy waters below."

"I can't swim," Corbett said.

Odelia sighed.

Paisley just had time to tell Corbett not to worry when the pod hit the frozen water, jolting them all upward as they smashed through the layer of ice.

The pod plunged deep into the thick, churning river, the portholes covered in darkness before it sprang back up to the surface like an aquanaut's submarine, chunks of ice floating around them.

"That was brilliant!" Dax declared. "Can we do it again?"

"Yes, the very next time we are running for our lives," Odelia said as she pressed the seat belt release and jumped out. She approached Dax. "Right, my Lord, I promised you a job worthy of a copilot." She removed her goggles and placed them on Dax's head.

"Wow," he said. "I can see everything as clear as day; it's as if electrica lights are shining on you all but only I can see them."

"It's a form of alchemy. We Dragon Walkers have learned to build many devices, just as the Great Dragons built the universe."

"They're amazing," Dax said, twisting his head from right to left.

"Sit in my seat," Odelia said. "You can navigate us to the shore."

"We don't have to swim?" Corbett asked, not bothering to hide the relief in his voice.

"No, no swimming. Not all dragons do well with water," Odelia said, and something about the way she said it reminded Paisley of the way that Dax spoke about spiders. He was fine with the little ones, but the thought of a big one worried him.

Paisley felt the pod begin to move smoothly as Odelia showed Dax which controls to use. Through the porthole, the lights on the banks of the Thames grew bigger as the pod moved closer to dry land.

"What do we do next?" Corbett asked Paisley.

"Next," Paisley said firmly, "we visit the Natural History Museum."

"I like museums as much as the next person, but I'm not sure that that is such a good idea," Odelia said.

"It's a *great* idea," Dax said. "I love the Natural History Museum."

"I've never been," Corbett said.

"You've been missing out," Dax told him. "There's so much fantastic stuff there. There's this exhibition on at the moment..."

"We're not going on a sightseeing tour; we're going to see Doc Langley," Paisley cut in.

"Who is this doctor?" Odelia asked.

"He's a Dragonologist."

"And he is one of your mother's friends?" Even in the dull light from the torches on the bank of the Thames, Paisley could see that Odelia was raising one disbelieving eyebrow again.

"Sort of," Paisley said. "Corbett said that Doc Langley and she were working on a project together: OORT. I think it might have something to do with Mother's experiment, and the more information we have, the better chance we have of finding the Heart Stone. Besides, I found a book in Mother's study; it would seem that my father had been a student of his."

"Father studied *dragons*?" Dax asked, a look of excited bewilderment on his face.

"It appears so," Paisley said.

Dax shook his head in disbelief. "Wow, how exciting this whole adventure is, don't you think?"

"Oh yes, Master Dax. I think it is all very exciting—after all, we Dragon Walkers live for such things as death-defying adventure. The fear of dying makes it all the more exciting." Odelia's eyes glinted.

"Dying!" Corbett said.

"No one is going to die," Paisley told him.

"Besides, you saw the way Odelia can fight; she'll keep us safe," Dax said.

"I promised my service to you alone, Master Dax, not to your sister or friend," Odelia said, flicking a few switches and bathing the interior of the pod in harsh electrica light.

"Well, Paisley's a great fighter anyway, but Corbett is useless. No offense, Corbett."

"Oh, no, none taken, I'm sure," Corbett muttered.

"You will save them?" Dax asked as he pushed the goggles up on his head. "If they need saving. I mean, I wouldn't want to be saved if Paisley wasn't . . . and Corbett, I guess."

"Thanks, it just gets better," Corbett said in a small voice as he unfastened his restraints.

The pod rocked as it bumped into the riverbank.

Odelia began to twist the locking handle on the pod. The door opened with a hiss.

"It's not far to the bank; a short jump should do it," she told them before moving to one side.

"I'll go first," Paisley said, pushing an eager Dax behind her. "I'll catch you on the bank."

Paisley leaped from the bobbing pod and landed on the slippery ground, her legs buckling as she hit. She quickly stood and turned to look at the pod, sitting in the water like a giant buoy. The soft light from inside joined the light from the gas lamps and bounced off the lapping waters of the Thames in glowing, rippling pools.

She looked up and saw the small glow of Kensington Above, a fast star against the midnight black beyond. To think they had been all the way up there just a few minutes ago. Paisley took a deep breath and let her legs wobble before rallying.

"Come on, Dax," she whispered into the darkness.

Dax's head appeared, silhouetted in front of the light.

"Geronimo!" he cried as he leaped straight into Paisley's outstretched arms. She caught him and then held him close.

"Are you all right?" she asked as she hugged him.

"I will be, once we find Mother," he said, hugging her back. "We *will* find her, won't we?"

"Of course we will."

"Look out!" Corbett landed on Paisley and Dax, pushing them both to the ground in a tangled mess.

"Corbett!" Dax said. "We didn't just plummet from a floating borough so that you could squish us."

"I'm sorry, I didn't mean to." Corbett rolled to one side, pushing his glasses back up his nose. Paisley stood and helped Dax to his feet.

"It's all right, Corbett. But we'd better move to one side before Odelia knocks us all down again," Paisley added as she took Corbett's hand and pulled him to his feet.

"Odelia wouldn't land on us; she'd do some Dragon Walker trick and somersault right over us," Dax said. Paisley imagined it in her head just as Odelia landed soundlessly behind her.

Corbett let out a little yell and grabbed Paisley's arm as he saw Odelia's shadow loom down on them.

"Relax, Corbett, it's just . . . Odelia?" Paisley paused, unsure as she looked into the darkness.

"Odelia, is that you?" she said.

It *was* Odelia, but she looked just like any other Lower Londoner. She wore a long, dark traveling cloak. The hood was pulled up, and underneath she wore an elegantly curled wig. At the bottom of the cloak, Paisley could just make out the blue and red of her trousers billowing out over the top of her boots. There were no signs of the weapons she had carried, but Paisley bet she still had them on her, concealed just like her wings.

Paisley thought that she looked both trapped and magnificent. She could still see the power of the Dragon Walker, barely contained within the shell of societal conformity.

Odelia reminded Paisley of her mother, completely herself beneath the disguise that she wore to make others feel comfortable around her. She hoped that one day she would be strong enough to look like them both.

"I'm in disguise," Odelia told them.

"Aye, we can see that," Corbett added as he admired Odelia.

She ignored him and pushed a curl from the wig back under her hood. "If any Dragon Walker is caught in the Empire, we are killed immediately. We dragons need to be cunning," she added, with a look toward Dax. "You need to change your trousers. Someone might see your Touch."

"I don't have any spare clothes," Dax said, looking down at the burned hole in his trousers and the unmarked dragon scales below.

"Ah, not to worry, Dax," Paisley said, digging in her pocket. "I have your spare long sock." She helped him put it on as Odelia looked up at the sky, her Dragon Touched eyes adjusting in the light and focusing in on Kensington Above.

She saw a small metal spark falling from the borough.

"We aren't safe here," she said.

"Well, in that case"—Paisley reached for Dax's hand—"let's go see a man about some dragons."

26

THE DRAGONIAN WING

Dax scampered up the steps at the front of the Natural History Museum and banged on the large wooden double doors, Paisley and the others following. Stone creatures watched them from their lofty homes around the stained-glass windows and the tops of the towers. Paisley felt their dead eyes on her and shuddered.

"They're closed. No one will answer; you will have to come back tomorrow," Odelia said as Dax continued to bang on the doors.

Paisley could have kicked herself. "I didn't even think that no one would be here," she muttered. "Even if we could get in, I don't suppose Doc Langley would be there."

"I doubt it," Odelia said as she crossed her arms in front of her chest and raised an eyebrow at Corbett, who was also banging on the double doors, calling for attention.

"But there might be a home address for him, a personnel file or something." Paisley looked to Odelia. The hood of her cloak was still up, and she was scratching at the dark hair of the wig underneath it.

"You could get in, couldn't you, Odelia? Maybe fly up and find an open window," Paisley asked.

The Dragon Walker turned and looked at Paisley. "Of course I could," she replied. "But there's no need."

"What makes you say that?"

"Because the way those two are going, they'll have the Great Dragon bones awake and answering the door in no time."

Odelia was almost right as moments later a light moved steadily toward the doors.

Paisley darted forward as one of the doors opened a crack.

"The museum's shut—clear off!" said a rough voice. As Paisley's eyes adjusted, she saw a large man in a guard uniform holding an electrica lantern.

"Excuse me, sir, we're looking for someone; it's extremely important," Paisley said.

The guard looked at her, then beyond to Dax and Corbett. Paisley shot a glance over her shoulder; Odelia was gone.

"I 'spect it is mightily important, the racket you was making."

"Oh, it is, sir. It's a matter of life or death," Dax added.

"Really? Whose?" the guard asked.

"Our mother's," Paisley told him. "Do you know where we might be able to find Doc Langley?"

"I might, but I think 'e's the wrong type of Doctor for that." The guard's face softened as he looked between the three of them, his eyes coming to rest on Dax. "It's a bit late for him to be out, ain't it?" he said to Paisley, gesturing to Dax with his lantern.

"Yes," said Paisley. "I suppose it is, but like I said, it's an emergency."

"Best you come in, then. The Doc usually keeps late hours; I reckon he's still here. Besides, it's getting a bit nippy out here."

The guard held the door open, and the three of them hurried inside.

Corbett looked around and realized that Odelia was gone. "Where's...?" Paisley abruptly shook her head, and Corbett fell silent.

"Where's what, now, young man?" the guard asked.

"Where's, um...the dragons?" Corbett asked.

"Ain't you never been to the Natural History Museum before?" Corbett shook his head.

"Blimey! Most of the dragons are in the Dragonian Wing." The guard gave a chuckle. "Dragonian Wing, get it?"

"Oh aye, very funny," Corbett said, and gave a false laugh.

"But she's just up here."

"She?" Corbett mouthed to Paisley, who smiled and nodded after the guard. He bristled with pride as he jogged up the short flight of stairs and clicked an electrica switch on the wall. Bright white lights filled the vast vaulted ceiling.

Below the cathedral-like hall, in the center, was one of the last Great Dragons to have walked the Earth.

She was perfectly preserved. Her green-gray scales looked like pebbles in a riverbed, each one glistening as if she had just leaped from the water.

Her wings were outstretched, threatening to beat at any moment as she reared up on her legs, mouth open, teeth bared.

Fyrdhwæt, the small brass plaque at her feet named her in Old Celtic.

"She's . . . magnificent," Corbett said in awe as he moved forward and reached out a hand.

"No touching, lad," the guard said, and Corbett slowly moved his fingers back.

"Yep, she's something, ain't she? Although I don't mind telling ya that I'm mighty glad her and her kind ain't about today. Swallow you whole they would, 'specially a little 'un like you."

Dax looked at the man sternly. "They would never eat me," he told the guard, who laughed and ruffled Dax's hair.

"'Spect you fancy yourself as one of these Krigare, a Dragon Rider, aye? Yeah, can't say I blame you. When I was your age, I dreamed of running away to the North too," the guard told them as he began to lead them out of the hall.

"I don't know why everyone is so eager to go North. Take it from me, it's blooming cold up there," Corbett said.

"Yeah, but I'm sure those dragons keep 'em warm."

Paisley shot a look at Dax as they followed the guard. Dax's cane tapped on the smooth floor as his foot fell in its twisted motion, rocking him from side to side.

As they exited the hall, Dax caught the glimpse of a shadow on the balcony above. He discreetly pointed. Paisley had already seen Odelia flitting from exhibit to exhibit as she followed them through the museum, as silent as the dragon in the entrance hall.

The guard led them through the galleries before they came to the doors of the Dragonian Wing. The doors were tall and covered in cogs, reminding Paisley of the doors of the Mechanist chapel. It seemed like a long time ago that she had received her stars. But in fact it was only yesterday. The Mechanism had seemingly begun spinning out of control from that moment.

The guard pulled a ring of keys from the chain on his waistcoat and began to search for the right one. They jangled loudly, but Paisley was still able to hear the delicate susurrations of Odelia leaping from the balcony and landing softly behind them, her wings outstretched to soften her fall. Paisley turned her head just in time to see the wings fold back on themselves, and for a moment, she wished she had been Dragon Touched like Odelia, like Dax.

The guard pushed open the door, and Dax eagerly hobbled forward.

Paisley's cheeks flushed as she saw his face set in grim determination as he moved his leg forward.

She stepped close to him as they entered the room.

"Is your brace still rubbing?" she asked. He nodded and continued walking. "I could piggyback you for a while?" she offered.

"I'll be fine," he said. "I can rest when we find Mother."

"You can rest when we find Doc Langley," Paisley said gently.

They walked past glass cases full of Pigmy Dragons. Corbett stopped now and again, marveling at their diversity.

"Those are Papillion Dragons," Dax told him as he peered into a case of dragons no bigger than a moth or butterfly. They ranged in color from puddle gray and moss green to jewellike sapphire blues and lime greens.

"They can get quite big," Dax continued as he pointed to a glass display case that had a tree standing in the middle with rocks all around it; to one side was a puddle of water.

Small, bird-sized dragons ranging from the size of finches and sparrows to swans and geese filled the exhibition.

"Most of the bigger ones are extinct now, some of the smaller, brighter ones too. My friend Marcus said he once saw a Golden Crested in Covent Garden." Dax pointed to a small golden-yellow dragon, with a long tail and amber horned scales on its head that looked like a crown.

"They're ... magnificent," Corbett said, giving his glasses a quick clean on his waistcoat before putting them on and peering closer. "Back home we sometimes saw small flocks o' Loch Leeder." He pointed to one of the larger dragons with mottled brown scales and flashes of white on the underside of their wings. "If we saw them, we were supposed to report them."

"You didn't, did you?" Dax looked at Corbett in earnest.

"No, I'd never," Corbett said, holding Dax's gaze.

Dax nodded, and Paisley watched as his shoulders relaxed a little.

They had reached the back of the wing, where the larger dragons were displayed. There were four of them, the size of Shetland ponies, each a different breed. Dax made a beeline for one of the dragons.

She was frozen in space and time. Corbett couldn't work out if she was just about to land, or had just taken off, her talons curling several inches above the ground, her wings mid-beat.

"Isn't she magnificent? She's my favorite," Dax said, his eyes fixed on the dragon.

Paisley and Corbett walked around the dragon. Her scales were all the grays and blues of a winter storm; her eyes were as bright as a lightning strike, and her twisting talons and claws were as white as snow.

When Corbett reached her tail, he saw a three-pronged barb, like a trident. Each barb, like the claws and talons, was sharp enough to slice a man in half unless he was wearing nightsilver armor.

"To think, all that stood between a knight and a dragon was his nightsilver," said Corbett wonderingly. "And that my family was part of the chain that reached back to the First George and the start of the destruction of the Great Dragons. I can't decide if I feel pride for the skill and bravery of my forebears or guilt at what had become of the Great Dragons."

"Maybe a bit of both," Paisley said.

"Aye, I think you're right."

The guard rattled his keys once more and opened a door at the back of the exhibition hall.

Paisley held the door open and signaled with her head for Dax and Corbett to follow the guard. Corbett passed her with a confused look.

"Odelia," she whispered.

He nodded and hurried along the corridor with Dax, throwing a look over his shoulder to see Paisley walking fast behind him, a shadow larger than her own trailing her.

"The Doc's a good man; I've always liked him," the guard said. "Full of interesting stuff. Most of them are smart, but Doc Langley takes the time to talk to you. The others are far too busy and important.

"Did you know that a dragon can hold its breath underwater for over four hours and that Great Dragons are thought to have been able to hold their breaths for nearly a day?"

"Yes, I knew that," Dax said as he walked beside the guard, his cane tapping as they began to walk up a set of plain stone stairs, less grand than the public areas of the museum.

"Ahh," the guard said, scratching his chin. "Well, did ya know that in the East—China and the like—they never had Great Dragons like what we had in the Empire and the North? They had Dragons that were longer, like they'd been stretched out."

"Yes, I knew that too," Dax replied.

"Um, and I guess you already knew that those dragons had smaller wingspans and were thought to be more genteel?"

"Yes, and I know that they all died from a curse back in the early days of the Empire, when one of the kings before the George made a gift of a Great Dragon to the people of China."

The guard snorted like a disgruntled dragon. "You know a lot then, don't ya?" he said as they reached the top of the stairs.

"It certainly sounds like he does," said a deep controlled voice from above them; the soft Amerikan accent was unmistakable. "Except it wasn't a curse that killed the Asian Dragons, but disease. There are no such things as curses."

Doc Langley was standing at the top of the stairs, holding open the door that led to his vast workroom.

He was just as Paisley had seen him in the book, a little older but nonetheless a small neat little man, with white hair and a beard. He wore the many trinkets and tools of his trade strapped to his leg and waist.

"Thank you, Hammond, for showing my guests up. I can take it from here."

The guard nodded. "If you're sure, Doc, I do have other things to be getting on with."

Paisley looked worriedly down the stairs as the guard passed her. Odelia was nowhere in sight.

Doc Langley waited a few minutes, listening to the retreating guard and holding up a finger to stop Dax from speaking, his mouth half open.

The door to the exhibition hall echoed as it closed, and Doc Langley let out a long breath.

"Quickly, follow me; we've got a lot to discuss," he said as he turned and entered the workshop. "And, Miss Fitzwilliam, tell your Dragon Walker friend that she need not skulk in the shadows on my account," he called back over his shoulder

✦ ✦ ✳ ✦ ✦

On the banks of the Thames, Roach stood looking at the abandoned escape pod.

"They couldn't have gone far," he said as Lorena leaped out of the pod, followed by her four Dark Dragon Walker faithfuls.

Lorena turned on Roach. "We must find them."

Roach reached inside his pocket and pulled out a handful of cogroaches. The soft light from the gas lamps glinted off the metallic black wing casings. "We'll have hold of them before you can say *Dark Dragon*."

"I hope for your sake that you are right," the Mistress of War threatened. Roach opened his hand flat, and a group of beetles flew off into the night.

27

OORT

Jars lined the walls of Doc Langley's workshop, each one carefully labeled in clear cursive script. The different-sized jars were full of clear liquid, and suspended within each one floated a specimen.

Some contained tiny Papillion Dragons, their jewellike bodies glistening from within their liquid prison. Others contained pieces of dragons.

Paisley noticed Odelia curling her lip in disgust as her eyes skimmed each of the jars. Odelia's hands tightened into fists.

Doc Langley led them toward the back of the workshop, where a large wooden bench ran across the room. Laid out on it was the skeleton of a bird-sized Pigmy Dragon. The bones were as dark as nightsilver.

She looked down at her brother's encased leg and wondered if the bones in his Dragon Touched leg were made of the same dark material as the dragon bones on the bench.

"Come on through," Doc Langley called as he opened the door to a messy study. Papers and books, instruments, and small specimen jars littered the shelves.

On the wall was a map of the Empire of Albion and beyond. Colored pins scattered the landmasses in certain areas along with elegantly written notes, which Paisley assumed must belong to Doc Langley. Amerika contained the most pins, but Paisley looked to India, where she knew Doc Langley had been with her father. She tried to decipher the handwritten scrawl next to the pin that was placed there, but she was too far away.

Somewhere in the middle of all the clutter was a desk, covered in anatomical drawings and written papers, all in the same neat font that labeled each of the jars in the workroom and the map on the wall.

"Just clear the papers from the chairs," Doc said, adding with a little sigh, "I don't get many visitors."

Paisley looked around and found a chair covered in books. She lifted them up and placed them on the top of an already over-burdened bookcase, then signaled to Dax to sit on it while she found another place to perch.

Dax gave a sigh of relief as he took the weight off his leg.

Corbett followed Paisley's lead and cleared a small stool of its burden. Odelia waited for Doc Langley to close the door before standing with her back to it, her cloak unbuttoned, her hands rested on her hips, within easy reach of her belted weapons.

Doc Langley smiled at Odelia. "Of course, if you don't feel like sitting, that's fine by me."

The Dragon Walker looked as if trouble was about to rush forth again. Paisley couldn't help but think of Lorena, of the way the fire burst out of her.

Paisley took her mother's watch from her pocket and held it in her hands, the warmth radiating out into her fingers, keeping her hope alive and her will straight.

"Now, I understand that you children have had a busy day of it," Doc Langley said as he moved a battered old brown fedora hat and picked up a copper pot that had been nestling underneath it. He bustled about near the little stove that was beside his desk and dangerously close to a pile of papers.

Paisley wondered how the whole place hadn't yet caught fire.

"Doc Langley," she said, "how do you know what we've been up to?"

"Well, for starters you can just call me Doc—everyone else does, makes me feel more comfortable. And as for me knowing what you've been up to, Miss Paisley, well . . . you see, there are a great many things that I know about you. You and your brother," he said with a nod and a quick gaze at Dax's leg.

He knows, Paisley thought as a bolt of fear ran through her. She locked eyes with Dax, whose face had gone white.

In the space of a day, the number of people who knew about Dax's Touch had doubled, to Paisley's mind.

She proceeded with caution. "And how is it that you know so much about us?"

Doc Langley poured water from a flask into the copper pot and set it to boil while he started to fuss about with a tin of powdered cocoa as he spoke.

"Well, I knew your parents pretty well. We were old friends, you see."

"Friends." Paisley raised an eyebrow. "As I understand it, you and Mother had fallen out." She looked at Corbett.

"I heard the two of you arguing a few weeks back. The professor was . . ."

"Angry with me." Doc Langley sighed as he sank back into his chair, the pot warming on the stove. "I know she was, and I was giving her time to calm down and see reason. But now—now that she's . . ." He looked from Paisley to Dax and gave a little cough as he rallied himself. "Now that she's dead, of course I wish we hadn't had words."

"What were you arguing about?" Paisley asked.

The Dragonologist took in a long breath, then leaned forward in his chair. "What I'm about to tell you children must stay in this room. You must never speak of it to anyone—I'm trusting you. Do you understand?"

"I think so," Paisley said as the others nodded, even Odelia.

"I first met your father many turnings ago—"

"When he was a scholar of Dragonology," Dax interrupted.

"Ah, you know about that, do you? Well, yes, that was when we first met, and I could tell at once that he was a bright fellow with a bend in his track and stars that burned with the biggest of questions.

"It seemed to me that our meeting was fated; we had a bond in common, you see. My forefather, Sir Kenneth Langley, was one of the First Knights of the George, just as your father's forbearer, Sir Lucan Fitzwilliam, had been. Sir Kenneth and Sir Lucan, along with three other founding knights, Sir Jasper Selby, Sir Yellen Crane, and Sir Penvrill Foster, all formed a secret order, the Order of Right Turning."

"OORT," Paisley said.

"Quite. The Order has been going for centuries. Over the turnings, members of the founding families have come and gone and others have joined in their place. I was a member, I still am, as is my brother. When I met your father, he was not a member, no Fitzwilliam was, but I invited him to join. And soon after he married your mother, she too joined the Order."

Doc Langley turned to the stove and gave the liquid a stir. The smell of warm cocoa filled the air.

"What does the Order of Right Turning do?" Paisley asked.

"We are seekers of the truth. When the first knights assisted in the Great Purge, they discovered something, something that the

Order has spent thousands of turnings trying to understand."

He took the pot from the stove and poured the creamy brown cocoa into five tin cups. As he spoke, he handed out the cups, then offered them each a piece of rich-looking fruit cake.

"Have you ever realized that in the whole world there have only ever been eighteen Great Dragon bodies recovered? Eighteen, from a species that numbered in the tens of thousands.

"Granted, it was a long time ago; if it had been any other animal on Earth, I would make allowances for deterioration, but we are talking about *dragons*." Doc Langley paused and took a sip of his cocoa.

"Only eighteen. Are you sure?" Paisley asked.

Doc Langley smiled. "Yes, I'm sure."

"But their bones and claws last forever, stronger than nightsilver even in death," Paisley said.

"Aye, and their hides too. Just look at the one in the entrance hall of the museum; she looks as if she's still warm. How can it be that so few have been found?" Corbett asked.

"Precisely." Doc Langley raised both eyebrows, his eyes twinkling. "It is a puzzle. Some, no doubt, have been stolen; dragons are valuable things. In fact, they are worth more dead than alive. Many have looked for the missing bodies of the Great Dragons, but as I said, only the eighteen have been recovered—that we know of.

"The theory of OORT is this." Doc Langley rose and pulled a book down from his shelf.

It was old and dusty, the title declared in Old Celtic: *Tales of the Veil.*

"As I said, the founders of our Order were with the George during the Great Purge. There are no direct accounts of what happened, not even in the Order's records; we only have written laws and duties, which I will get to, but I want you to understand it as I have.

"When I was a boy, not much older than you, Dax, my grandpa showed me this book. Our descendants had lived in Amerika since the George sent his knights westward to follow the Great Dragons that were fleeing the Purge. I've always been fascinated by dragons, but I don't think that was the reason my grandpa showed me this book."

Doc Langley thumbed through the musty pages and opened it to an illuminated page near the end.

He turned the book around to face the children and pointed at a section of text below a picture of the first George. He was on horseback; both he and his steed were covered in nightsilver, and in his hand he held his lance, Ascalon, pointing at the heart of a Great Dragon.

"What does it say, Paisley?" Dax asked.

But it was Corbett who answered. "It says, *The Banishment o' Dragons.*" He dragged the book toward him and traced his finger under the old-fashioned Celtic script as he translated it into English.

"And from the West rode a knight from Albion and in his hand he held a lance called Ascalon and from its tip all dragons did flee.

"And when that mighty lance did face its foe, it would pierce the Veil and into that would flow the life and heart and soul of the dragon."

Paisley sank back in her chair, as the words formed a solid meaning in her head.

"After I read that, I asked my grandfather a single question. Is there anything you would like to ask me?" He looked at them each in turn.

"Where did the Dragons go?" Dax asked, his voice rising as he posed his question.

"They went into the Veil, Dax; the text tells us that. What it doesn't tell us is *how*," Paisley said. "How did the lance—Ascalon—pierce the Veil?"

"That is exactly what I asked and that is what the Order has been asking for all these turnings. How did the mighty lance Ascalon pierce the Veil, and what is the nature of the Veil itself?"

"You are saying that the Great Dragons passed into the Veil? This is not possible," Odelia said. "The Veil is not a place of flesh and blood and bone; it is for the spirit, the consciousness only. We Dragon Walkers know how to walk in the Veil; we speak there with our ancestors, with ancient teachers. There are no Great Dragons in the Veil."

Doc Langley tipped his head to one side, took a sip of his cocoa, and brushed cake crumbs from his beard.

"Corbett said you hadn't wanted Mother to perform her experiment. Why?" Paisley asked.

"Ahh, that is a tricky one to answer." Doc Langley thought for a moment, stroking his beard. *"There is only one track,"* he said, quoting Mechanist scripture. Paisley could hear the muted Amerikan in his accent. "The Mechanists believe that we all follow our tracks, from start to finish, from birth to death. Our track is set in the stars. The Mechanism brings order and order is life. It gives us structure and contentment. Take it away and many would be lost and overcome. Take that away and the Mechanists would lose the power and control that they have."

"But how would that impact on the Order?" Paisley asked.

"We operate within the system; we have some answers but not all of them. If we present the truth to the world now, we have nothing to replace it with, and people need something to believe in."

"Wouldn't they believe in the truth?" Dax asked.

"What is the truth?" Odelia took a step closer.

"There is no set track," Paisley said, the force of the words hitting her. She had believed it as soon as she had seen the photograms at the lecture. Mother had looked at her and Dax and told them straight, but she hadn't believed it was as easy as that. "Mother used intention to move the comet; she made it happen. We can all move comets; we can make our own destiny." Paisley looked over at Dax, finally understanding the enormity of what her mother was trying to achieve.

Paisley sensed the atmosphere in the room shift and thicken.

Odelia moved to stand behind Paisley. "That is impossible. The

Great Dragons forged the Mechanism. Only they can bend the tracks to their will."

"But what if your will was great?" said Paisley.

"Aye," said Corbett slowly. "And you had a machine of your own to amplify it."

"A machine that could bend the Celestial Mechanism, a machine that could do anything," Paisley said. "Even . . ."

"Even open the Veil," Doc Langley added.

28

SLEEPING DRAGONS

"We need to rescue Mother," said Paisley. "If the Dark Dragon makes her perform her experiment again, but this time with the Dark Dragon's intention, who knows what might happen."

"Indeed, the Dark Dragon must be stopped at all costs," Odelia added, clapping a hand on Paisley's shoulder in agreement.

"I'm sorry, but we cannot get your mother back; she is with the Veil now, and as for this Dark Dragon, I am at a loss."

Paisley held the watch out and passed it to Doc Langley. "No. Mother is alive."

"The nightsilver in this watch was bonded with Violetta; it's warm and strong," Corbett said.

"Ah, of course, the marrying of silver and host, the promise of life that the warmth holds as opposed to the knowledge of death that cold nightsilver brings. It's a little-known nightsilver law—but I still don't understand. How did she survive the accident?"

"The accident was a ruse to cover up that Mother was taken." Paisley proceeded to tell Doc Langley all about the Dark Dragon, Roach, the attack in the Dragon Vault, the Soul Sisters, Grandmama Fiona's necklace, and why they needed to find the Heart Stone, to trade it for Mother's life.

Doc Langley paused and thought about this for a long moment. "If this is true," he said at last, "and I have no reason to doubt you, except that it does all sound a little fantastical, although no more fantastical than lances that can pierce the Veil, I might add . . . But if it is true, then why come to me?"

"We are out of ideas, Doc. Our last hope was that the Heart Stone was in the Vault, but it wasn't. We need help," Paisley pleaded.

Dax pulled the egg out of his pocket and placed it on the desk, then tugged out the chain and the empty setting that he had retrieved from the floor when Lorena fell.

It swung in his hands, and through the vacant ring of gold, Paisley saw Doc Langley's face light up.

He was staring at the silver-covered egg. His hands reached out tentatively for it.

When he spoke, his voice was breathy and full of awe. "Where did you find this?"

"It was in our family trove," Dax said as Doc Langley reached out a hand and gently picked up the egg. He hastily scooped up his glasses with his free hand and clicked several of the lenses on his spectacles into place, making his left eye magnify several times.

"I never thought I'd live to see the day."

Doc Langley swung around an electrica lamp and shone it on the egg. The nightsilver looked dull against the egg's shell. It shone in the electrica light as if it were crushed glass, twinkling like a sky full of starlight.

Doc Langley snatched up the egg and rushed out of the room.

"Come, see this," he called to them as he entered the workroom and turned on the electrica lights. He made his way to a workbench near a side door, placing the egg gently down on the bench.

He turned and searched the drawers of a large cabinet behind him, pulling from the drawers several cardboard boxes, each one labeled in his thin, looping script.

"Do you know what this is?" he asked as he opened the smallest of the boxes. It contained two eggs: one was very small, smaller than the tip of a pencil; next to it sat a bigger egg, about the size of Paisley's thumbnail. The smaller egg looked as if it was made of the same sparkling black shell as Dax's egg; the bigger one was gray and dull like a stone.

"These are both dragon eggs, eggs from a Papillion Dragon. When the egg is first laid, it looks like this." Doc Langley pointed to the glistening black egg. "A dragon will only lay a few eggs in her lifetime, two, maybe three if she is lucky, and she will lay them all when she is young. Much too young to look after any dragons that may hatch from them. So, she hides them like a squirrel storing away for winter.

"When she feels the stirring of maternal instincts arise, she will recover one of the eggs and fire it."

"Fire it?" Dax said, looking up from the tiny egg. "You mean she'll set fire to it?"

"No, not set it on fire; but she will burn it in her breath, and that short, sharp introduction of heat will set the egg growing. It will grow many times the size of the original egg, as you can see." Doc Langley pointed at the gray egg. Paisley guessed that the dull egg was about eight times bigger than the smaller one.

"Why does it change color?" she asked.

"Two reasons. Firstly, the firing process changes the chemical structure of the eggshell. And secondly, the dragon may need to leave the egg for periods of time to hunt and socialize, so the gray stone-like appearance acts as camouflage."

Doc Langley opened the bigger cardboard box from the drawer.

"Now, these eggs are from a Northern Dragon. As you can see, they start off about the same size as a chicken's egg and then when they are about the size of a rugby ball, the egg opens and the dragon hatches."

"But Northern Dragons are big," Corbett said. "Like small ponies. They can't come from an egg the size of a rugby ball."

"Well, they can, and they do; they grow very quickly, doubling in size each month until they reach maturity at about six to eight months.

"Now"—Doc Langley reached for Dax's egg—"if this is what I think it is, an unfired egg, if it were to be exposed to a dragon's fiery breath, it would grow to be the size of . . ."

"Paisley's satchel?" Dax asked.

"Yes, good, maybe a little bigger than that. Now, think of the size of the dragon that would hatch out of an egg that large and how big it would be after six months or so of doubling and doubling again . . ."

Dax's eyes grew as big as his egg. "A Great Dragon," he whispered.

"Indeed. Whoever it was in your family who found this treasure was very smart; encasing it in nightsilver would have protected it from any heat. Even with parts of the shell showing through, there wouldn't be enough of the surface exposed to start the chemical reaction that would cause the dragon to start gestating in the egg."

"How do we get it out of the nightsilver?" Dax asked.

"Dax, we don't want to do that." Paisley scowled. "We have enough to deal with without a Great Dragon to rear."

"Not *now*, but maybe when I'm older," Dax said.

Corbett was staring at the egg too; he reached for a magnifying glass on the desk and held it close to the nightsilver casing. "I've never seen such fine nightsilver work," he said admiringly. "Here, look at how thin the wee cogs and gears are, how intricately they connect to create the pattern on the egg; 'tis beautiful." He ran a finger over the nightsilver cogs. "If I didn't know better, I'd say that those wee cogs could move and open."

Paisley stood up and leaned toward the egg. "What makes you think that they can't?" she asked.

"There isn't a motor, no winding spring. Nothing to drive it." Corbett puzzled over the egg.

"Maybe there's a secret winding pin," she suggested. "Or maybe it's like Mother's watch. That has no way of winding it either." She fumbled for the watch, then reached it out to show Corbett. As she did, her hand grazed the egg, and the delicate nightsilver cogs began to move.

"What did you do?" Dax asked.

"Nothing. I just touched it."

"Do it again," Doc Langley said in a hushed whisper.

Paisley tentatively reached out her index finger and touched the egg. Nothing happened. She swiped the back of her hand over the egg in the same motion as she had when the metal had stirred. Nothing.

"Try the watch," Odelia instructed from behind her.

Paisley hung the watch from its chain and moved it closer to the egg. When it was close to the surface, the cogs began to move again. Paisley quickly pulled the watch away.

"Do it again," Dax said.

Paisley did, this time touching the watch to the silver casing and holding it steady. The delicate cogs around the egg whirled silently.

The nightsilver folded away from the top down, like petals of a flower unfurling, and then pulled down to the bottom of the egg, so that it sat in a solid silver cup.

"Wow!" Corbett said.

"Wow indeed, Grubbins," Doc Langley said. "Violetta's watch—could it be made out of the same nightsilver as the egg casing?"

"Aye, it could," Corbett said excitedly. "That would explain the connection."

"The egg belonged to Mother, and she never told us?" Dax's face was horrified.

"There are lots of things she never told us, Dax."

Odelia leaned forward. "When the two get close to each other, they recognize each other and interact?"

"Aye," said Corbett, frowning. "But that doesn't explain everything. There has to be a power source. A clockwork watch can't generate an electrica field."

"That's because this watch has its own power source, just like an electrica lamp, but . . . greater." Paisley stood up straight as the revelation hit her. "The Heart Stone!"

"Aye, of course, it all makes sense now. Violetta always had her watch with her for safekeeping, but she'd left it in her office the night she was taken. She asked me to fetch it before the experiment began because she needed it to power the machine. I never got to the laboratory in time to give it to her before the explosion happened, before she was taken—and *that's* why the Dark

Dragon needs it. They can't power the machine without it."

"So that Mother can perform her experiment, again." Paisley ran a long finger over the warm metal of the watch. "I had it all the time?"

"We can free Mother now," Dax said.

"Stop," said Odelia gently. "You can't hand that over to the Dark Dragon. What will she do with the machine once she has the power to change our track? To open the Veil?"

"I don't care what she'll do with it; I want my mother back." Paisley pulled the watch close to her heart.

"Odelia is right, my dear," Doc Langley said. "I want to get Violetta back too, but we must think of the bigger picture. Think of what the Dark Dragon might do with your mother, her knowledge, her machine, and the power of that stone."

"If the Dark Dragon thinks that the comet is a Great Dragon, then she would want it, right?" said Corbett.

"Yes, she would," Odelia answered darkly.

"Then, instead of pushing the comet away, she'd want your mother to pull it *toward* her, toward the Earth."

"But that's just crazy," Paisley said. "It's a comet."

"To you, maybe, but to her, it's a dragon—the Dragon Malgol no less, real and true," Doc Langley said.

Corbett drew in a sharp breath. "Dragon or comet, either way it'll destroy the world all right."

Everyone was silent as Corbett's words sank in.

"You forget, that is what the Dark Dragon wants. To destroy the world as we know it," Doc Langley said at last. "She won't care much about who gets hurt, as long as she gets all that she wants."

Paisley reached out a hand for Dax, and he laced his tiny fingers in hers. We can't let that happen, Dax." Paisley felt her eyes sting with tears and her chin wobble.

"But Mother?" Dax was already crying.

Paisley kneeled so that she was level with him.

"I know, Dax, I know. But Mother wouldn't want us to save her if it meant that the Dark Dragon won."

"So, we're just gonna leave her, leave her to die?" Dax sobbed, and Paisley's tears ran down her cheeks.

"No, no. We're going to try." She held up the watch. "But we can't use this to get Mother back; we can't give the Heart Stone to the Dark Dragon, understand?"

Dax nodded and ran the sleeve of his jacket under his snotty nose. "In that case, what's the plan?" he asked.

29

BATTLE AND BETRAYAL

Roach crouched in the shadows of the mighty dragon Fyrdhwæt and watched as the guard strolled through the dark corridors of the Natural History Museum, his electrica lantern sending out a searchlight that hit the glass cabinets as he passed.

The guard wasn't really concentrating, though; he held the *King's Herald* folded onto the crossword page and was reading one of the clues as he made his way back to his office. His voice echoed through the corridor. "Immovable but always moving. Unbreakable but always bending. Unknowable but always knowing."

The main hall was cold. Fyrdhwæt looked down at the guard as he shivered and turned off the electrica lights that he'd left on. The Dragon looked majestic in the shadows and moonlight cast by the high arching windows.

The guard shone his lamp over the dragon, squinting in Roach's direction.

Roach held out a hand to still Lorena as he felt her stiffen beside him, her hand gripping her spear.

Just then the guard turned—the front door was open. He swore loudly and hastened to close it, not noticing Roach and the Dark Dragon Walkers racing up the back of the Great Dragon and leaping onto the balcony above.

"Spread out," Lorena instructed. Roach and the Dark Dragon Walkers nodded as they slipped deeper into the museum, seeking out their quarry.

Silently, they traveled through the museum, through the Dragonian Wing, and up the steps to Doc Langley's workshop.

Roach stood to one side of the frosted glass door and listened as Paisley and the others discussed the Heart Stone.

Lorena started to move, but he held her back again. The look on the Dragon Walker's face would have made anyone else wither, but Roach had faced worse than an angry Dragon Walker before. He heard the Fitzwilliam children discussing whether they should save their mother or the world. For a moment, he was jealous of the way they could put the lives and happiness of others before their own. But then he remembered Clara. He was putting her first.

With a shove, the workshop door banged open. Roach swept in, followed by Lorena and an army of mechanical beetles.

"Give me the Heart Stone or I'll take the blasted thing from you,"

Roach said, his hand outstretched, his eyes seeking out Paisley's.

Odelia cast off her cloak and spread her wings out, forming a barrier between Lorena and the others.

"Very touching, Odelia, but misguided," said Lorena. "Join us. Help us restore order to the world. Give me what my mistress seeks, or I will burn you along with your friends."

Odelia pulled her swords from her belt. "Really? After that worked so well for you last time!" she taunted.

Lorena let out a roar of rage and charged at Odelia.

"Run!" the Dragon Walker shouted behind her.

Doc Langley opened a side door. Paisley scooped the egg and watch into her satchel and grabbed Dax's hand as she ran from the room.

"Quickly, this way," Doc Langley called. Corbett followed as they ran blindly down the service corridors. Dax stumbled as his leg landed awkwardly with each stride, Paisley pulling him along.

"This way." Doc Langley led them down a set of stairs. When they reached the bottom, Paisley paused.

"Can you hear that?" They were all silent, holding their rapid breaths as they heard the metallic clicking of tiny legs.

"Roach—he's sending his cogroaches after us," Corbett said as he rummaged around in his pocket and pulled out the gadget that he had used to stop them on the roof. "Go, I'll be right behind you," he told Paisley.

She hesitated for a moment, holding his eye. "Make sure you are," she said to him.

He waved Paisley and Dax toward Doc Langley, who was holding open a door that led back out into one of the main visitors' corridors.

"He'll be fine," Paisley told Dax as the two of them followed along behind Doc Langley. "He'll be with us in no time; they both will."

But when they reached the end of the corridor, there was still no sign of Corbett or Odelia.

"We have to keep going," said Doc Langley. Paisley looked back over her shoulder as she turned into a larger exhibition space showing how the continents of the Earth had been formed from a single landmass. The fallen body of the First Dragon, the Mighty Mother Anu, stretched across the globe, breaking up and changing as the cogs of the exhibition moved. Anu, whose breath still warmed the planet, and whose shriveled heart beat in the watch in Paisley's satchel, had broken apart and formed the continents of the Earth.

Two young Dark Dragon Walkers stepped from the shadows. Paisley pulled Dax toward her as she saw them.

She let her satchel fall from her shoulder and onto the hand that was clasped in his. She gave her brother's hand a tight squeeze, and she flipped the satchel onto his forearm.

"Run," she told him as she released his hand and unsheathed her sword.

Dax turned; Doc Langley was by his side, helping him along. "Here, take this." He threw his cane at Paisley, and she caught it in her free hand.

"Run, Dax!" Paisley screamed as she moved toward the two Dark Dragon Walkers, releasing the bottom of Dax's cane with a twisting motion. She pulled out the sharp, thin nightsilver blade.

Doc Langley pulled Dax along the exhibition space, supporting him as they made their way toward the staircase that led to the entrance hall.

Paisley moved in the opposite direction, along the banister that looked over the Great Dragon Fyrdhwæt.

The Dark Dragon Walkers moved apart, flanking Paisley.

She remembered the instructions that her father had given her on facing multiple opponents.

"Always use their strengths against them," he had told her.

Both the girls were older than Paisley, one taller and broader than the other, but both strong and powerful, with the shaved heads of initiates, like Odelia.

The bigger of the two girls was turning her head from side to side as if she were listening to Paisley rather than seeing her. In the dull light, Paisley noticed that the scaled skin of the Dragon Walker's eyelids had been fused shut over the sockets.

The other Dragon Walker opened her hand, splaying her fingers. From the index finger on each of her hands grew a deadly-looking claw that curved like a scythe.

Without seeming to communicate, the Dark Dragon Walkers simultaneously began their attack, moving in on Paisley from both sides.

Paisley ducked low, swiping out a foot and knocking the bigger Dragon Walker off her feet. She hit the floor with a resonating thump.

Paisley made to swerve over her but wasn't fast enough as the second Dragon Walker lashed out with her claw. She cut Paisley's back, slicing through her woolen coat, dress, and flesh as if it were butter.

Pain pierced through her and she cried out.

Dax screamed her name. He and Doc Langley were on the grand staircase below her running for the entrance doors, the guard coming up toward them.

"Go!" Paisley yelled as she rose to her feet, blood soaking the back of her brown coat black.

She lifted Dax's blade and sliced out at the Dragon Walker in a wide arc. The girl jumped back, her hand trailing. The nightsilver blade sliced through the long claw, cutting it clean in half. The Dragon Walker howled in pain and fell to her knees, holding her hand.

Distracted, Paisley hadn't heard the other Dragon Walker rise; she placed her strong arms around Paisley like a tight band— holding her in place and slowly crushing her.

Paisley struggled to breathe as the girl lifted her into the air and over the railings.

Paisley felt her legs dangle in nothingness as small stars started to form at the edge of her vision. She dropped the sword from the vault but squeezed her fingers around Dax's nightsilver blade.

She kicked her legs and felt the edge of the balcony behind her, but it was too late to get any purchase. The girl let go of her, and she fell toward the ground, toward the Great Dragon with its wings outstretched. Paisley stabbed wildly at the wing with Dax's sword as she fell; the point of nightsilver dug in between the scales and held her in place.

She held on to the hilt of the sword with all her might, her back stinging.

There was a scream from below.

The guard lay in a bloody pool below her.

Paisley looked over her shoulder; Dax was too far away. She let go of the sword with one hand, swiveling around to see Lorena and Roach grab Dax and Doc Langley and drag them out through the main doors of the Museum.

"Paisley!" Dax yelled as he locked eyes with her one last time.

"No, No, NO!"

Paisley let go of the sword. She fell along the outstretched wing like a steep slide and landed in a crumpled heap not far from the guard.

Winded, she rolled onto her hands and knees before pushing up and running for the door. Her legs wobbled, her back ached, but she pushed on, shoving the double doors open, just in time to see Dax's face looking through the back window of an electrica car, calling to her.

"Dax," Paisley screamed. She ran after the car as it sped away from her. "No," she sobbed as she slowed to a halt.

Another car was coming toward her. Paisley stretched out her arms, throwing herself in front of it, bringing it to a halt.

The driver's door opened.

"My flower! What's happened?"

"Uncle Hector." Paisley fell into her uncle's arms as he stepped from the vehicle. "They've taken Dax; they're getting away!"

"Who has taken him? Why, you're hysterical; what's going on?" he asked as he held Paisley at arm's length, his hands wrapped around the tops of her arms.

"There isn't time to explain." Paisley took a shuddering breath. "Mother is alive. The Dark Dragon has her, and now she has Dax too—she wants something . . ."

"The Heart Stone?"

"Yes, and we found it, but then the Dark Dragon's henchmen found us and they've taken it and Dax. We have to go; we have to find them!"

"Quickly, get in." Uncle Hector pulled open the door, and Paisley climbed in. "Goodness, Paisley, you're bleeding!"

"I'll be fine. Please, we have to get after them; we have to save Dax." She gestured frantically down the street. "They went that way."

Uncle Hector seemed to make a decision. "Don't worry, we'll catch them." He hurried around to his side of the car and jumped behind the wheel.

The car began to move. Paisley blinked and focused on the road ahead. The wound on her back was bleeding freely, and waves of pain made her feel sick.

Uncle Hector grabbed hold of Paisley's hand and gave it a squeeze. "I'll get you to Dax."

"How do you even know which way they went?" Paisley asked as she looked out at the warren of streets in the dark. "I can't see them."

Just then a vehicle darted out erratically into the oncoming traffic. Paisley gave a little yelp as it swerved back in, narrowly missing an omnibus.

"Don't worry, everything will be fine," Uncle Hector said as he put his foot down and darted through the night in pursuit.

"No, no, it won't. The Dark Dragon is going to destroy the world." Paisley struggled to speak through the pain in her back.

"Poppycock, Paisley, you can't destroy the world; the Chief Designer would have never put that in anyone's track." Uncle Hector pulled sharply around a bend; Paisley cried out as she shifted in the seat, her back bursting into a deeper agony.

He looked over at her; Paisley could see the deep lines of concern on his face. "Gosh, you really are in pain, my dear. Not to worry, once we get there, I'm sure we'll be able to patch you up a bit."

"Once we get there?"

Paisley's head swam.

"Uncle Hector? How . . . how did you know about the Heart Stone?"

Uncle Hector looked over at Paisley, then back to the road as he crossed Lambeth Bridge. "You told me. You said the Dark Dragon wanted it."

Paisley shook her head. "No. No, I didn't."

"You're in pain; you're misremembering." He kept his eyes on the road, his hands gripped on the steering wheel.

"You knew where I was; you knew where to find me." Paisley knew that the dawning realization would crush her, but she was in too much pain to care.

"Corbett said that you were at the observatory that night, but I... I never thought it could be you. But it was. You're working with the Dark Dragon. Why would you do this to Mother, to us?"

Paisley watched her uncle. In spite of everything she knew to be true, she wanted him to tell her that she was being silly, that she had it all wrong, that he was there because it was in his track to save her and Dax.

Uncle Hector turned and looked at her, his face alight with excitement, and in that moment, Paisley's heart broke. She didn't know if there was a limit to the amount of pain that a person could carry, but she was sure that her track was bending under the weight of hers.

"The Dark Dragon is everything, Paisley," her uncle said. "Just wait till you meet her; you will see that she is the most magnificent being in the Celestial Mechanism. She is going to set us all free."

Tears streamed down Paisley's face as she fought to steady

her breathing. "You're wrong. She's going to kill us all."

"Just think about it, Paisley. She is going to open the Veil, and all of those who have left us will return. The Great Dragons, but others too, like your grandmama Fiona, like your father. I can't wait to see him again. I *need* to see him again. I need to explain to him. He'll understand; I know he will."

Paisley was trembling. "What do you need to explain? What will he understand, Uncle Hector?"

Uncle Hector smiled as though he could see the Veil opening in front of him and all those he loved were coming back to him.

"He will understand that I had to kill him."

"No," whispered Paisley. "You couldn't have." Paisley felt as if all the cogs in the mechanism had stopped turning. She looked up at her uncle slowly, shaking her head. "No, you didn't; you wouldn't. Father was killed—" And suddenly Paisley's memories failed her as her mind flooded with pain and darkness.

"He will understand because the Dark Dragon will set his track in motion once more and then he will see that the Mechanism is to be honored, not broken as his stupid Order believes."

The world began to drift away from Paisley. Her fingers curled into weak fists, anchoring her to the here and now.

"You killed my father," she said. "You took my mother, and you told me she was dead, when all the time you knew she wasn't. I trusted you and you betrayed me."

"I have not betrayed you, can't you see? All that I have done was in my track. I was destined to do it; the Chief Designer made it so."

"I thought you loved us. Dax and me and Mother," Paisley said.

"I do love you, Paisley; can't you see I'm doing this for you? For Dax, for all of us. We need never fear death again."

Paisley looked at her uncle, and she saw him clearly for the first time in her life. Her voice was cold. "You're not doing this for me or Dax or anyone else but yourself. You're nothing but a self-obsessed, narcissistic coward, and I hate you."

Uncle Hector flinched.

Paisley gathered the last bit of strength that she had and flew at him. Her fist connected with Uncle Hector's jaw, and the car swerved. Then the darkness rose up and pulled her under.

As Paisley lost consciousness, she heard Uncle Hector say, "I will prove to you that my actions are noble."

30

GREENWICH BELOW

When Paisley woke, she thought she was back in the museum.

Above her was a large Orrery, suspended from the ceiling. Each of the planets was placed upon the golden tracks of the Celestial Mechanism. Around the planets operated smaller bodies, the companion planets, and in the center burned a low gas flame, representing the sun—the breath of the Mother Dragon Anu.

The solar system turned slowly, whereas the world felt as if it were rotating at a million miles an hour.

Paisley sat up. She flinched as her back bloomed into pain. Scrunching her eyes tight, she took deep calming breaths. The cold air caught in her lungs, and Paisley coughed into her hands. Thin, bright blood covered her palms.

This was it. This was what her stars had seen—the end of her track was close.

Her father's words rang in her ears. *"Physical pain is temporary. We must sometimes move past it if we are to save ourselves from greater suffering."*

She thought of Dax, of his face at the window at the electrica car as it had driven away. Fear gripped her as she thought of what the Dark Dragon might do to him if she found out about his Dragon Touch.

Then she remembered why this was happening, and more importantly who had made it all possible: Uncle Hector.

She balled her fists and opened her eyes.

She felt as if he had stabbed her in the heart; she had loved him like a father, trusted him like one too, and all the time he was the one who had robbed her of her family—first her father, then her mother, and now Dax.

Anger flared inside Paisley. It flowed through her like dragon fire, giving her cold, aching body strength. She would have her revenge. But first, she would find Dax and Mother. Finding them was all that she could allow herself to think of now. She couldn't see further along the track than finding them—maybe there was nothing after that for her.

Paisley pushed herself to stand. She reached out a hand to steady herself and felt something cold and metallic.

It was a telescope.

She ran her fingers over the brass instrument and found the bolt that held it to the tripod. Her fingers felt stiff as she began to turn the nut to release the scope, but as the screw twisted, she became more focused.

Below the gaslit sun shone a band of copper inlaid into the wooden flooring of the room. It ran from end to end.

She had been in rooms with a line like that before.

"The Meridian Line."

The imaginary line from which time ended and began.

She was in the old Greenwich Observatory. She held the telescope in her hand and felt the weight of it.

She remembered walking along the Meridian Line like a tightrope walker when she was little. Mother had worked here, many turnings ago, before she went to work on Greenwich Overhead like all the other scientists, leaving the original Greenwich Observatory empty.

Paisley walked toward the door and tried the handle. It was locked.

She crossed the room, to the other door. That was locked too. She kicked it and let out a groan.

Calm down, think, she told herself as she walked back to the Meridian Line, her boots sliding along the coppery surface as she moved back and forth. Her eyes scanned the room.

Besides the giant Orrery and telescope mount, it was empty. The two doors were the only ways out. She let out a long steadying breath as she thought of Mother, of Dax.

The night was fully dark now, pressing against the high windows. The stars winked at Paisley. Far above in the Heavens, the green comet goaded her.

The window, she thought. She reached up on her tiptoes and looked into the night. Her eyes just peered over the top of the thick stone windowsill.

She tucked the telescope into the waistband of her skirt and tried to pull herself onto the ledge.

She gave a little jump, her boots scrabbling against the wall as she desperately tried to climb up, the rough brickwork biting into her knees.

Paisley dropped back down to the floor. She could feel the wetness on her back as the wound the Dragon Walker had given her reopened.

She took a sharp breath, sucking the air in between her teeth. She looked up at the window.

"Maybe if I had a bit of a run-up," she told herself.

Paisley walked to the Meridian line, then turned to face the window. She shrugged off her coat and let it fall to the floor, not looking at the large dark stain. Her arms felt cold but free.

She eyed the window; then, dipping low, she steadied herself before running hard and launching herself into the air. Her boots pushed off the wall as first her hands, then elbows, made contact with the windowsill.

The pain stabbed through her as she heaved herself up onto the sill.

It was wide enough for her to stand on comfortably.

The fitted panes of clear glass towered above her in an arc. There was no latch to open. Paisley took the telescope from her waistband and smashed the glass.

The noise echoed through the room, then below her as the glass fell to the ground. A cold north wind whipped in, sending Paisley's hair whirling. The flesh on her arms rose in small bumps as she shivered.

She held on to the window frame and leaned out into the night.

She was on the second floor of the building. Outside, there was a large stone ledge that ran along the length of the building. A little way along the ledge in either direction were more windows.

Paisley looked out into the night, at the lights of Lower London reddening on the horizon. Above, small points of light from the floating boroughs danced among a backdrop of stars. Paisley's eyes drifted down toward the open dome of the observatory across the way. Light was shooting out of it like a sword blade.

"That's where they are," she told herself.

Papillion Dragons fluttered in Paisley's stomach as she stowed the telescope in her belt and stepped out onto the ledge, her boots crunching on the shattered glass. She ran her fingers across what remained of the windowpane, sliding them over the freezing glass.

Inside the room, the door banged open, and the smaller Dark Dragon Walker from the museum, the one with the dragon-claw Touch, tore into the room.

Paisley and the Dragon Walker locked eyes, before the girl turned and ran out of the room.

Heart beating fast, Paisley shuffled along the ledge, leaving the alcove of the window, her fingers finding purchase on the brickwork as the ledge got narrower. Just the balls of her feet were making contact, her heels hanging over the edge.

The Dark Dragon Walker erupted through the main door of the building directly below.

"We have a debt to settle, you and I," she shouted up to Paisley, lifting her broken claw. Paisley held on to the wall, not looking down, focusing on getting to the next window.

Something struck the wall very close to Paisley's head; she let out a little scream and halted.

Below, the Dark Dragon Walker was throwing stones, trying to knock Paisley off balance and down to the ground, like a bird in a tree.

The Dark Dragon Walker reached down, scooping another rock up. Using the bloodstain on Paisley's shirt as a target, she threw the stone, hard.

The pain tore through Paisley—her hands slipped, her legs wobbled, and the balls of her feet fell away from the ledge. Paisley's shins scraped the ridge of the windowsill, and her fingers scrabbled against the brickwork before she came to a halt with her forearms and chest resting on the ledge, the bottom half of her body dangling.

The Dragon Walker smiled as she tossed, then caught a sizable stone. She lined the struggling Paisley up in her sights.

Paisley tried to pull herself up. She could see her face reflected in the corner of the window in front of her, hair wild, her eyes wide in fear; then something moving behind her caught her eye.

Odelia!

She swooped toward the ground, and Paisley heard a familiar scream followed by a thud.

Just as she lost the strength in her arms and let go of the ledge, she heard the beating of wings from below and then felt Odelia's strong arms catch her.

Odelia swept Paisley up and turned a loop in the air before gently landing next to Corbett.

He sat on top of the crumpled Dragon Walker, his glasses at an angle. "You dropped me!" he said to Odelia.

"I needed to save Paisley; my master would have never forgiven me if I had let his sister die." Odelia narrowed her eyes and searched the shadows as she released Paisley. "There are bound to be more of them."

"How did you know where to find me?" she asked.

Corbett climbed off the Dragon Walker. He looked at Paisley, shivering and bleeding. He took off his coat.

"We followed your uncle." He placed his coat around her shoulders. "Well, Odelia followed him; I just came along for the ride," Corbett added with a shrug and a smile.

Paisley grabbed both Odelia and Corbett in a huge hug. She didn't care that her back hurt or that Odelia stood as stiff as night-silver armor.

"Thank you," said Paisley as she released them both, dashing the tears away with Corbett's coat sleeve. She pulled back, her face fierce. "My uncle. I trusted him. But he did all of this. He took Mother. He's been working for the Dark Dragon all this time; he killed my father too," she said, wiping the last of her tears on the coat sleeve.

"I can't quite believe it," Corbett said with a shake of his head.

Odelia took a step closer to Paisley and leaned a little toward her. "I will help you take your revenge, Paisley," she said, her face full of earnestness.

Paisley smiled; she appreciated the sentiment and was sure that whatever was to come, Odelia would be right there beside her, fighting for them all.

"Did your uncle take the Dragon Lord too?" Odelia asked.

Paisley shook her head. "No, Roach and Lorena took Dax and Doc Langley, but they're here." She nodded at the Dragon Walker on the floor. "If she's here, then so are they." Paisley turned and pointed. "I think they're in the observatory over there; it's the only building that's lit up."

Odelia was already striding in the direction of the dome, her swords pulled out.

31

A MEETING OF HEARTS

The Dark Dragon paced around the machine, the tail of her coat flowing out behind her, her hair plaited over one shoulder, and on the other sat a mechanical dragon. It flapped its wings and opened its mouth, letting out a little glow in frustration.

Roach stood next to Dax, holding him in place as he watched the Dark Dragon.

"Faster," she yelled. Her high voice echoed around the dome of the observatory. "I want my dragon!"

Roach watched as Professor Fitzwilliam struggled with the internal workings of her machine. Every now and again she would glance in his direction, her eyes fixed on her son, the worry plain to see on her face. It was so much easier to be brave and honorable when it was only her safety at risk, but now it was her son's fate that was at stake, in more ways than one.

Roach looked down at Dax's leg, remembering the dark green scales that he had seen. He hadn't told Dax's secret to the Dark Dragon, and Roach was convinced that she had no idea that the boy was Dragon Touched. If she had known, she would have been treating the Dragon Lord very differently.

Dax looked up at him, and he set his jaw. He looked small and scared, but defiant too, just like Clara the day the Men of the Yard had come for her.

Doc Langley was beside him, shabby and crumpled. Lorena guarded him, standing close to the railings that shielded the stairs from the entrance room below.

Standing a little away from them all, by a large desk next to the levers that once controlled the mechanism of the telescope, was Hector. He was avoiding looking at both his nephew and his sister-in-law.

"Hector, please," Violetta said, her voice breaking as her fingers trembled. "Let Dax go; he's just a little boy. He—"

"Silence," the Dark Dragon cried. She turned and looked at Violetta. "We children are capable of more than you think."

"You are not a child," Violetta said, her voice cold and full of disgust.

"True." The Dark Dragon smiled sweetly. "But I am eternal; I am chosen. I will restore the greatness of the Dragons to the world. I will destroy the George and all his knights and anyone who gets in my way. That includes you and your family."

Roach felt the determination rushing off the Dark Dragon as she paused in front of Dax and ran a small, sharp fingernail down his cheek. "Now, unless you want to see your son suffer, I suggest you get back to work. And if anything goes wrong, if you deliberately fail to bring me the dragon, then I will kill him."

Dax spat in her face.

The Dark Dragon's reflexes were sharp; she clenched her hand around Dax's neck, her nails biting into his flesh as she lifted him from the ground, his legs swaying as he tried to kick her with his braced leg.

"Let the boy go!" Doc Langley shouted as Lorena restrained him.

Violetta shouted, "Don't. I'll do it! I promise I'll do what you want."

The Dark Dragon opened her fingers, and Dax fell in a heap on the floor.

Roach instantly crouched and lifted him straight back up, his grip a little looser around the top of his skinny arm.

The Dark Dragon turned to face Violetta.

"I will do you this small kindness, for I am magnanimous; if you do as I instruct, both you and your son may leave unharmed. The same, however, I cannot promise for dear Paisley."

"What have you done to my daughter?" Violetta tightened her grip on the wrench in her hand, her eyes dangerous.

"I haven't done anything—yet. But she had a run-in with one of my loyal warriors." The Dark Dragon pulled a faux sad face. "She's lost quite a lot of blood, poor thing. It's a pity, really; I admire her strength and determination. I had hoped that, in time, Hector may have been able to persuade her to join us."

Roach tightened his grip on Dax as he lunged forward. "You don't know my sister very well. She would rather die than help you!"

The Dark Dragon turned. "How fitting. I don't think she'll live long, not with a wound like that." The Dark Dragon shook her head, her jet-black hair glistening like nightsilver.

"However, I promise that as soon as I get my Great Dragon, I will ensure that Paisley sees a doctor. How long before she sees that doctor is up to you, Professor."

Violetta gazed at Dax, then turned her attention back to her machine.

The Dark Dragon signaled for Roach to follow her back across the room to the workbench. He tugged Dax, holding the top of his arm as he struggled to pull away, supporting him a little as he moved forward without his cane, his braced leg hitting the floor. Lorena followed, bringing Doc Langley with her.

Hector stood next to the workbench. Roach saw the way that Dax looked at his uncle, hurt and angry. Hector avoided his gaze as he concentrated all his attention on the Dark Dragon.

She was rummaging around on the workbench where she had upended Paisley's satchel.

She lifted Paisley's journal and began to thumb through the

pages; she paused every now and again to read, or look and giggle, or frown.

Roach followed Dax's eyes; he gazed first at the watch, which sat in a fine filigree nightsilver bowl, and then at a large replica dragon egg, half-covered by a book.

The Dark Dragon closed Paisley's journal and placed it back in the bag, along with a box full of loose letters.

She lifted the watch from the nightsilver bowl by its long chain.

"Is this it?" she asked.

Roach nodded and then watched in amazement as the tiny decorative cogs on the bowl began to move, changing shape to that of an egg.

"That's a fine trick," the Dark Dragon said, lowering the watch.

"But how is it doing that?" Hector asked. "It's just a watch."

"It is not just a watch, fool. This is what you have been searching for."

Hector's eyes widened. "All the time I spent rummaging through Violetta's study, searching Greenwich Overhead, and it was inside the watch."

"Indeed, I am surprised that you did not realize," the Dark Dragon chastised.

"Yes, I'm sorry," he simpered. Roach looked down at Dax and saw a twinge of disgust cross the boy's face.

"How can I make it up to you?"

The Dark Dragon turned her attention back to the nightsilver egg. "I wonder if it works with the other one?" She reached her hand into the breast pocket of her coat and pulled out a handkerchief. Slowly she unfolded it to reveal a stone so red it looked black.

"Soul Fire," Doc Langley spluttered. "You stole it from the Northern Realms!"

"I did not *steal* it," the Dark Dragon snapped. "It is mine by right. I am the Dark Dragon. It is my heritage, my birthright. All the stones belong to me, as does all the power of Anu."

Roach felt Dax twitch.

The Dark Dragon lowered Soul Fire toward the egg, but nothing happened. She repeated the action.

"I ain't no expert, Your Darkness," Roach said. "But maybe it has something to do with the silver and not the stone?"

"Quite right," she said. "And I think it's about time I liberated my stone from this case." The Dark Dragon ran her fingers over the surface of the watch. "How do you open it?"

"You don't," Violetta said, looking up from her calculations. "It was encased in nightsilver to keep it safe. No one can open it."

The Dark Dragon whipped her head toward Violetta and smiled dangerously. "Wrong, Professor. No human can open it, but for a Dragon, nightsilver presents nothing more than a challenge."

She placed the watch on the bench and stepped back.

"Lorena, fire it," she instructed.

Lorena stepped away from Doc Langley and stood in front of the desk. Flames erupted, engulfing Paisley's pencil case and the book of Dragonology. Paisley's dragonhide satchel glowed in the heat, as did the egg and the watch.

Lorena stopped and used her cloak to put out the small fire on the bench, knocking the glowing egg to the floor as charred pieces of paper flew into the air like black confetti.

The Dark Dragon lifted the hot glowing metal. The watch fit perfectly into her cupped palms. She began to squeeze. A gentle stream of black sand-like particles fell from the bottom of her hands. When she unfolded her fingers, she held Soul Fire's twin.

Roach watched with an open mouth as she reached into her pocket once more, then moved the two Heart Stones together. They glowed from within as they got closer to each other, and as they touched, a bright light fused the two to form half a heart.

It started to pump, like an engine. But the rhythm was slack; it reminded Roach of the noise Dax made when he walked, the sound of his brace echoing while his other footstep was silent.

The other stones, he told himself; they would make the heart whole and real. There were four parts of the Dragon Heart. What would happen when she had all four parts?

He felt a deep and ancient terror stir within him. He remembered the way that Paisley and Dax were ready to sacrifice their mother to save any wrong done in her name.

Clara, he thought. *Clara, what have I done?*

32

THE PARTING OF PAISLEY

Paisley slipped her arms into Corbett's coat and turned up the cuffs as she rushed toward the Observatory. High above the dome, the comet looked down on the world.

Paisley gave a little shudder. The night sky had always made her feel small and insignificant but at the same time so full of wonder. Now she felt scared. The green eye of the universe was looking straight at her, into her, weighing her worth and judging her actions.

Odelia led them in the darkness, creeping toward the Observatory like a shadow fleeing from light. The door to the Observatory building was open and unguarded.

Their footfalls echoed softly in the empty lower portion of the Observatory as they moved upward toward the dome.

Odelia paused on the stairs. She turned and placed a finger to her lips. Paisley nodded. Corbett was right behind her.

Odelia turned and began to crawl up the stairs that led straight up through the floor of the dome.

Paisley crawled alongside her, the two of them peering over the top step.

The telescope that should have stood in the center was missing. In its place stood a machine made of nightsilver. Paisley traced the complex array of cogs with her eyes. It was bigger than she had been expecting; she guessed it was about as big as the telescope that had once stood in its place. She noticed that the machine was attached to the same base that the telescope had used to pry the secrets from the Celestial Mechanism. And that, just like the telescope, the mechanism had a limb that protruded up through the gap in the dome, a finger pointing toward the Heavens, aimed directly at Comet Wolstenholme.

Movement caught Paisley's eye, and her cogs slipped as she saw her mother move from behind the machine. Odelia clamped her hand down on Paisley's wrist.

"Not yet," she whispered as she looked across the room.

Paisley followed her gaze and saw Dax and Doc Langley being held by Roach and Lorena. Dax's little hands balled into fists.

Next to them was a girl, a little older than Dax, with long dark hair. She was dressed in black taffeta from head to toe. Paisley had seen her before; she was the little girl from Mother's lecture, the one with Roach, the one she thought had a clever face.

Paisley instantly felt sick.

She realized that everyone was looking to the little girl; everyone was taking their instruction from her.

"It's her...the Dark Dragon. How is she so young?" Paisley asked Odelia.

"Do not be deceived. Remember, she has the eternal Touch. It is very rare; she would not have aged past the time her Touch ripened—for most of us that is at the start of adolescence, for some after, others before." Paisley felt a fiery blast of hatred roar up inside her, and she narrowed her eyes.

This child was the Dark Dragon. And she had taken everything from Paisley.

Odelia's grip on Paisley's wrist tightened.

"Wait," she whispered as Paisley tensed, ready to pounce. "When we strike, we will do so together."

They watched as she placed the watch on the bench, and Lorena breathed fire onto it, burning it red hot.

The Dark Dragon reached out and took the watch in her hands. Fine black silt drifted to the table. When she opened her fingers, Paisley's breath caught. The Heart Stone.

"What's that?" Paisley whispered as the Dark Dragon raised Soul Fire from her pocket and combined the two parts of the dragon's heart.

A gasp escaped Odelia's lips. "No," she whispered.

Paisley snapped her head to Odelia and then back again.

The Dark Dragon smiled in triumph.

"Glorious," she pronounced as she held the beating stone above her head. It pulsed with a soft red glow. "Glorious dominion." Her expression of childlike innocence twisted as she saw before her all that was to come.

The Dark Dragon walked over to Violetta and held out the heart. "Take it; make it work. Bring me my dragon, my Malgol."

Violetta shook her head. "No."

The Dark Dragon's eyes shone as she reached up and slapped Violetta across the face with the back of her hand.

Dax could stand it no more; he kicked Roach as hard as he could in the shin with his braced leg, then ran across the room and leaped onto the Dark Dragon's back.

"You want a dragon; I'll give you one," he yelled as he clung tightly to her, his arms around her neck, his brace striking her as he kicked.

The Dark Dragon flung Dax from her. He landed in a pile by her feet.

Violetta lunged forward and pulled him to her, tight and fierce.

Paisley untangled herself from Odelia the moment that Dax had leaped on the Dark Dragon. She ran across the observatory in a blur and brought the telescope down on the back of the Dark Dragon's head as she stood back up, Dax at her feet.

"Let my family go," Paisley told her as she pulled the telescope back over her shoulder.

The Dark Dragon sank her hand into her hair. There was blood on her fingers and a look of surprise that soon shifted back to her mask of innocence. Paisley instantly regretted striking the beautiful child.

"I will never release your family," she said sweetly as Paisley felt the telescope wrenched from her hand. She turned to see Uncle Hector holding it.

"Don't do this," Paisley pleaded with him as he dropped the telescope with a clang and grabbed her by the tops of the arms, holding her still as she writhed and bucked like a lassoed dragon.

"Help us, Uncle Hector, please," Paisley begged as she twisted to see her uncle's face.

Uncle Hector shook his head. "Don't you see? This will help us all."

"You're wrong, Hector," Violetta said. "This will destroy us all. There is no dragon; it's a comet, a huge ball of rock and ice, and if you pull it toward us, it won't grow wings and land gracefully. It will smash into us, obliterating us all."

"You are a wonderful woman, Violetta; Edmund chose well. But you have always been a woman of cold, hard fact. Facts can be manipulated. They can lie. Faith is always true, and I have faith in the Dark Dragon and her vision. I have faith that I will see Edmund again. I have faith that I will be rewarded."

Paisley saw the conviction on Hector's face. How could anyone make a man like this see reason?

The Dark Dragon smiled. "I will bring back the Great Dragons; I will control all the tracks. I will open the Veil and all those that we have lost will be restored to us."

"Uncle Hector, even if she could do all that she promised, Father wouldn't want you to bring him back, not like this, not when it will cause so much destruction. Think of the Great Dragons—think of how many they will kill under her command." Paisley nodded toward the Dark Dragon.

"But she and I have that in common, Paisley—killing. I killed your father, and that is why I need her to open the Veil."

"No," Violetta cried. "You killed Edmund—your own brother. Why?"

"Edmund told me all about your mission for the Order. He told me everything. I knew I had to stop him. It's just . . . I miss him so. And once the Dark Dragon restores him, he will see the error of his ways and serve her as I do."

"No," Paisley said. "Father would never give up on what he believed in and thought was true; he would never join you and the Dark Dragon."

"ENOUGH!" the Dark Dragon roared. Her hair was disheveled and clumped with blood. She shook her head from side to side.

"For centuries, I have tried and failed to restore the world to its rightful owners. This time I shall succeed. I will save us all from the lies of the Mechanists, from the heresy of the Chief Designer, from the abominable actions of the George, and the weakness of the Dragon Walkers.

"I will be victorious; I will bring back the Great Dragons to the world. I will rule the Mechanism. And you, Violetta, will help me." The Dark Dragon kept her eyes turned on the professor as she walked over to Paisley; Uncle Hector was still holding her firmly by the arms.

Paisley moved her head back as the Dark Dragon stroked a twisting red lock away from her face.

"I'm so sorry that it had to come to this." She put her small hand into the folds of her coat and pulled out a nightsilver blade. She kissed Paisley on the cheek and thrust the knife deep into her chest.

"No!" Dax and Violetta yelled as Paisley's eyes grew wide and fearful.

The Dark Dragon twisted the blade as she pulled it out.

Paisley crumpled to the floor, clutching her hand to her chest.

A dark shadow passed over her.

33

THE NIGHT BETWEEN THE WORLDS

She felt no pain.

She felt nothing at all. No hope or joy. No sadness or anger. She just felt that she was. *Where* she was, she didn't even try to question at first. It was just enough that she was.

It was not, however, until she began to question that she began to feel.

"Who am I?" she asked.

At first, she felt déjà vu. She had been here before.

The darkness was everywhere; she was sure she had been in it many times, only she couldn't recall when or where.

She thought that she might *be* the darkness. But as she thought more about it, the more she could feel herself coalescing out of the inky blackness, forming into a distinct and separate part until she was in the dark and not part of it any longer.

I am me, she thought, and at that moment, she saw a lightening, like a candle flickering from far away.

She moved toward the light as water moves in a stream.

She could not tell if she were a pebble and the water moved around her or if she were a leaf and the water carried her.

Either way, the light stayed where it was, never getting any closer or farther away, a constant glow, ever-present while she moved in the dark space.

She knew that the darkness went on forever in every direction, and yet she knew that it didn't.

"Where am I?" she asked.

The darkness shuffled around her, arranging itself, thickening into something more.

A stone floor below her feet; a narrow passage on either side of her; rough-hewn walls. She stretched out and felt the cold of the stone, comforting and familiar.

She knew this place. She was in between. But she was not in between the two walls of the secret passages that ran through her home as she felt she had so often been before, but in between two worlds. On one side lay the world she had just slipped from, and on the other lay the Veil.

This small passage of space and time, she knew, was the edge of both of these worlds.

The light still glowed, small and steady. She knew that it would always be that way, never getting any closer or farther away, if she wanted it to.

"Why am I here?" she asked.

And in her heart and mind and soul, life rushed in. It pressed into her being from both of the worlds.

She remembered everything and felt it all.

As if she had existed with her eyes closed, she now opened them. The darkness was replaced with the light and the dark, and every shade of gray between the Veil and the world.

The soft glow was still there, still shining out of reach. But there was a closer light now.

It filled the passageway behind her, reminding her of the opening of the secret passage in Dax's bedroom. The light from her world slunk in, pale and weak through the low secret entrance.

She knew that Dax's bedroom did not lie beyond, just as she knew that in that light lay her mother and Dax, huddled together in the Observatory of Greenwich below. In that light lay pain and suffering and hard choices.

She looked back at the soft glow, constant and peaceful. To move toward it would be to move into the beyond, to enter the Veil. There would be no pain there. There would be no suffering.

She reached out and felt warmth radiate through her body; she felt her soul expand. And from out of the soft glow of the Veil came her father.

"Paisley?"

"Daddy?" She ran to him and threw her arms around him. He felt whole and warm and real. He held her back, hugging her so tight and kissing the top of her head.

"Oh, how I have missed you, my darling girl." He brushed Paisley's flame-touched curls from her face and held her cheeks in his hands.

"You have grown so much." He hugged her tight again, and she cried into his chest while she smiled. She had missed him more than she had ever realized.

"Paisley, what are you doing here?"

"I . . ." Paisley looked back over her shoulder at the light—it was still there, bright and steady. "I think I died." Paisley looked up at her father and felt her loss in the look of sadness on her face.

"No, Paisley, you must go back. It isn't your time."

Paisley looked down at her chest, and as she did, a bloodred stain bloomed.

Edmund took in a sharp breath. "It will be all right." He reached his hand up and away toward the light of the Veil. Although he was nowhere near it, he cupped his hand and scooped some of the light into it. It shimmered and pulsed like a star as he brought it close. The light bathing them felt warm and comforting. He stretched out his hands and gave it to Paisley, and as she took it, the light changed from bright to black, an orb of shifting black that radiated with all the colors and none at all at the same time. The orb lost its smooth structure and began to fray at the edges till it looked like a rip in the world.

Edmund guided Paisley's hands toward the wound in her chest. Paisley let out a startled gasp as the light from the Veil slipped into her body.

"There, you can go back now," Edmund told her as he reached up and stroked her face.

Paisley threw her arms around him. She clung to him harder than she had ever done. "But I don't want to leave you again."

"Nor I you, but Dax needs you, Paisley. You're not supposed to be here, not yet. We'll be together one day: you, me, your mother, and Dax. But for now I need you to go back and I need you to promise me one thing: that you will listen to your heart and follow its melody. Even when it is at odds with the song of your stars."

Paisley looked up at her father, bewildered. "I don't know what that means."

Edmund leaned forward and kissed her forehead. "You will. Now go; your brother needs you."

A voice echoed behind her. "Paisley!"

"Dax?"

She turned to look at the light, and when she looked back, her father was gone and all that remained was the dull glow of the Veil.

An eon passed in an instant, and Paisley fell toward the light.

34

THE SECOND STARS OF
PAISLEY FITZWILLIAM

She felt only pain.

She heard it too. Dax was next to her, his leg sticking out at an awkward angle, her head in his lap, tears running down his cheeks as he rocked back and forth, moaning, "Please don't be dead. Please don't be dead."

Violetta was there, angry sobs escaping her as she dashed the tears from her face and turned to the Dark Dragon.

"Please, don't pull the comet toward us; we will all die, every last one of us."

The Dark Dragon's voice was as cold as dead nightsilver. "Only the undeserving will be cleansed in the fire of Malgol."

Deep within the machine, Paisley could hear the half dragon

heart beat out its powerful rhythm, its electrica energy pouring into the metal cogs like blood.

Paisley felt life flowing through her, weak at first but then stronger. The warmth that she had felt from the constant glow of the Veil had not left her. It began to move through her body, tracing her veins, filling them with heat, vitality, power, and fire.

Her eyes were still closed, but in her mind's eye she could see the room; she could see past the room. She could see the whole world and all its tracks. She could see the possibilities permeating in the Veil, exploding into life, like stars being born.

She saw all that had been, and now she saw all that could be, both terrifying and wondrous.

In her mind, she traced back along the tracks, playing out what had happened when the Dark Dragon had stabbed her, like watching a moving picture.

Mother and Dax had rushed to her as she fell. Corbett and Odelia had leaped up and flown for Sabra, Odelia with swords drawn and mouth open in a scream of vengeance.

Lorena and two of the Dark Dragon Walkers set upon Odelia; she was bested from all sides, her wings tied, her swords scattered across the room.

Paisley stretched her fingers a fraction and felt the cold blade of one of Odelia's curving swords where it had come to rest. Almost as if it had been placed there, waiting.

The images in her mind caught up with the now, and Paisley could see it all; Corbett was sitting at the controls of the machine, his face bloodied and bruised from Roach's handiwork.

The Dark Dragon stood close behind him, a hand on his shoulder, her voice in his ear, her waterfall of black hair trailing over her shoulder.

"Bring him to me," she told Corbett. "Bring me my dragon."

Corbett hesitated.

The Dark Dragon moved to Violetta, coiling her fingers in her hair as she dragged her away from Paisley, toward the machine. She held the knife, still coated in Paisley's blood, to Violetta's throat.

Corbett looked from the Dark Dragon to Violetta. Her eyes were red, her hair disheveled, and her dirt-strewn face was white with grief. "No," she mouthed.

Corbett's mind was whirling through possibilities just as Paisley's mind was seeing them. She saw what would happen a moment before Corbett thought of doing it.

"Do you have the information on the position of the comet?"

The Dark Dragon nodded to Uncle Hector, who pulled the observation logbook from his pocket.

Corbett looked at the log. He was looking at the position where the comet had been last night. The machine would be off. It would move the comet off course, perhaps, but it wouldn't send it hurtling directly toward Earth. It would be close, and he couldn't rule out some type of contact, but it was better than pulling the Comet straight toward them.

Corbett made a show of tracing his finger along the numbers and read each one out as he put them into the machine, twisting the dials to match the coordinates printed out. He looked at Violetta as he did so. Paisley could tell that she was running through the numbers in her head. Her brows contracted as she concentrated. And then her face went blank, and she chewed the corner of her lip before she gave Corbett the smallest of nods. His jaw tightened, and then he entered the last digit. The machine began to move into position.

Maybe, Paisley thought as she saw the golden tracks shift, the unseen cogs moving them ever so slightly. *Just maybe, it will be all right.*

The Dark Dragon moved away from Violetta, leaving her kneeling on the floor.

"Rejoice, for you are the witnesses. This night the Great Dragon Malgol begins its descent and the mighty of the Earth will return." The Dark Dragon pulled the lever on the side of the machine.

From deep within the machine, a whirling sound began. It started quietly, then rose in volume, maintaining the same pitch, a deep low resonance.

The vibration increased, moving through the air, moving through everything.

Paisley could feel it pass through every cell in her body as her eyes opened.

The Observatory looked as if it was a mirage on a hot summer's day. The edges of everything oscillated.

She closed her eyes again, looking for the paths of the Mechanism that she had seen in the Veil before, but instead of paths, now she saw a rip. A gap in the track.

She felt a shifting, coalescing.

Now was the moment to rise.

35

THE INVENTION OF NIGHT

Paisley seized Odelia's fallen curved sword and pushed up from the floor with the speed and strength of a mighty dragon. Her body felt both fluid and robust, as if the touch of the Veil had made her new.

Dax barely registered what had happened; he opened his mouth to call out to her, but his words halted in his throat as Paisley bore down on the childlike dragon.

The Dark Dragon sensed the stirring of the air and turned, but not fast enough.

Paisley swung the sword through the air from high above her head, bringing it down in an arc, slicing along the Dark Dragon's tunic, into her ribs, laying her broken flesh bare.

The Dark Dragon raised her knife and staggered back. Her eyes widened in fear and confusion. "I killed you."

Paisley shone like vengeance, her hair flaring as she matched the Dark Dragon step for step, hounding her backward.

The Dark Dragon swung her knife from side to side, Paisley's blood still glistening and wet along the long blade. Paisley held the knife mid-strike with the curved blade of Odelia's sword.

"I was dead. I have seen beyond. I have risen."

The Dark Dragon's beautiful face trembled, and she pushed Paisley away from her.

Lorena moved forward.

"No." The Dark Dragon held up her hand. "This is between Paisley and me."

Paisley lowered her head in a mocking bow, her eyes fixed on the Dark Dragon.

Paisley cast the sword in a large arc, dipping and turning to deflect a head-on attack.

She passed behind her, bringing the hilt of her sword down hard between the Dark Dragon's shoulder blades.

Paisley felt in control, her movements graceful and exacting. The fire rose up inside her.

Paisley let out her anger and frustration in a mighty roar and leaped toward the Dark Dragon, who scrabbled to regain control.

"You are nothing," the Dark Dragon said. "I have everything within my reach. The machine is pulling my Dragon forth; the world will soon be mine. I have seen the stars you were born under. I have read your track. Your destiny is to die."

Paisley felt a rage explode inside her, the heat and fire becoming solid and real. She launched at the Dark Dragon, dipping her shoulder and knocking her hard into the machine.

The Dark Dragon's body crunched as Paisley drove her harder into the metal. She dropped her weapon, her already bloody head leaving a dark sticky mark on the nightsilver behind her.

Paisley's face was inches away from the Dark Dragon's. "I already died," Paisley told her. "I fulfilled the destiny of my stars; I get to choose what I do now, and I choose to destroy you."

Paisley kept her eyes locked on the Dark Dragon's. She did not see the rip in the world form or move silently toward them like a never-ending storm of darkness, but she felt it: She felt its track and instinctively called it near.

The power of it flowed through her, and she smiled as the Dark Dragon's eyes widened in terror. The rip Paisley had witnessed in the Veil manifested in the world, a cloud of impenetrable night, moving swiftly and silently, and Paisley stepped back to watch it.

The Dark Dragon stood rooted to the spot, her back against the machine. "Paisley, please." She reached out a hand.

Paisley sent her intention forth, the cloudlike rift passing over the Dark Dragon's arm, taking it into the Veil.

The Dark Dragon screamed, and Paisley felt the world refocus. She lost her grasp on the rift and watched as the dark cloud drifted away and struck its own course, shooting off upward and through the machine, taking a part of it before dissolving as quickly as it had formed.

The Dark Dragon fell to her knees, clutching the stump where her arm had been and writhing in agony. There was no blood, no open laceration. The Veil had taken her flesh and sealed her wound.

Paisley stumbled back. She dropped Odelia's sword, her eyes wide.

"Paisley." Dax's voice was small and shaky as he looked at his sister. She moved toward him, but he stepped back, his eyes wide and wary.

Paisley swallowed down a sob as tears tumbled down her cheeks like liquid regret.

She looked back at the Dark Dragon, writhing on the floor and howling with pain; Lorena was by her side, lifting her up as she mourned her ruined arm.

Paisley felt the room rushing back to her. Her chest felt tight and the air thick. Her ears were ringing. The machine's vibration had changed. It was deeper, menacing.

She stood looking at Dax, a lump rising in her throat, her mind racing in desperation. *What have I done? What have I done to the machine, the Dark Dragon, the Veil, the world?*

Dax let out a yell as he fell to the ground, his braced leg shooting outward as he hurtled toward the machine like a pin to a magnet.

Paisley leaped after him, holding his hands as he scrambled to stay still. Dax clung to Paisley, and they halted for a moment, both looking into each other, both knowing the world had changed, both terrified.

The vibration deepened a notch, and they slid along the floor, Dax hitting into the machine, his brace stuck to it like bonded atoms.

"Paisley, what happened? What did you do?" he asked, his eyes searching for an answer.

"I . . . I don't know."

"That thing?"

"It was the Veil." Paisley felt herself tremble as she recalled the blackness of the rift.

"Look out," Dax shouted, and ducked as metal projectiles flew at them and hit the machine. Paisley moved fast, covering his body with hers, hugging him tight, shielding her brother.

"We need to move." Paisley put her hands under Dax's arms and tried to pull him away from the machine. She was aware of her body; her muscles felt strong, her back didn't even twinge, and her heartbeat was sure and steady. But the machine was stronger.

"It's no use. Undo the brace," Paisley said. They both struggled to undo the clasps and buckles of the brace.

The vibrating intensified as the low pitch deepened once more. As the machine began to fail, it started to tug metallic objects through the air.

Dax pulled his leg free; Paisley slid him out of the way, just as all the mechanical beetles flew from Roach's pockets, dragging him with them and pinning him in place.

The vibrating sound was punctuated by another, a soft tearing sound.

Paisley looked up and saw another distortion in the air, like a rippling of darkness. It sucked in the light from around it, and then it was gone. Paisley looked at Dax; his mouth was as wide as his eyes. He gulped. "Did you?"

Paisley shook her head. "It's free," Paisley said. "I don't know how, but the Veil is free in the world, our world." She gave a shudder.

They stayed still for a moment; then Paisley took Dax's hand and pulled him to the curved walls of the observatory. Another dark rift had opened, and it shimmered like black oil on a puddle.

Uncle Hector was staring into it, close by, his face pale with terror. From the darkness came a familiar voice. "What have you done?"

Uncle Hector reached out a hand. "Edmund?"

Paisley didn't hesitate; she ran for her uncle and tackled him to the ground. He pushed her roughly to one side, his hand still outstretched toward the rift in the Veil as it moved above his reach, drifting through the room and crackling like an electrica storm cloud.

"Edmund!" he cried.

The rift moved through the machine again, breaking the long projecting arm in two, absorbing the part it had touched and leaving nothing behind. As the large spike of metal fell, the dark rift continued to drift across the room like a stone sliding on the surface of ice. It headed straight for Odelia, who was still on the floor as Doc Langley loosened her bonds.

"Watch out," Paisley yelled. Doc Langley ducked as the rift rose and passed above them.

Violetta screamed.

"Mother!" two voices cried out.

The machine grumbled and began to break apart from the strain of the rifts and its own failings.

As it fell the vibrating stopped, and another sound replaced it, a roaring harsher than the wind and deeper than a lion.

"Dragons!" Dax said as he pointed upward "The machine worked!"

Paisley looked up. Through the opening in the top of the dome flew not a Great Dragon, but a dragon of the Krigare.

She was deep-sea blue with bronze-colored horns and talons. On her back sat a boy about the same age as Paisley. He had blond hair and a patch on his left eye, and he smiled down on the scene as if the whole world amused him.

Behind him swooped in another dragon, smaller than the first, and as green as spring grass. A little girl, no older than Dax, in full Dragon Guard uniform, sat majestically on the dragon. Her white hair shone like moonlight, her Krigare marks light blue against her creamy skin, making her look as cold as ice.

Three more Krigare dropped through the opening on long wires connected to their dragons above. Each one was no older than

Paisley, or younger than Dax, dressed in the uniform of the Luft Krigare and armed with nightsilver.

Dax raced to Paisley's side. "What are they doing here?" he asked her.

"They've come for Soul Fire," she said as the boy clumsily dismounted his dragon and headed straight for the broken machine.

Paisley shot her head around as Lorena called to her initiates and struggled to hold the Dark Dragon up. They rallied behind her, weapons in hand.

Lorena opened her mouth and let out a huge fireball as the girl on the green dragon swooped in, protecting the assembled Krigare with the underside of her dragon's belly, wings outstretched to beat back the flames.

She shouted orders to the Krigare in a language Paisley did not understand as they moved against the Dark Dragon Walker.

"Where's Mother?" Dax asked, looking around the room.

"I . . . I don't know. I can't see her; she was on the other side of the machine before it broke apart. I heard her scream."

Paisley and Dax climbed over the wreckage of the machine that littered the floor. They began to work together, lifting pieces of nightsilver and tossing them aside as around them the Dark Dragon and her Walker battled the Krigare of the North.

"Corbett," Paisley cried as she saw his arm under the wreckage. She tried to pull the metal away, but it was too heavy.

The Krigare boy who had left his dragon was at her side, helping her lift the debris before she even realized.

Corbett crawled out from underneath, covered in dust and coughing.

The Krigare reached out a hand and pulled him up.

"Thanks. Wait, who are you?"

Corbett looked at his uniform, then at the blue dragon beating its wings above his head. "Wow!"

"I am Hal, and this"—he motioned to the dragon—"is Sterk-Natt. Sterk-Natt, come," he commanded, lifting his arm in the air. The dragon stayed where she was, glowering down at him.

Hal looked at Corbett and raised an eyebrow. "We are having issues at the moment," he said. "Sterk-Natt, now!" Then, through gritted teeth, "You're making me look bad."

The dragon flew a lap of the observatory, screeching in a mocking tone and gnashing her teeth at the Dark Dragon and Lorena as they made for the stairs. A coatless Roach was already at the top of the stairwell.

"Paisley," Dax yelled.

Paisley turned to see Dax struggling to lift a piece of the wreckage. "It's Mother; I found her."

Paisley, Corbett, and Hal climbed over the fallen metal to Dax's side.

Hal and Corbett lifted the metal while Dax and Paisley got down on their hands and knees, calling to their mother. She reached out a hand, her fingers searching for her children from under the broken nightsilver.

Paisley and Dax grabbed her hand as Hal and Corbett cleared the wreckage from her.

"Hal, vi behöver dig!" the girl on the dragon called out from above.

Hal looked over at the fighting. The Krigare were struggling.

Paisley looked up to see that Uncle Hector was now carrying the Dark Dragon as tears ran down her beautiful face, white with pain, and Lorena had joined her initiates. Odelia had broken free; she was shielding the Krigare from Lorena's fire with her wings. Doc Langley was also fighting; he had found a fallen piece of the broken machine and was using it as a club to aim blows at anyone who came close enough, friend or foe.

Hal patted Corbett on the shoulder and shot a look at Paisley before he leaped into the action, pulling his sword from his belt as he went.

Paisley kneeled by her mother. There was something wrong with the way that her chest fell to one side. Blood was trickling slowly from her mouth.

"Mother . . ." Paisley began, her lip trembling.

"There isn't much time, my darlings." Violetta ran a hand over her daughter's face, then down to her chest, where blood stained her shirt. "I thought I had lost you."

"I'm . . ." Paisley shook her head. "I can't explain it, but I'm fine,

Mother; I'm better than fine. Something happened...but I don't know what it was."

Dax whimpered.

Violetta grasped Dax's hand.

"Listen to me. I want you to run. You hear me? Never stop running. Get far away from here. Take this." She thrust the combined soul stones from the machine at Dax; he held it close, the half dragon heart pulsing against his chest.

"Destroy it if you can, hide it if you can't, but never let her get it, or the other pieces. The other two stones. If she had all four she would be unstoppable. Do you understand? You must find them before she does!"

"Yes," Paisley and Dax said, through salted tears.

"Promise me. Promise me you'll do this and that you will stay together. Promise me."

"We promise," Paisley said.

"I wish...I wish I had more time to tell you all you need to know. I wish I had time to watch you grow, to love you more." Violetta coughed.

"Mother, please. Please don't leave us," Paisley pleaded.

"I don't want to go," Violetta whispered. "I don't ever want to leave you." The light in her eyes turned dull; tears ran down her face as her hand fell from Paisley's cheek.

"No," Dax said, in a small voice. "This isn't the way it was meant to be. We found her. We're supposed to take her home and have a happily ever after, forge our own destinies; that's what we're supposed to do." Dax clutched the heart in one hand and Violetta's limp hand in his other. "Why doesn't she come back, Paisley? You came back."

Paisley sobbed, holding Violetta's other hand to her cheek. "I don't know, Dax. She's gone; she's..."

"She's dead," Corbett said, his voice thick with loss as he placed a hand on Dax's back.

Dax shrugged him off, rounding on him. "NO! I won't let her die," he shouted. "She moved the comet; she made a new track. This doesn't have to be her end. I have the heart." Dax thrust his hand up into the air, the blackened heart clenched in his fist, glowing red between his fingers as it beat.

"Dax, what good can that do?" said Paisley. "It won't bring her back."

"It might. The Dark Dragon was going to use it to break the Veil. She's going to bring back the dragons and the dead. She can bring back Mother too; we can get her back, Paisley."

"No, Dax, we promised. We promised not to let her have it."

"I don't care. I want Mother back, now," Dax said, his anger flaring. Paisley moved to soothe him, but as she did, a swooping movement descended on Dax, and the green dragon hoisted him up in her claws.

"Krigare, retreat," the girl on the dragon called. "I have Soul Fire; our mission is complete, retreat."

The Krigare halted in their fighting and ran for the ropes that were still dangling from their waiting dragons.

Paisley reached after Dax, scrambling to her feet, running to the gap in the observatory roof and watching helplessly as he disappeared up into the night.

Paisley roared her brother's name into the darkness.

The sea-blue dragon flew after them. In her claws was Doc Langley, and on her back was an empty saddle.

"No!" the Dark Dragon yelled. "They have the Heart Stone; I need it, I need it." She was still being carried by Uncle Hector, cradling the stump of her arm.

"Don't worry, Your Darkness, the Great Dragon is coming. By his fire, he will restore the light. We will retrieve the heart. We will have our revenge for what they have done to you, but now we must leave. We need to heal you," Lorena told her.

"He's coming," the Dark Dragon repeated. "Yes. He's coming." She locked eyes with Paisley. "Mark me, when he arrives, I will feed you to him first." A dark delight danced in her eyes. "This is not over between the two of us," she told Paisley.

"Far from it," Paisley promised.

36

THE TURNING BEGINS

Dawn rose slowly.

In the sky, the Comet Wolstenholme was following a new track. Despite Corbett's hurried calculations, Violetta's machine had been as efficient as one might expect. It had succeeded in turning the course of the comet toward the Earth in a path of motion that over the coming weeks would alarm the good people of London, who had no idea that the course of history had been replotted in their fair city.

Across the waters from the ruins of the astronomical dome of the Greenwich Observatory, the stirrings of the black rifts continued to radiate out, small rips into the Veil striking their own course in the world. Most would vanish as quickly as they formed, unknown and unwitnessed. But not all would be as benign.

Less than two miles away, a ginger alley cat hissed and curled at a shadow so black it shone with all the colors of the rainbow.

The cat fled as the dark rift moved, hitting the side of the house, absorbing the bricks and leaving a gap as it sucked the matter from the world.

The cat waited a while before hopping through to the exposed kitchen beyond.

Back in the old Greenwich Observatory, Paisley held her mother, wishing she could pull her back from the Veil. Behind her, she could hear Odelia whispering to Corbett as they sat side by side on a blackened bench, Odelia ignoring her wounds, Corbett nursing his.

"We need to get going," Odelia told him.

"Give her time; her mother just died. She lost everything she was fighting for."

"Every minute we spend here is a minute that Dax gets farther away. We need to get moving, fast."

"Maybe you can fly after him, but the rest of us can't. We'll sort something out. But not right now. Now Paisley needs to say goodbye."

Paisley stroked her mother's hair and spoke to her in hushed tones.

"How is she not dead?" Odelia asked. "The Dark Dragon stabbed her in the heart; *how* is she not dead?"

Corbett shrugged. "We'll figure that out later too."

"The Dark Dragon said that she had seen Paisley's stars, and that they said she would die, yes?"

Corbett pulled his broken glasses from his nose and examined the damage. "I thought Paisley was trackless."

"We all have stars guiding us, even if we can't see them," Odelia said.

Corbett shrugged and put his glasses back on. "Maybe, though I guess nothing is certain anymore—I think what has just happened proves that. Violetta could move a comet with a machine; what's to say Paisley can't steal her fate from the stars?"

They were both silent for a moment.

"And what about him?" Odelia nodded toward Hal. He was lying on the floor, where she had gagged and bound him. He had long since stopped struggling.

"Aye, he'll have to wait and all."

"Why do you think they took my Lord?" Odelia asked.

"I don't know, but we can ask the Krigare if you'd just untie him. He seemed like a decent sort to me."

Odelia snorted and folded her arms across her chest. "Looks can be deceiving. I used to think Lorena was one of the good ones." She set her jaw, and Corbett could hear her teeth slowly grinding.

"I can't believe the Krigare just left him."

Odelia shrugged. "It is the way with warriors. If they are worthy, they will return under their own steam; if not, well, it isn't worth them returning."

"So much for loyalty," Corbett said. He leaned back on the desk, knocking Paisley's satchel to the ground.

He got up and bent to retrieve it. A little way under the bench, he saw something glittering. At first he thought it was another of the dark Veil rifts, but when it stayed still, he reached out a hand and rolled the egg toward him.

He stood up, slinging the bag over his shoulder, holding the egg in his hand.

"Does it look different to you?" he asked.

Odelia glanced at it. "Not really. A little sooty, maybe."

Corbett ran his sleeve over the egg, but the hard surface didn't return to the black it had once been; it stayed a dark gray.

"Weird," he said.

"What isn't right now? The ground is a troubling place. I prefer the floating boroughs," Odelia added.

Paisley kissed the top of her mother's head as she finished making her silent promises.

She slowly rose to her feet and shrugged off Corbett's coat. She placed it over her mother, then walked toward her friends.

"Paisley, I ... I just wanna say ..."

"Don't, Corbett, please, don't."

Corbett shuffled awkwardly from one foot to the other as Paisley put her hands up in surrender.

Early morning light came streaming through the gap in the dome, glinting off the debris of the machine. Dust motes danced above Violetta's body.

Paisley felt another rift before she saw it. Disturbingly dark, it sucked in the dust motes as it glided toward Violetta's body.

Paisley watched as the rift passed over her mother and took her.

Corbett cast a sideways look at Odelia, who was staring at the hole that had been left in the world.

Paisley took a deep breath, her shoulders dropping as if a huge weight had just been placed on her.

She reached out a hand to Corbett and took her satchel from him and slung it over her shoulder, then went to Hal and untied his feet.

"Get up," she told him.

He slowly stood, hands behind his back, gag still in place.

"I'm going to get my brother back, and you are going to help me," Paisley told him. Hal mumbled at her through his gag; she threw a hand up to silence him. "I'm sorry, but you're my prisoner now; I need something to trade for Dax, and you're it."

Hal started murmuring again.

Paisley fixed him with a stare. He was quiet once more. His face was expressive, his un-patched eye imploring her.

She turned to Corbett and Odelia. "You two should go home; it's not safe. The Dark Dragon will be after the Heart Stones, which means she'll be after Dax; she'll probably be after us too. Her and Roach and . . . my uncle."

"Paisley, we're in this with you," Corbett said. "We're not going to let you do this on your own."

"Agreed," said Odelia. "I swore allegiance to my Lord, and I will not rest until I am by his side."

"Right," Corbett said. "We're coming with you, whether you want us to or not."

Paisley felt a small glow of hope, like the light she had seen in the Veil.

She would find her brother, and she wouldn't do it alone.

✦ ✦ ✳ ✦ ✦

In the dawn-lit sky of the far North, Dax sat behind the white-haired girl, clinging on for dear life. He shivered from the cold and pressed himself into the warmth of her back.

He knew that he would have felt excited about riding with the Krigare if he didn't feel so hollow and empty.

He kept seeing Paisley standing in the rubble, crying up to him, Mother dead on the floor behind her. He felt his tears turn to ice on his cheek as the dragon heart beat in his pocket.

"Paisley," he whispered into the wind.

Read on for a sneak peek as the adventure continues in *The Doomfire Secret*.

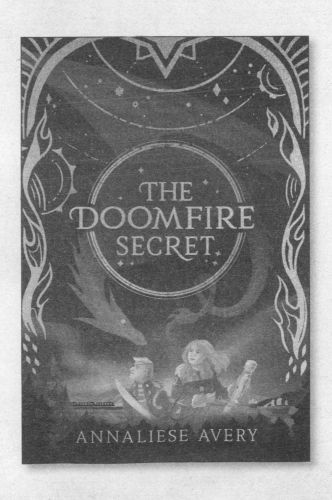

1

THE LANGUAGE OF SORROW

Sorrow was speaking to Paisley Fitzwilliam. It called to her from deep inside as she led Odelia and the others through the crisp, cold streets of Lower London. Keeping to the shadows, they moved swiftly.

"Paisley, are you all right?" Corbett asked.

Odelia tutted loudly at him. "Of course she's not all right. Would you be, if your mother had just died and your brother had been carried off by Krigare to the icy Northern Realms on dragonback?"

"No, I guess not," Corbett said in a low voice. "But it's what people ask, isn't it—'*Are you all right?*' not '*Would you like to talk about your loss and grief?*'"

Paisley said nothing, then looked away from him, glancing over at Hal. Odelia was by his side, one hand firmly wrapped around the top of his arm as she guided him through the streets. He was still in his Krigare uniform: dark-colored, dragon-scaled leather trousers and a military tunic. It got cold riding high through the air on the back of a dragon, and the leathers were warm, offering protection from the elements as well as from enemies; there wasn't much that could pierce a dragon's hide.

Hal smiled sadly at Paisley, his single eye glinting in the early morning light, the angry red scar that ran from the top of his head under his eye-patch and all the way to his jaw puckering. "In the Northern Realms, when we lose a loved one, we celebrate their life, we remember the way that they lived, and we tell the stories of their deeds—the same deeds that are recorded in their Krigare marks, if they are lucky." He gestured to the icy-blue tattoos that ran up his neck and up into the shaved sides of his hair; the band of dirty-blond hair that ran down the center of his head was long and braided in a way that reminded Paisley of the older Dragon Walkers she had seen in the vaults of Kensington Above.

Paisley took a step toward him. "You don't get to tell me how to grieve. You don't get to tell me about loss. My brother isn't here because your people took him! I will not allow him to become another blue mark on anyone's body. You, Hal Northman, are going to help me get my brother back—I'm sure I'll be able to trade you for him. But if you do anything to jeopardize me getting Dax back, if you add to my grief in any way, we won't take you north with us; we will leave you here for the King's Men to deal with."

Hal had stopped smiling. He set his jaw and looked solemnly at Paisley.

"That seems like a sound plan. Similar to something I might do myself, if I were in your position."

Paisley turned away from him and the others and closed her eyes tight. Her head filled with images from the night before: the fight in the observatory at Greenwich, Mother's machine, the experiment. The Dark Dragon stabbing Paisley in the heart.

She remembered what it had felt like as she had slipped into the Veil—distant and vast. How she had seen her father, and he had sent her back, back to face the Dark Dragon, back to watch her mother die and Dax be taken, back to the realization that Uncle Hector had betrayed them all.

When she thought about her mother lying in the rubble, her eyes closed to the world forever, it was as if she could see it but couldn't feel it just yet. It felt distant, as if it had all happened to a different Paisley: maybe the one she was before she went in the Veil. She found the distance comforting and was scared of what would happen when she felt her loss.

The freezing-cold streets of Lower London felt as if they were pressing in on her. Mother was dead, Dax was gone, and deep within herself, she felt empty; it was as if the black Veil rifts had reached in and taken away a vital part of her, as they had done to the Dark Dragon's arm, leaving a sticky patch of nothingness in their wake.

"Paisley?" Corbett touched her shoulder.

She turned on him. "Look, I'm not okay, Corbett. I mean, obviously I'm not okay. My mother . . ." She took a deep, rattling breath in, then breathed out slowly, her breath fogging like dragon smoke in the chill morning. "But Dax needs me, and I need him." She could hear her voice tremble, and coughed as she pushed down the lump at the back of her throat. "So, right now that is what I'm focusing on: getting to Dax."

Paisley glared over at Hal. Everybody knew that the people of the Northern Realms were barbaric, uneducated, and not to be trusted. History was full of their treachery against the Empire of Albion and the Chief Designer, and now they had Dax.

Paisley felt her anger rise as she looked up at the floating borough of Kensington Above drifting overhead, its large snow-globe-like dome glinting in the clear, bright blue winter sky. So much had changed since they had left the floating borough. How would her track have bent if she and Dax had never visited the Dragon Vault, never set out to save Mother? Would Mother still be alive? Would Dax have been taken? Paisley sighed. There was no escaping one's track; whatever she would have done, she was sure that eventually the cogs of the Celestial Mechanism would have brought her here.

"Where are we going?" Odelia asked, alert, her body tense, as she held on tight to the Krigare. Paisley looked from Hal to Odelia and realized that the streets of Lower London were just as unsafe for her as they were for him.

"Home's not far," Paisley said.

"Are you sure that is wise?" Odelia asked. "The Dark Dragon might try to find you there."

"True. But I don't know what else to suggest. We shouldn't be out in the open like this, just walking around on the streets. If the King's Men find us . . ."

"I agree with Paisley," Corbett said, looking over at Hal and Odelia. "And we can always check out the house to make sure the coast is clear when we get there."

"And once we know we are safe, we can come up with a plan to be reunited with Dax," added Odelia.

Paisley gave a small smile to both Corbett and Odelia. She knew that there was a gaping hole inside her that her mother had left, even if, at the moment, she couldn't feel it. She also knew that when she did, Odelia and Corbett would be there to help her from falling into it.

She gave Hal a wide berth as they continued on, but she kept her eyes on him, checking that he wasn't putting any of them in danger.

"What are you looking at?" Paisley asked as she glimpsed Corbett staring up at the sky. He was wearing the coat that Roach had left behind after the fighting at the observatory, and it looked large and bulky on Corbett's smaller frame. The collar was turned up, and so was his face, as his hands dug through the many pockets before pulling out a small pair of binoculars and peering through them.

"What is it?" Paisley asked.

Corbett lifted an arm and pointed into the early morning sky. "You see that star?" Paisley nodded. "Well, it's not a star!"

"Is it Comet Wolstenholme?" Paisley asked. Something tightened in her chest as she thought of the comet that her mother's machine had just pulled toward the Earth.

"No, it's not a comet either. It's a planet, and it's not supposed to be there."

"What? How is that possible? Where is it supposed to be?"

But Corbett never answered. As he had been looking through the binoculars, he didn't see that Odelia had suddenly paused at the curb ahead of him. As he bundled into her, she swiftly twisted to one side, but his inertia carried him into the road. Corbett fell, arms out, ready for impact, but he never reached the ground. Hal grabbed the back of his coat and held him suspended above the road, his feet still on the curb. Paisley turned her head in unison with Corbett's to see the fast-approaching omnibus heading straight for him. He let out a scream as she lunged forward to help just as Hal promptly pulled Corbett to safety. The omnibus passed in a blur.

"That was close!" Paisley said as she placed a hand on Corbett's arm. Paisley's heart was racing as she looked at the receding omnibus. "Are you both all right?" she asked. If anything had happened to Corbett or Odelia, Paisley was sure that she would be in even more trouble than she already was. She needed them, and not just to help her get Dax back, she realized.

"You saved me!" Corbett said to Hal as he stood staring at him in disbelief.

"Yes, thank you, Krigare," Odelia said to Hal with a nod of approval, before she snapped her head to look across the street.

Paisley saw what had made Odelia halt: Two Men of the Yard in their black-and-red uniforms were making their way across the road toward them. They were staring at Hal; his ice-blue Krigare marks and dragon-hide uniform made him an easy target to spot on the quiet early morning streets.

Odelia stepped in front of the Krigare, shrugging back her cape and resting her hands on the hilts of her curving swords.

"Stay where you are, in the name of the George!" the Men of the Yard called.

"Run!" Odelia yelled. The four of them turned and ran back the way they had come, pounding through the streets of Lower London with the Men of the Yard behind them, blowing on their whistles for assistance.

Odelia swiftly outran them all, taking the lead, steering them away from danger. Paisley was not surprised to find Corbett close behind the Dragon Walker, the fear of the situation making him run fast. Paisley ran along behind Hal, making sure he was following the others. She wasn't about to let him use this as an opportunity to escape.

Paisley glanced over her shoulder: The Men of the Yard were in hot pursuit as Odelia led them toward a covered market full of stallholders setting up for the day.

Paisley grabbed her satchel as it swung out wildly, knocking a passer-by, who yelled at her. She noticed how her body felt strong and agile, better than new. She was sure that if she wanted to, she could have easily outrun Odelia, the pain of her wounds from the previous night a distant memory.

She glanced behind her and saw that the man she had hit with her satchel had stumbled into the Men of the Yard, holding them up.

"Stop those kids! They're Krigare!" one of the Yardmen shouted.

The stallholders rallied then, and Paisley realized that she and Hal had been cut off from Odelia and Corbett, who were both running for the exit on the far side of the market building, being chased by a man holding a baguette and another in a butcher's apron.

Hal came to a stop, looking about. Paisley pulled him along with her as she skidded left between the stalls, avoiding the group of people in her way, as she headed for a smaller side exit, Hal following close behind now. She leaped up onto a flower cart and turned to help Hal. He jumped up after her, and the two of them ran along the adjacent stall before jumping down on the other side.

Paisley could feel a strange electrica surge in the air, as if her fear and anxiety were stretching their way out as she and Hal ran for an open side door. When they were just feet away, the door slid into place, trapping them. Paisley looked at Hal, his breathing coming fast, his blond braid whipping about him, his single blue eye narrow and searching as he crouched a little, arms wide and ready for trouble. Then he straightened up and his face became smooth, and his eye widened.

Paisley turned to see that between her and Hal and the people chasing them was a black Veil rift, large and looming and incredibly dark as it sucked in all the light around it.

Paisley stepped away from it, feeling the door at her back and Hal beside her.

"It looks like the things from the observatory. Do you think they followed us?" Hal asked.

Paisley stared in disbelief. "I don't know. I mean, maybe. I've never seen anything like them before last night. I think they might be the Veil—not the whole thing, just pockets of it, like little drops spilling into our world . . . or something."

Paisley remembered that she had heard her father's voice inside one of the black clouds as it had moved close to Uncle Hector in the observatory. Her father, who had died four years earlier; her father, whom she had seen when she was in the Veil.

Paisley unconsciously reached her hand toward her chest, feeling the space where the Dark Dragon's blade had sliced into her body.

She watched the fear in the faces of the people on the other side of the black rift as it grew and split in two. She felt something tug her toward it.

She realized that she was tethered to it in some way, connected on a level that she could not understand or make reason of, but that she knew to be true just as she knew that water was wet and that love sometimes hurt. Paisley's eyes grew wide as one of the clouds shot toward the crowd; they ran and jumped behind stalls for cover as the other rift headed straight for Paisley. She stood stock-still as the cloud of seemingly unending blackness glided toward her, smooth and undaunted in its approach.

Hal threw her down to the ground and out of the way as the Veil rift glided over her head, buzzing like the low hum of an electrica light. As it made contact with the door behind them, Paisley watched with fascinated horror as the rift absorbed the parts of the door that it touched, pulling the matter from the door into the blackness with the crackle of an electrica spark. Then the hum was gone and so was the rift, leaving behind a large hole in the door. The edge of the hole in the wood was smooth and precise, as if it had always been there, this gap in the world.

Hal was straight back on his feet, pulling Paisley through the gap. She froze, watching in terror as the other rift grew and made its way silently forward. The stallholders and early morning shoppers were screaming and running as the rift sucked in everything it came in contact with, before vanishing as quickly as it had arrived.

Outside was chaos, people running away from the market, calling and screaming.

"Come on, we have to get away! More of your Yardmen will be here soon." Hal dragged Paisley down a nearby street. Then another and another. They ducked into an alley to catch their breath. Paisley doubled over, her flame-red curls falling in front of her face.

"Those things, you think they are, what? Gateways into the Veil?" Hal asked, a single eyebrow raised over the top of his eyepatch.

"Yes— No, not gateways . . . I don't think you would want to travel through them; you saw what happened to the door. I don't think that anything good lies within them," Paisley said. "If Mother were here, she would be conducting some kind of experiment, trying to find out how they ticked, and what they were made of." Paisley's hands were over her heart again as she remembered the pull of the rift and the string of connection that she had felt.

At that moment, Odelia dropped from the heavens, carrying Corbett in her arms. Paisley was relieved to see them both, safe and unharmed.

Odelia let go of Corbett, and he moved away awkwardly as she folded her magnificent dragon wings smooth to her back and threw her cloak over them.

"Here." She thrust a large moss-green shawl at Hal. He took it, wrapping it to form a hood, his Krigare marks hidden in the shadows, his dragonhide uniform covered as the shawl reached down to his knees. "What happened? Why was everyone running away from the market?" Odelia asked.

Paisley looked at Hal and shook her head. "The Veil rifts, the ones from the observatory . . . they were here."

Odelia gave Paisley a serious look. "Curious," she said. "The Men of the Yard are distracted; we should make the most of the confusion."

Paisley led them once more, but this time she stuck to the backstreets and twisting passages, and they headed to her home in bursts of motion between the shadows.

Despite the empty cobbled walkways, Paisley kept looking all around her, not for the Men of the Yard but for any sign of the black Veil rifts. She thought of the connection she had felt to them, and shuddered at the way they had obliterated everything they touched, as if what had been there never was, leaving behind that same gaping hole in the world that Mother had.

ACKNOWLEDGMENTS

I was lucky enough to be born under a few bright stars that have guided my track well over the years. Sure, there have been moments when the light has dimmed and I couldn't see my way, but when that happened, I was blessed enough to have people around me who lent me their light and helped to guide me.

Joining the Golden Egg Academy and connecting with the fabulous Imogen Cooper was a guiding moment for me. Meeting my GEA editor, Nicki Marshall, helped me to figure out so much about the writer I wanted to be and the stories I wanted to tell. Nicki has become more than just a mentor to me; she has become my friend and dragon sister!

A few years ago, my fabulous friend Anj Medhurst and I set off along a track together as we embarked on a creative writing MA.

Over the two years, there was lots of chatting and tea and cake at our favorite café while discussing books and writing and assignment. All those things taught us so much about what we wanted to write and what we didn't (especially the cake and chat), allowing us to choose the light that we put out into the world.

Stars are often born in twin systems, and two of the brightest orbiting stars in my Celestial Mechanism are my fabulous friends Jane Martin and Debbie Edwards, one a multifaceted rainbow of light, the other a dragon! They have been constant stars, guiding me on—dragging me when needed, the light and warmth of their friendship has given me comfort and inspiration, shenanigans and joy. My night would be dark without them in it.

I have been so lucky to have many writing and bookish friends who have helped to straighten my track; Linda Spendlove, Mike Ellwood, Ashleigh Hambling, and Abigail Tanner have all been mighty cogs that have aided my turning over the years with the guidance of true friendship.

My track would be half as much fun as it is if I didn't have my lovely friend Vanessa Harbour to giggle along the way with. Vanessa, along with the gorgeous Teara Newell and John Malone, were the first to read *The Nightsilver Promise* and join Paisley on her epic adventure.

Jennie Sandberg is a mighty Krigare; hailing from the Northern Realms, she has been my guide to the language of the Dragon Riders. "Tack så mycket, Jennie!"

The dedication at the front of the book is for my grandfather Buster, who sadly passed away as I was writing *The Nightsilver Promise*. And although he is no longer here, I can still feel his gravity pulling me on. He, along with my grandmother Sheila, and my aunties, Jane and Sue, have been lighting my way with love and support, and I am so glad that I have them in my track.

Over the past year, I have been lucky to connect with some of the most talented writerly friends I have ever had. Together with Debbie, Jane, and Teara, this band fearless of dragon women equal the Dragon Walkers for strength, wisdom, and heart—Janet Baird, Elizabeth Lawson, Olivia Wakeford, Simone Greenwood, Elizabeth Frattaroli, Nicola Whyte, Vikki Marshall, Alice Ruth, Victoria Benstead-Hume, Kay Weetch, Amy Kitcher, Kirsty Fitzpatrick, Butterfly Hartley, Naomi Conran, Vikki Spreadbury, and Fran Benson—you are all amazing, and I love the floating borough of magic, friendship, and writing that we build together as The Fairy Book Mothers.

Another group of amazing writers that I'm lucky enough to share my track with are my fellow UV2020 finalists, Michael Mann, Urara Hiroeh, Harriet Worrell, Helen Makenzie, Angela Murry, Anna Brooke, Adam Connors, Sharon Boyle, Yvonne Banham, Clare Harlow, and Laura Warminger. Our shared experience has bonded us like nightsilver, and our monthly meetings are a constant source of light.

Blueprints are very important to the Celestial Mechanism; they require not only a skillful eye for detail but a boundless imagination that can see endless possibilities. Stephanie Yang has used that same energy and commitment to greatness to create a cover and visuals for *The Nightsilver Promise* that rival the most precious Blueprints in the Mechanists Repository!

Melissa Schirmer and Jacqueline Hornberger have given *The Nightsilver Promise* the same meticulous attention that the Celestial Physicists apply to the Celestial Mechanism, with their copy and proof edits helping to make the world shine.

Two of the most twinkling stars in the Celestial Mechanism are Victoria Velez and Rachel Feld, who, over the past few months, have added all the sparkles to this amazing journey that I find myself on and have shone their lights brightly—telling the world about *The Nightsilver Promise* and guiding me along as I navigate this new stretch of my track.

A little over a year ago, the Society of Children's Book Writers and Illustrators lit up my track with the supernova that is Undiscovered Voices. I am still riding on the glorious shock waves of the amazing opportunity that Sara Grant and the Undiscovered Voices team created; without you, I would never have found Helen.

If I am the Chief Designer of this story, then my agent, Helen Boyle, is Anu, the Great Mother Dragon who creates the universe. Helen forges all the tracks and guides me on my way. I am ever grateful for her light and counsel, and cannot even begin to tell you how much I value her wisdom and friendship.

Scholastic is the most amazing publisher and I am so proud to be traveling my track with them. The mechanism was definitely gleaming on the day that my track crossed with those of publisher David Levithan and editor Jeffrey West. Both have been a constant glow of support and inspiration to me—their belief and passion for this story and the world of the celestial mechanism has been a guide to me when the skies have darkly obscured the stars. I am looking forward to lighting up the night with them as we continue Paisley's journey together.

The world of the Celestial Mechanism would not have existed if it weren't for my amazing family: my partner, Jason, who gave me a room of my own to write in, my own space that he still supports and encourages; and our awesome children, Liberty, Krystal, and Oak, who have provided me with the best inspiration I could have ever wished for. Together the four of them keep me honest and true: my pointer stars, ever constant, showing me where my true north lies.

And finally, to all the people who have journeyed with me in my track to publication, I thank you, all the Eggs, and the SCBWI members, all the Twitter friends too, and to you, reader, I hope your stars are bright and constant and that Paisley's story has entangled with you to create a bond as strong as nightsilver.